PRAISE FOR WAYNE JOHNSON AND *DON'T THINK TWICE*

"An audacious debut . . . Johnson deftly mixes the components of a thriller with a complex character study, and Paul is a difficult, tormented figure, but also a compelling one. The language, while terse, is exact and vigorous. . . . An original, wonderfully assured, and powerful work."

—*Kirkus Reviews* (starred review)

"This novel crosses boundaries of cultures and also of literary genres. Although this is a murder mystery, the polish of the language, the pacing, and the characters make a fine literary fiction. . . . Johnson's terse descriptions are as poetic as the best of Raymond Chandler."

—*The Kansas City Star*

"Johnson has written a book that manages to make the wide, airy spaces of the Land of a Thousand Lakes feel claustrophobic with tension. . . . He gives the reader a brilliant sense of place, even as the plot tightens a noose of anxiety."

—*Library Journal*

Also by Wayne Johnson

The Snake Game

DON'T THINK TWICE

a novel

WAYNE JOHNSON

POCKET BOOKS
New York London Toronto Sydney Singapore

POCKET BOOKS, a division of Simon & Schuster, Inc.
1230 Avenue of the Americas, New York, NY 10020

Published by arrangement with Crown Publishers, a division of Random House, Inc.

ISBN: 0-7434-0632-X

First Pocket Books trade paperback printing November 2000

10 9 8 7 6 5 4 3 2 1

Cover design by Brigid Pearson, front cover photo courtesy of the author

Printed in the U.S.A.

As always, for Karen

Acknowledgments

This book would not have been possible without the support and encouragement of a number of people, first among them my wife, Karen, who patiently (and at times with humor) saw me through it. Thanks also to Makwa, Mike and Mary Farrell, John Buck, James Alan McPherson, Kevin Cooklin, Clay Bedford, Leola Bergmann, Richard and Kathryn Jefferson, Gerald Davey, Thom Cowan and Meredith Stricker, C. Neske, Vik and Raj Vohra, and J.F. Chapman II, friends, all who helped move things along.

I would like as well to thank my agent Wendy Hashmall, whose sharp reading and comments helped me discover connections in the book that needed discovering, and whose efforts got the book to the right place; and my editor, Shaye Areheart, who believed in the book from the first, and helped, with her especially insightful editing, to bring out the best in it.

Finally, I acknowledge the workings of the Spirit in all of this, be whatever its name; or, as my friend John Buck said: Ogotcit-ci'yane siwa'wigane, Like a bird, it appears.

Anawi'na nimo'kinina'
tibick'nandawen'damig.
What lies buried in desire,
bring to light.
—*Na'waji'bigo'kwe* ("Woman dwelling among the rocks")

The heart wants what it wants,
or it doesn't care.

—EMILY DICKINSON

BOOK I

1

It was the way Gwen was standing, head tilted admiringly, that made my heart leap, that got me wondering. But then, with a cough, I came down the path, and the two of them, laughing, turned from the lodge stoop. Gwen, her hands on her hips, hair done up over her head in a dark knot, eyes bright. Clark, my old friend, tall and stoop-shouldered, grinning.

"Hey there, Paul," he said, or at least that is what I think he said, and something shot away, like a night bird, a shadow.

"What's up?" I asked.

I was carrying a stringer of walleyes; they thumped against my leg as I walked. It was a good feeling. I put a foot up on the stoop, and Gwen and I exchanged glances. We had a variety of signs we used around guests—a certain flat look, for example, meant, keep it moving; a narrowing of the eyes warned we needed to talk alone.

Gwen gave me that warning look now. It was after eleven and I had a party to take out early, so I had no intention of chitchatting. Clark pointed to the fish.

"Gill netting again?" he teased.

"Nah," I replied.

There had been some rough weather earlier, only it had moved off to the south. Now the air was damp, with electricity in it; thunder rumbled in the distance.

"You hear that?" I said, hefting the stringer with one hand and reaching for Gwen with the other.

"Dynamite," I said. "Brings 'em to the top every time."

On the path back to the cabin, Gwen stopped now and again. There was something in her step, a lightness I wasn't sure I liked.

"Clark's funny," she said.

Yes, he was that all right, I agreed. Clark was very funny, in that offhand, dry way of his. We climbed the spine of the island. Down toward Hayes Junction lightning flashed. The cobalt-blue rectangle of Gwen's shirt bobbed ahead of me in the dark.

Gwen said something I didn't hear.

I was thinking about the money, and where I'd get it. I was trying not to let my near panic show. I had just days to come up with our next payment or we would lose the cabins, lodge, everything. I'd lent my old, and estranged friend, Al, a small fortune and had little hope of getting it back. Gwen had no idea.

And there was this, too: I got the feeling that something had changed around the lake, and in town, while we'd been gone over the winter, and the change wasn't good. People weren't talking to me, crossed the sidewalk in Pine Point when I approached.

It was as if something dangerous had attached itself to me, and getting too close meant trouble. *Tchibai,* the old ones called it, or walking shadow.

Following Gwen now, I wondered who'd put it on me. If it was fatal.

"Al call this afternoon?" I asked, trying to sound casual.

"No," Gwen said. She gave me a quick glance over her shoulder.

I pulled a face. For my old friend Al. A boogeyman face, tongue out, eyes wide. In short, trouble. Al had gotten deep into everything I'd run from up there on the reservation. All that Medicine Society hocus-pocus and politics.

"Stop it," Gwen said, laughing.

Yet there was little consolation in that. Al would call; I don't have it, he'd say. I'd lie, to Gwen, and to some officer at my bank in the Twin Cities, who'd want to know what the trouble was—Why is your payment late?—and then I'd begin the scramble to turn things around.

I watched Gwen's hips shift as she climbed, her legs sinewy and slender.

"The washer died," Gwen said.

"Again?"

Gwen chronicled the day's losses. I knew them all. In November, when we'd shut down for the year, I'd taken inventory. Things did not look good. Now, the end of May, we'd been up at the lake two weeks and the lodge was coming apart around us.

"The pilot light goes out on the Hobart—"

That was the industrial-size oven I'd bought at an estate sale.

"—the thing in the bottom of the washer—"

"The impeller—" I said.

"Well, whatever, it doesn't work."

She stopped on the path where the spur angled off to our cabin, and I very nearly bumped into her. I thought she was going to ask me why I wasn't doing anything about it, but it was worse than that. She turned her face away; the moon shone in her hair.

"Gwen—"

"No, don't. Don't say anything," she said, her eyes shiny in the dark. "Please don't be funny now, will you? I just couldn't bear it. I mean it, Paul."

I got a sick feeling in my stomach. Now, here it was all over again.

I thought, standing behind her, just say it. Or shout it. I was to blame. Get it over, now. Just not all this—*distance.*

Our boy, Bobby, had died the November before; we'd all had a hand in it, Gwen, Clark, and I, though, it seemed then, Clark had had the deciding one.

"It'll get easier."

"No," Gwen said. "Stop. Just stop. You're always—you're always *thinking* things. You've always got some *angle* going. Can't you just let things be? Do you always have to tangle everything up?" Her eyes were hard; I'd never seen her look so bitter. "I don't *want* to be convinced things are different. That they aren't bad."

"I'll fix it," I said.

"You *can't—fix— anything,*" she cried. "So can you *please just stop it?*"

"Gwen," I said, reaching for her.

She stepped back, shaking her head. She was lovely, and crying again. She'd misunderstood. I wanted to explain. But how could I? I hadn't meant Bobby, but Bobby was everywhere and in everything. Our winter down in St. Paul seemed not to have helped one bit.

"I'll have the old Taj Mahal—"

"Jesus—*stop—please.*"

"I'll fix it," I said, taking her hand. "Really."

"Like *what?*"

"Like what? Like all of it."

"Oh, *god!*" Gwen said.

I pulled her close. She laid her head on my shoulder, the weight of the world there, and gritting her teeth, tried not to cry. In seconds she had me doing it, too.

"I'm sorry," I said.

"It's not your fault."

"It is," I replied.

"Oh, *shut up!*" Gwen said, pushing me away and running up the path.

. . .

At our cabin, in bed, Gwen propped herself on her elbow, toying with her hair. The room was stuffy and I opened one of the windows overlooking the lake. It was one of those molasses-dark nights, the trees outside the window rustling in the breeze off the lake.

We were trying to be cheerful again.

"So," Gwen said. "You're going to take the money from Clark?"

Undressing, I kept my back to her. I nearly laughed to myself, relieved. So that's what it had been there on the stoop.

Earlier, over breakfast, Clark had been hedging around something but had never gotten to it. I'd wondered about that most of the day, his embarrassment.

"Am I?" I said.

I wanted to go easy here. I didn't want to rule out the possibility offhand.

"He said you were."

"I'm thinking about it," I said.

And I was, just then. I was trying this thing out, getting a feel for it. It made me sad to see what Clark was doing, trying to help, by going through Gwen.

"Well, anyway, I didn't ask," I said.

"Because he offered?"

"Something like that," I told her.

It would be an in-between thing, I said. Just a month or two, a stopgap deal. Why bother with the bank, I said. We talked about it all very matter-of-factly, what it would take to get by.

"But I'd rather not," I said.

Gwen coiled her blue-black hair around her finger and tugged at it. She didn't seem convinced. She was working on something. Those fine, Irish eyes of hers had a distant look in them.

"What if Clark lent it to me?"

Somehow, just the thought of her owing him anything, much less a substantial outlay of cash, cast Clark's offer in a new and especially unattractive light.

"We can make do without putting ourselves in hock to Clark," I told her.

I sat on the bed, springs creaking. I'd been toying with the idea of selling a boat I had in storage, at my old place on the reserve. Now the possibility took on real proportion. The room seemed suddenly smaller for it, the knotty-pine paneling, Gwen's bric-a-brac, cobalt glass and beading she collected, what had been in the past warm and inviting, all oppressive, poorer.

"So you won't," Gwen said.

I wasn't sure what she wanted me to say.

"No," I said.

"Money and friends don't mix."

"Something like that."

Gwen lay back, the covers pulled up around her waist.

"We're in some kind of trouble, aren't we?"

"No, not really," I lied.

I tried not to be aware of the clock ticking on the dresser. The curtain billowed in. I watched. This is the way you lose things, I thought. They get by you, like wind. Rarely did we have anything to say to each other now, these months since November. The slightest upset, it seemed, might finish things. So I said nothing.

Gwen ruffled my hair, laid her arm across my chest, squeezed me.

"Hey."

"Hey, you," I said in return.

2

I rose early, before Gwen woke.

Mornings, when there are guests, I'm up by five, down to the lodge for coffee, and there I might exchange pleasantries with an early riser at one of our dining room tables, red Formica top, chrome ringed, from the fifties, rocking slightly, so that I'll slip a folded page from my scratch pad under one of the legs, just to start the day out right.

Now I sat by myself, doodling on my scratch pad, trying to make the figures there add up to something they wouldn't. I tried not to take in too much around me.

Always, in the dining room, I am reminded of repairs. Endless repairs, electrical, mechanical, some mysterious. Why was the floor suddenly bulging in that corner? Did I smell something burning? What was that grating sound in the kitchen? Still, though, the lodge is charming. The dark log walls are festooned with photographs of trophy catches, going back to the twenties, when the lodge was built, names and dates scrawled across them. Fake moccasins, but old ones—the beading all wrong, and colors such as my mother would never have used—hang here and there. Lakeside, the ceiling rises a good twenty feet to dark oak beams, windows across the wall, a fireplace opposite, ten tables, all built to last; under them, linoleum floor, that late forties mint green, warped, but friendly.

Home, to me.

I thought that, and doodled some more. My guest was late. And so, as if nothing were wrong, I began to go about my morning.

I eat quickly, hot coffee and a roll, then, screen door creaking, clunk down to the lake. I make a circuit of our cabins along the shore, fourteen, all log on stone-and-mortar foundations. I head up by the generator, where I check the oil and radiator before we start it for the day. I never spend much time there; I don't like the smell of electricity, or the big, angry-looking diesel and generator gear, and I regard the ropy, frayed power lines as one might rattlesnakes. Left to themselves, they're harmless.

That done, I hike the west side path, a good three-quarters of a mile to the point, then loop back to the boathouse. When Bobby was alive, he'd help me with the tackle. In the boathouse I assemble first the live bait: fathead minnows, frogs, leeches, worms, and when in season, lacewings. Then artificial lures: Rapala, Hula Poppers, Mepps spinners, Nos. 01–09, daredevils, jiggers, sinkers, leaders. I sort line, different tests—eight, twelve, twenty pound—check the ferrules on the rods, repair them if necessary. In the supply shed, I heft orange-red gas tanks and greasy rubber hoses, gasoline and wood rot and water smell, and outside again, clean the boats, fifteen Lund runabouts, candy wrappers—Snickers, or Mars, or Nut Goody—underfoot and slippery.

I hate myself for loving it. Love myself for hating it. I am trapped, but free.

Home.

On the dock, my cleated boots make wooden, musical sounds, exquisite. On quiet mornings, a light mist rises off the water. There is something new about it all. Life here has just a toehold on these glacier-scarred basalt and granite islands.

Waiting, that morning, I felt some buoying hope, some certainty of things turning around. They had to. It was spring, after all. And there was the usual:

I love mornings.

I love mornings, I think, because even rain, a light rain, in a land of lichen, and basalt, and circling eagles, can be a promise. Maybe it'll clear up? Or maybe it'll stay cool and the fish will bite better for it? In gray light, bass will hit on anything that approximately looks like a frog. Or sunny days, early, one can hope for a breeze. Sounds are muted. Birds call, or maybe they chatter all day?

Mornings, though, you hear them.

The boat rigged, tackle boxes set in the bow and midships, the boat rocking underfoot, here is possibility itself. The water stretches wide and flat beyond the point, a mass of stone there, and farther out, a series of buoys, high and painted white, mark the channel.

Beyond that is a labyrinth of thousands of lakes, deep water and shallow, and just as many islands, a hundred different habitats, reaching far, far north.

A wasteland, or a frontier, depending on how one thinks of it.

To the east, the bay runs ten miles to Falcon Island, and beyond that, another twenty-five miles to the Grassy Narrows. To the west, ten miles distant, is Pine Point, population seven hundred and eighty—a farm town and border watering hole—and the government docks. The landmass there, the Northwest Angle, as it is called, abuts Manitoba and encompasses the Upper Red Lake Reservation, where I was born. The lake runs seventy miles in all, north south; fifty miles east west.

Our fourteen thousand acres lie just off shore of the reserve, yet remain in Minnesota waters, forty small islands in it. "Not fit for development" the original lease stated. Which, back then, meant not fit for timber or mining interests.

Only on a rare day do you see another boat out on the lake. The islands are still and quiet. You'd never guess nearly eight thousand members of the Big Grassy Band of Chippewa live in and around these islands. We are, for the most part, invisible, and not ones for laying concrete or clear-cutting forests.

Now, this morning, I paced the length of the dock, waiting. Bright sun cut off the water. My guest was late, very. So I was smoking.

Only if guests are late do I succumb to the temptation to smoke around the boathouse—too many flammables, and some guests don't like it. For the late ones, it is part of my ritual. Then there is the crush of gravel underfoot, the guests threading down through the pines, and taking one last tug on the cigarette, I drop it in the lake, hissing, and loose the boat.

All that follows is theater:

Women in first, and a hand down.

There is a moment when all the graciousness of the world is bestowed on my person, or the worst of bitchiness. The gracious ones I love. The others, I do my best not to let them rankle me. And the men? Men bring with them politics, money, power. Men bring with them hierarchy, accomplishment, class. I read it in their clothing, their handshakes, their voices.

I steady the boat for them, unassailably affable.

"Some place you got here."

I have heard a number of variations of that greeting, all subtly, or not so subtly, inflected to communicate the inexpressible to others in the party. But the message is usually this: Who owns it? Certainly not you. Occasionally someone is rude enough to ask,

"Where's the owner live?"

"Right on the island."

"Does he?"

"He does," I'll say then, and add, "You're looking at him." Which, I'll grant, is pretty close to the truth, as far as that goes.

In the boat, there follows an exploration of a number of habitats: lily pads and marsh for bass; rock inlets and deeper water for walleye; open lake for muskelunge; sandbars and submerged deadwood for northern. If we catch anything, I'll find a suitable island, build a fire and throw a shore lunch: bacon fat in cast-iron skillet sizzling; lots of salt, and fresh fish, breaded in cornmeal and lightly fried; Texas toast; cowboy coffee. Sometimes canned peaches or apricots or cake.

I don't eat, as to do so, sitting like that, guiding, I would balloon. Always beer, then dozing. The islands are covered with moss, soft blue-green moss. One bed of it after another.

I might pick gooseberries. Chokecherries.

Tin cup, or mess kit. Plunk, plunk, into the cup. There are black bears, lots of them, and at times not so much to pick, the bushes raked down and torn at. Then I arrange tackle, again, or if it is uncomfortably hot, stay in the shade and read. Nights, too, after dinner and an intentionally bad hand of poker, I'll retire to a corner and pick through Marcus Aurelius's *Meditations,* or a good history.

Guests are amused at my reading.

3

But not the guest I'd been waiting for—not Clark.

"Why do you waste your time on that crap?" he was saying now. He was stretched on a swatch of moss, hands folded behind his head, the picture of leisure. "It'll rot your brain. Jesus."

"Leibniz," I said, trying to interest him in it. "You ever hear of him?"

But this kind of diversion did not work with Clark, especially after the ritual of lunch was over and there was nothing to be done. (And I couldn't hide my irritation from him. I was gritting my teeth, knocking things together without meaning to.)

"Me?" Clark laughed. "I got through my bar exams and haven't opened a book since." He settled his head, pulling his cap over his eyes. It was a beautiful, cloudless May afternoon, the lake still and bright.

I was biting my fingernails. My heart galloped from cigarettes. Too much coffee. I set the book down; it was no use trying to read.

"Ah, what luxury!" Clark said.

"You can afford it." There, I thought, I'd said it.

"What do you mean?"

"Nothing."

He wriggled his toes. Black socks. Gold toe. "Really."

"Really *what?*" I said. I was thinking of the way Gwen had been looking at Clark, my old pal. Even now that I knew what it was about, it rankled me. Still, I wanted things to go on the way they were; I wanted it badly. Maybe it could work out, I could take the money, and it wouldn't ruin what was still good between us.

"You worry too much," Clark said.

"Do I?"

"Your face gets all scrunched up. All that bullshit. This... *obsession* with things."

"It comes with the territory," I said.

"All work and no play...."

"Play for you, work for me," I corrected. But there, I'd done it again. Clark did pay me for my time guiding, after all.

"Is it?" he asked.

I told him, no, said it was no use explaining. I'd taken out my gear and was putting together a black lacewing. It was slow going. My guests would lose most of the flies; the others they'd take for souvenirs. I felt ashamed, then angry. I broke one hook, then picked up another, trying to still my hands.

Clark dozed off, then snored.

I was tempted to throw something in his open mouth. A pinecone, or a fish head. Or a rock, a big one. But that was just envy, I told myself: I was barely making ends meet, while my old friend, boyish Clark, could afford to fool around. It had always been like that: Once, he'd taken up flying and bought himself a Beechcraft Bonanza (an expensive plane the older pilots in the area called "Lawyer Killers" for their unique, but untrustworthy, combination elevator/rudder) only to lose interest, luckily for Clark, before that airplane did it for him. There followed sports cars, all exotic—first English, then French, and finally Italian—none of which he kept.

It was an odd sort of reversal, our fortunes, since Clark had been so easily overrun as a boy. Our friendship had started like that.

The day I met him, I'd shot him in the side with an arrow. A few other kids and I were out screwing around; I had a cheezy fiberglass bow I'd stolen, but no arrows. So we were pulling dried nettles from the ground and notching them.

At some point we passed Sadie Debundunk's.

We'd all been disgusted with Clark, left out on Sadie's stoop like that, with a *Lil' Hot Stuff* comic book, and told to sit, while his father rooted around inside. We didn't feel sorry for Clark; we hated him.

"Hey, you," I had called.

I told him, joking, to run across ahead of us and I'd shoot at him. "Why?" he asked. That was how you got into the club, I explained. His forehead wrinkled. We could see he was deciding what to do. And just like that, Clark took off, legs akimbo, sprinting for all he was worth, stumbling, and charging, crossing that rough ground between us.

Shoot him, one of the kids with me said.

I drew the bow back. I followed him and let fly. The arrow was crooked and augered through the air, but it stuck smack dab in his side. There was a matter-of-factness to it, how noiselessly it stuck in him.

He looked at me, incredulous.

I looked back at him, the same. You couldn't hit the broad side of a barn with a nettle stalk, but here I had done it, and then some. The other kids ran. I expected Clark to start bawling.

He didn't. And so I took him home.

Remembering all that, I poked him with the toe of my boot, but he just settled in, one long swatch of white cotton and khaki on the green moss.

"Clark," I said, but he didn't answer.

We had this small matter of the liberties he'd been taking with Gwen to settle between us; I wanted to get it over and done with. But I worried there. What cost love? What cost friendship?

Clark scratched at his side, the shirt riding his waist, that star-shaped scar there.

Even now, nearly thirty years later, it amused me, the thought of it. I'd bandaged up Clark's side. He'd had a roll of fat around his middle, which, I suppose, saved him. My mother sweetened to him immediately, and like that, he became family.

All of that seemed another world now, and I ached for it, Clark sleeping there, bright light, the lake stretching, broken by islands, in all directions, blue and deep.

Lake of the Woods; or, as my people call it, *Nin'godonin'djigan,* The One Swallow Land—meaning, a place you could never take in.

This was where Clark and I had spent our childhoods:

In town, at the bowling alley, there'd been kids back of the pins, setting them by hand, chugging bottles of Sunrise Soda—grape, orange, or lime—or Pepsi. There was a big red, white, and blue dispenser against one wall of the Pine Point Alley. On the side was written: *Pepsi Cola hits the spot, Eight full ounces, that's a lot!* in the brazenly optimistic lettering of the day.

There'd been Main Street, stores with facades from the late thirties, or at the earliest, brushed aluminum, from the first few years of the fifties, the stores chock-full, hanging from the ceiling, sleds, varnished wood and steel frames, green hoses coiling like snakes, hardware in tall, sheet metal trays, oily outboards, a repair tank in back, speckled strips of flypaper, rakes of all kinds, and Indian mementos, most of it junk, but brightly colored. When it rained, the roads turned to thick brown muck. There were hunters and fishermen year-round—summer, army green rain gear; fall, red wool—but for the middle of the winter, and then things froze solid, the temperature dipping to fifty below, and that without windchill.

There were immense, fiberglass fish, painted to look scaly, erected on the roofs of the breakfast places, always just off lakes known for good angling. The cars? Battered station wagons, old Oldsmobiles, and Fords, and Pontiacs. Green, or red, or that industrial blue, dream catchers hanging from the rear-view mirrors, a daring, and some thought foolish, declaration of pride.

I always walked taller going by those cars if I was with my father, and shrank, if I was alone.

It was dangerous, to do something like that back then, because there was an undeclared war on, everywhere, barbed wire strung between trees, girdling them, bristling with resolve. *Stay Off, Private Property,* and always, the signs riddled with buck-shot, or holes in them from high-caliber rifles. The signs changed from year to year, depending on how the land changed hands. The barbed wire moved, from here, in a field of oaks, to there, a stand of deep, tall pines, and back again.

I'd tried not to get caught up in all that, the battle the Big Grassy Chippewa were waging, silently, with encroaching private interests, most of them timber and mining—I'd learned not to, from what had happened to my father, and my grandfather.

But the land!

The land rolled, and there were bluffs, buttes of solid rock. Standing on top of one, the wind blowing, you'd swear you heard voices. What they said haunted you, and so Clark and I didn't listen; but, too, we were distracted.

With Clark around, I was set free, if only temporarily; if only for an afternoon.

There was machinery, in those barbwire-girdled fields, to play on, old threshers and balers, and tractors, settling into iron red and aluminum gray humps, trees growing up through it, even as it settled.

In the lakes, the timber companies had scuttled launches, and we'd dive in them, the wrecks, and it was all mysterious. The old, heavy brass fittings, the enormous ruined engines, the glass, old coins, and now and then a bottle of booze, hidden. The timber companies had pulled out in the early twenties, no profit in islands, and then the resorts had set up, the earliest, Barney's Ball Lake Resort, in 1923.

So the woods were full of strange things: old one-lung engines, generators, thick glass insulators the most intriguing colors: cobalt, teal, sea green, red, burgundy. My mother collected them.

There were abandoned mills outside the reserve, all gutted and airy with ghosts, only swallows nesting there. There were cars in ravines and riverbeds and behind barns: Hudsons, Franklins, Packards, and once, an old Cord, one that had hit something, and at a high rate of speed.

The accordion car, we'd called it.

All of that was ours, a place of infinite horizons. In summer, hill after hill of black-eyed susans. Ladyslippers, bitter-smelling cow parsley. Sunflowers, six, eight feet high. Aster and touch-me-nots and redbud. Paths, everywhere; deer, and around swamps, moose, and bear markings, always nearby blackberries, raspberries, blueberries. The roads were sandy farther north, so much so, you could take your shoes off, and if you dug under a little, on a hot day, the sand would loam up around your ankles, cool underneath, and refreshing.

The whole sweep of the land was either crushing—in rain, or snow, or August heat—or more than inviting. It was, on some days, a paradise.

Enormous, flat-bottomed and billowy clouds sailed by overhead. Dome of brilliant blue, and below it, as far as the eye could see, island after green island, set in the bluest water, sparkling, blue-gray rock outcropping, dark forest, elms, oaks, bright-barked birch, and on high ground, in rocky soil, sharp pine, tamarack, cool underneath, and the needles there, smelling of dampness, and must, and time and quiet.

That was it. What the Big Grassy had been fighting for all those years. What the Red Lake Band of Chippewa would not give up.

Quiet. On a hillside, if you really listened, you could hear a mother calling.

Thomas Pahpasay! Thomas! The clank of a cowbell.

Then—nothing.

Wind in your ears. Warm sun on your face. A life on the lakes, fall, ricing; winter, timber and trapping; spring and summer, hunting and berrying. But even those hot summer days, high up, on the ridge of an island, or in Indian summer, you knew that soon it would be twenty below zero, there would be three feet of snow where you were standing and a starving moose, just below, would be trying to kick a hole through the ice, to get something to eat. A red-tailed hawk would circle overhead, hungry. Your nose would be chilled, then so cold you'd cover it with your mitten, or, if you had a scarf, you'd wrap it around your mouth and nose—to hell with the nasty stink it made. In the trees, distant, deer would paw at the poplar, gnawing.

That bird would circle. Did circle, something as old as time in each watchful pass.

Back then, I'd think of raising mice to put out for that hawk, but I never did, for feeling sick at the idea of killing them. Standing there, you were a mouse, wanting to be a hawk. The domain of weather seemed infinite, the lake and islands consuming, yet in every direction, a mirror.

You meet yourself in silence, my grandfather, Nita, had said. Just then, perched behind Clark, the possibility of truly losing everything—Gwen, the resort, my very life—caught my breath short.

Sitting there, my heart hammered, as if it were trying to come out my mouth.

> > ◈ < <

"Ah, my fine feathered friend," Clark said, peering up at me, sleepy-eyed. His hair was squashed flat on one side, a copper wave in arrested motion.

I was reading again, or trying to.

"What does it say in there, Einstein?"

I turned the page. "It says we're like little universes. All variations of the same thing, like a chip of crystal. You know? Says... you should be able to deduce all aspects of a substance from just one attribute, like—take that hair of yours: you'd be kinky, red, and tangled."

"Christ," Clark said. "How come you can't be a normal Indian?"

"How come you can't mind your own business?"

"What's with you today?"

"You think about it."

Clark tried to smooth his hair. I knew I'd cut him off. I wanted to say how this wasn't a good time for him to be palling around with Gwen. Or dishing out favors, or trying to get to me, either, through her.

If I'd just said it, just then, and straight out—Don't get too close to Gwen—maybe things would have turned out differently.

"Do I have to guess," Clark asked, "or are you going to tell me?"

I took the iron griddle down to the shore, Clark following. My stomach tied itself in knots. I squirted a quantity of soap into it and took up a handful of sand and began to scrub, sharp soap smell.

"All right, dammit!" Clark said. He stood behind me. "What is it *now?*"

I scrubbed in agitated circles. We'd always had these problems, when Clark had crossed some color line or didn't understand the politics of the area, but now all that had happened since Bobby died came between us, and it was impossible.

"Gwen said she liked your car," I said. "Is it new?"

"Ah!" Clark said, laughing, relieved. Not Bobby, so not so awful. "Is this a socioeconomic thing we're onto here?" He grinned. "Or is it something... *of a personal nature?*"

"You know what it's about," I said.

"You're angry because I gave Gwen a ride into town from the docks."

I worked the grime out of the pan. I could stand to lose the rest of it, but not Gwen, I thought.

"It's the old *he's got a Jaguar syndrome,*" Clark said, teasing.

I gave him a flat look over my shoulder. "Is it?"

Clark threw his hands up. "Oh, Christ! You weren't around, so we took the launch in. I gave her a ride to Fort Alexander. I bought her a tea, at that new place, and we talked about you. Every last minute. Paul this, Paul that—

"Come on, Paul," Clark said. "Do we have to do this? Who the hell do you think I am, anyway?"

He made one of those comic faces of his.

I glanced up from the pan, trying not to be amused. "I don't want you buying her things."

He made that puffing noise—a kind of snort—he'd made since he was a kid. "You make this all so hard when it doesn't have to be. She's just looking for *someone to buddy around with,* which would be you, if you weren't working all the time.

"I buy her a lousy jacket and you go ballistic."

"You call this ballistic?" I said, but something in the tone of my voice scared me.

I was angry now: the jacket wasn't just some jacket; it was an L.L. Bean that had cost five hundred dollars. Just the kind of thing I couldn't afford. Ever.

"I just want to help," he said.

"Don't," I told him. "It's more... *complicated* than you think."

I meant the problem with the resort, the money crunch, but it went for all of it.

"You mean worse."

I rinsed out the pan, our tin cups. I wanted to say *yes,* but couldn't bring myself to it.

"Why can't you just *take the damn money?*" Clark said.

"It's not that I can't. I won't." It surprised me, my saying it.

"Why?"

I was not about to explain it to him, couldn't: first, there was all that business with Bobby between us, and, too, friendship can't withstand humiliation. And anyway, it was decided now. I'd sell the boat.

"Thanks," I said, meaning it, and clapped him on the shoulder.

"Sometimes you're *fucking impossible,* you know that?" he said.

"Yes," I told him, I was aware of it.

4

Driving into Pine Point I was more than a little anxious. I'd eaten quickly at the lodge, and my stomach was uncomfortably full of spaghetti. The window open, I passed one tarpaper shack after another, immense rough and lovely pine, scruffy tamarack, the road heavy, ankle-deep sand turning loosely under my wheels, warm yellow lights in doorways, here and there someone reclining, chair tipped back, cherry glow of cigarette in the oncoming dark, a "Booshoo, Pauly Boy!" and I'd wave in return.

There was the warm complicated smell of wet earth. That sweet smell of maple syrup. Spring, it was that time of year for it. People were boiling down sap, galvanized tubs in yards on slow-burning coals.

It was all so familiar, yet, now, each thing jabbed, a sharp reminder of what I had already lost.

Here was old Henry Selkirk, and Thelma Eagle. Gray hair in braids, big smiles. "Hiya!" I shouted. I swung clear of old Thomas Kettle, marching alongside the road, heavy around the middle, braids, hand held over his head in greeting. As I passed, he recognized my truck, and the wave became a raised middle finger. I honked. Shouted out the window,

"*Booshoo, Ninamuch.*" Hi, Darling!

But I was underwater again. Something comes over my head, like a hood, this impenetrable something between me and the world, almost like thick glass. Back then, part of it was shame, for having cut myself off from that life (some said, after coming back from out east I thought I was too good for it, which wasn't true); part of it came out of fear, for having refused help from the Tribal Council Office, and from the local arm of the Bureau of Indian Affairs.

And why shouldn't I have refused their help? The Tribal Office had held up the sale of the lodge for eight years; and the BIA had made their help contingent on "interior improvements."

Still, my refusal had amounted to something like a slap in the face of both.

All I'd wanted was to be free, and not beholden to anyone. But what I'd done was cut myself off, and got caught in the middle.

I gunned the truck up a steep slope, then wound through a stand of birch, the last rays of sun cutting through, a brief kaleidoscope of light. I needed to get my boat, I told myself, just that.

The boat was an old Chris Craft runabout that needed a new engine, hull work, and a few other repairs. I'd dreamed about that boat. A lot. And so it hurt me to think of selling it. I just needed a little cash to make it happen: motor burbling, cutting smart and stylish across Pawaganak Bay. The hull glossy, polished mahogany. Red leather seats. That low, sporty windshield. Shiny brass controls and fittings. It had been built in '56, a year that seemed fat, and happy, in my imagination.

I loved that boat, too, because it had belonged to Dr. Piper, who'd been kind to me when I'd been at my worst, and who'd arranged for me to go to that school out east.

That boat represented a kind of providence then. A kind of godsend.

And now I was going to sell it. I had to.

That's what I was thinking, turning up that last stretch of road, there, in my yard, a couple ruined refrigerators, startling phosphorus white; an old, faded blue Ford sedan, no doors or hood, the windows broken out; what looked like a furnace, the heating ducts coming out the top like arms on an octopus; a tangle of ruined bicycles to one side of the garage, which was shedding paint.

The house looked no better. Tarpaper and a bent tin chimney, the stoop settling to one side, as if it had just gotten tired of it all.

I pulled up the drive.

"Hey, Pauly," my old man said, giving me a mock salute from the stoop. My father had served in the Big War, and never let me forget it.

I peered through the windshield and got an awful sinking feeling. I couldn't see my boat anywhere, not in the front yard, not in the back, not in the pines where I'd had it wrapped in canvas, thinking no one would notice it there. I was out of the truck and crossing the yard.

"Where's my boat?" I said.

"This isn't a friendly call?"

A ruckus was going on inside. Singing, what sounded like nightclub music, which I recognized as Sinatra, *Songs for Swingin' Lovers,* an album my father had played overmuch after he'd come back from his re-up in Korea, all those years ago.

There was a woman's startled shriek, my sister's. I rushed by my father, and inside, a burned smell, something on the stove, holes in my newly Sheetrocked walls, my sister holding her hand to the bridge of her nose.

"He threw that at me!" Larissa said, pointing. Tall, lanky Larissa. An LP lay at her feet.

Her boyfriend, Gerry, moon-faced, in red plaid, held his hands out, an album cover in the left. "I did not. I just waved it and it flew out and—"

"Just... *shut up,*" I said.

Larissa was crying. No one listened to her, she bawled; the house was impossible. Wasn't she always cleaning it? *And just look at it!*

All those things my mother had so labored over in order to make a home of it, the stenciled floral patterns along the walls, the hardwood floors burnished to a sheen, leaded glass, in the windows, some the deepest cobalt blue, now gathered dust or were coming undone.

I'd inherited the house from my mother, and let it go to my father and sister.

I put my arm around Larissa. I was trying not to get angry. Or too sad. I felt confused, and a little sick, and wanted to leave. The house did that to me.

"Hey, are you all right?" I asked. "Is it okay here?"

"It came out of the jacket," Gerry whined.

"I'm all right," Larissa said.

I snatched the album cover from Gerry, tossed it on the sofa. "So where is it, Gerald?"

"Where's what?"

"My boat."

Larissa looked between the two of us. "Isn't it back there in the trees?"

My father came through the front door. I caught his arm as he went by.

"Where's the boat?"

"It isn't here."

"Brilliant," I said. I was trying not to lose my temper. "So where is it then?"

"Al Eagle came and got it, a few weeks ago," Gerry said. "It's over at the Rambler's."

My father grinned. "I sold it to him."

"No, you didn't," Gerry said. He was pacing, his big shoulders rucked down, as if ashamed. "Al came over in a panic and took it. Said you'd told him to."

"*I* told him to do that? He said that?"

"That's what he told me. All I know is he came and took it," Gerry said, "who knows what happened to it after that."

I said, "Now wait a minute."

I'd gotten that thick feeling in my face. I was a little afraid of myself. Years earlier, I'd been one for violence, and I was at the edge of it now.

"Al did that?"

"Something's burning on the stove," my father said. "Can't you smell it?"

"You're not helpless," Larissa said. "Get it yourself."

I tried to turn them back to the boat, but the three of them were arguing again. Another LP dropped on the turntable. More strings, then the Crooner Himself taking up. There was this awful feeling of being outside something much larger than a missing boat.

I would talk to Al, that was the answer. And thinking it, I turned to Larissa, my baby sister.

"Don't stay here, Larissa," I said.

She set her hands on her hips, her face twisted into an angry grimace. "So, just where am I going to go?"

"I'll take you to the resort. We can work something out."

She knew as well as I did that I couldn't take on more help. I was operating on a skeleton crew already.

She looked at me, then Gerald, then my father.

"Go away, Paul," she said.

5

I drove around back of the Rambler's to see if the boat was there—it wasn't—then, gritting my teeth, spun around front and parked. I'd forgotten it was Friday, and there was a crowd and a half, wild hair, dinner-plate-sized rodeo belt buckles, ragged denim, spilling out into the lot, some of them dancing, fooling around happily enough.

I waited; Al would come out for a cigarette sooner or later. I tried out a few things to say to him, watched people come and go.

I worried about Gwen. It was getting late, and I knew I should call the lodge.

In the dark now, the Rambler's shone like some kind of shrine. An amalgam of things, part bar, on the north end, roller-skating rink on the south, and between them, a grocery, lit in blue white fluorescent bulbs, here was the heart of Pine Point.

Al's place: the Rambler's.

There was something ramshackle, falling-down about it, but vital.

It was ours now, where, years back, a sign had hung over the front door—NO INDIANS OR DOGS. We'd had to sit on the stoop, or the hoods of our cars, which a lot of people still did as they filled the lot nights.

A star, made out of a jumble of bicycle frames and lights, left over from Christmas ages ago, blinked on and off on the roof, inviting. Strings of colored lights, blue and green and red flashed along the gutters, too, from one end to the other. Signs—*Pa st, ohs, G ain Belt*—flickered in the windows.

The sound of skates, on hardwood, rose distorted, but cheerful, through the south windows.

I lit a cigarette.

Someone came up from behind, long-armed shadow cast on the dirt road, yards off to the side of the truck. I reached for the lug wrench under the seat. There was a smoky, floral smell, perfume of a heavy sort.

"Haven't seen you around here in ages," Gilby said, setting her slender arms on the door.

"Oh, it's you."

"Gee, that's nice." Gilby pinched the white cotton of her halter, pumped the fabric there, her breasts full and heavy. Dark and swoopy-eyed, she was beautiful, but tired-looking. "You know, somebody says he loves you, and later, you expect more than 'Oh, it's you.'"

I told her I didn't mean anything by it.

She said she'd gotten that.

And so it went. Years back, in that dark and pathetic part of my past, I'd dated Gilby, and we'd even lived together for a time. Since then we'd run into each other like this; always something more than friendly, yet melancholy in it. (And, too, there had been that week after Bobby's death, when Gwen wouldn't speak to me, and Clark had gone back down to the Cities, when I'd fallen into Gilby's arms; and she'd saved my life.)

"I'm looking for Al," I said.

I thought to start the car and drive away. Gilby touched my hair.

"Gilby, don't," I said.

The door of the Rambler's swung open, thumping of bass, some twanging Western thing, hump of bodies, a light on behind the bar, someone pouring drinks back of it, but not Al.

"So how's business?" Gilby asked.

She meant Gwen. That insane week, I'd told Gilby I wanted to marry her, that the resort thing was over, that it was over with Gwen. It had all been crazy-talking.

"Fine," I said.

A truck pulled into the lot, a few Strongholds out for a night of it. Terry and Simon and George. They went inside, and then it was quiet, but for the incessant hollow whoosh of skates, the occasional high-pitched child's laugh, and the incessant tangle of music, bubblegum from the skating rink, CW from the bar.

I put my hand over Gilby's. All that hardness in her face went away.

"Is Al coming in tonight?"

"He's up north," Gilby said.

"Where?"

She pushed her hands into her pockets. She had a lovely figure. I tried not to notice.

"I don't know."

A shout came from the front door of the Rambler's. Gilby craned her head around. George swung his arm up, a hook. He'd just gotten out of Stillwater and everyone was waiting to see how he'd take to life in Pine Point.

"Go on back in," Gilby shouted, and he did.

I hoped she wasn't with him, but knew from the look of it she was. (Once, all those years ago, when Gilby and I were just lying together, side by side, I asked her who her ideal lover would be. She squeezed me, that was her answer. No, really, I'd said. And when she told me "—a man who is boss, you know? Can take charge?" and smiling, added, "and I want to belong to him," I told her she had the wrong man, and she said, no, she hadn't. I was twenty-two then, Gilby seventeen.)

"Come on, Gilby."

I pulled her down and kissed her, alongside her mouth. My heart was in my throat.

"That wasn't a kiss," Gilby said.

"What was it, then?"

"A peck. I hate pecking."

George, blue plaid and thick-soled work boots, lurched out the door of the Rambler's.

"Is that that double-crossing Paul Two Persons?" he shouted, joking.

"You'd better go," Gilby said, and in that way of hers, looking right through me as if she'd never known me at all, strode from the car.

It hurt; which always surprised me.

She caught George's arm, aimed him back at the Rambler's.

"Try Kennebeck Lake," she called over her shoulder. "He should be up there."

I was trying not to drive too fast. The road was narrow and winding, bordered by tall pines. I rolled down my window and put my head out. Later, I told myself, I would remember this rotten night as just another snag in the fabric of May. I'd find the boat, work something out with Al, and that would be that. The truck lurched, another pothole, and I slowed.

I slumped in the seat. I was being silly, I told myself. What was there to worry about?

I smiled into the rearview mirror, to assure myself. I saw Trickster in my face, nervous, pock-jawed Hare, and laughed. That I was even thinking of old backwards/forwards was not a good sign: he was around just waiting to trip me up, and at the worst moment, whether I believed in him or not.

I told myself I didn't.

The road curved sharply to the right, gravel now, a long, loose stretch of it, then narrowing. I drove into a parking lot overlooking the lake, a dumpster with the top hanging down, off to the right, a sign: *Kennebeck Lake Community Center.* I parked the car and went down to what was once a campsite. A whip-poorwill called off in the woods. The gloaming was on the place, a going into deep, deep dark.

"Al?"

I lit a cigarette, my hands shaking. It had rained earlier, and there were fresh tire tracks all over. One set, mismatched truck tires, the other narrower. A compact car, or a trailer. I wanted to think, boat trailer. I followed the tracks down to the rushes bordering the lake, where they ended in water.

A boot, Vibram sole with the yellow rectangle in the center, lay off in the weeds, waist-high nettles and foxglove. I carried the boot up to the truck and threw it in the bed, clonging.

"Al?!" I shouted, my voice echoing across the lake. "Al?!"

6

On the lodge porch, three men from St. Louis were playing poker. They asked me to join them, and I declined. Opposite, back of the big screened-in windows, it was dark and cool and quiet.

Mardine, our cook, brought me a note. Clark wandered in, pulled up a chair, and sat.

"You got that serious look on your face again," he said.

I put the note in my pocket. I did not tell him about the Ostermans. A party of twelve. They'd reserved a six-day fly-in, to fish char, lake trout, and grayling. Now they weren't coming. At $1,795.00 a head, even my selling the Chris Craft wouldn't have covered it.

"What?" Clark asked.

"Just more of the same," I said, and saying it, tried to believe it.

> > ◇ < <

Mardine brought out candles and the porch took on a flickering warmth. A woman who'd flown up with her husband that afternoon sat in Clark's seat. She patted the cushion.

"Warm."

"Yes," I said.

She asked if I came from nearby. Had my family always been in the area? I told her pretty much so, and she said, How much so?

I lit a cigarette, squinting against the light, and a little meanly, launched into a ten-generation saga of trappers, French and English, hardy natives, superstition, and even my family's lineage, that being connected to Chief Hole-in-the-Day. It was all a lie, and I felt disgusted with myself, telling it. I concocted it all as I went along, making up dates, places, events—some violent now, shootings and whatnot—testing her.

I wanted to hurt her, but why?

All that with those guests years back, the liberties those women had taken, because I was *that kind* of person, came back to me in a rush.

I glanced at Janice's hands: tapered, sensitive fingers, polished nails. (I thought of Gwen, and the meanness in me became grief. We hadn't so much as touched one another, that way, since the fall.)

But I was being ridiculous.

It was possible my father was related to Crazy Horse, I told her, thinking to put an end to it. I had to.

"Is that so," she said. She reached for my pack of cigarettes and lit one.

I felt my face heat. I thought to say, I'm joking. We're not even the same tribe, Crazy Horse's people and mine. Nor had my family come from those noble strains I'd implied: Pillagers, or Morrisons, or even Babcocks—all well-known and revered Chippewa.

We were *Giwadiswin,* wanderers.

It was all so—*pathetic* right then. The whole stupid thing.

"I'm sorry," I said, standing and shaking her slender hand. "It's half past twelve and I've got to be up early. You are—"

"Janice," she said.

"Janice, are you in the party? Tomorrow morning?"

She did not let go of my hand; I pulled ever so slightly on it, to be free.

"I think so," she said.

I trudged down the path to the cabin. The light was on in the bedroom. I carefully opened the screen door. Gwen was propped up in bed reading, a thick strand of her glossy black hair knotted around her finger. She always looked lovely in blue, and she'd been swimming now, every day, rain or shine, and she'd gotten walnut brown.

"Hey there, beautiful," I said. I meant it.

(I thought all kinds of crazy things: in a look, saw myself kneeling beside the bed. Can you forgive me? Can we just stop all this? Do you know I love you? That every rotten bit of this is for you?

I was afraid, sick with worry. I wanted to explain things. The whole place is coming apart, I wanted to say. *That's* why I've been away.)

She pointed to the kitchen. I went in and ate; chicken and pie and cold coffee.

"Where were you?" Gwen asked. I'd come out with my plate.

"At the lodge."

"I know that," she said, making another coil of her hair. "I mean earlier."

"Pine Point."

"I thought you hated Pine Point."

That amused me. Hated wasn't the half of it.

"Somebody up here said she'd seen you," Gwen said.

I sipped at my cold coffee. Not now, I thought. I didn't want Gilby's name to come up. Gwen would never understand. I'd promised never to so much as speak to Gilby again, much less be off in the dark with her.

"Who was it?" I asked.

"One of the guests. That woman, Janice. She was 'taking in some local color,' she said, with her husband, Len. At the Rambler's.

"He seemed to know the place."

"Did he?" I asked. "I was trying to run into Al."

"Does Al owe you money again?"

I laughed, my heart kicking up. "When doesn't he?" I said. "That stinking crook. His business would be in the toilet if it weren't for me."

"How much?"

"Not much," I lied.

I undressed and got into bed. "Drove all the way to Kennebeck Lake, looking for him. Said he'd be there—"

"Who said?"

"Somebody at the Rambler's—you know that crowd."

"You should have called."

She was tugging at that strand of her hair she'd knotted. She carefully wound it about her index finger, her mouth pursed in concentration. She glanced up; Gwen has that lovely, Irish face, hatchet blades for cheekbones, freckles and those ice-blue eyes.

"Why are you doing this to me?"

"Doing what?"

"Testing me."

"Am I?"

"You know you are. I was—afraid something had happened to you. I wish you'd stop it."

She put her arms around me, her chin on my shoulder. I felt something warm and hard at the back of my throat. My eyes glassed up.

"Do you remember that first spring, I mean when we came up here?" she asked.

I told her I did.

"It was so quiet and it snowed, and we swam anyway, and after we were so cold and curled up right here?"

"Yes," I said.

"It was so easy then."

I reached for the switch on the lamp. The room was dark and quiet.

"Paul?"

I told her I was listening.

"Can it be like that again?" she said. "A little, even?"

I pulled her arm around my middle, said, "Yes, yes I think so," her breasts soft and warm against my back, rose scent in her hair.

And like that, for the first time in months, I fell soundly asleep.

Early the following morning, our parties ambled down from the lodge full-bellied and sleepy. I hopped into my boat, arranging cushions and whatnot. Hugh, my summer help—usually I would have four kids up but could afford only one now—got the engine in his boat started, oily burble of blue exhaust.

Janice, light on her feet, wove around the last of the birch trees on shore, her husband, this *Len,* broad shouldered and balding, directing her. He seemed to know the paths; I wondered how.

"Len Barthelowe," he said, dockside.

He passed Janice down—there was something duplicitous in it all, his overfriendly handshake, Janice's bright smile—then stood over us on the dock, hands on his hips, hunky gold watch, polished white shoes with tassels, well-creased pants.

"You coming?" I asked him.

"Jan wanted to go out by herself for once," Len said, shielding his eyes with his hand, his eyes dark pockets. "That okay?"

He was giving me a hard once-over, as if he'd seen me at a distance, and now, close up, was getting a new take on things. I didn't like him.

Still, I could only be cheerful.

"Whatever," I replied.

>> ◇ <<

No place was right. Now and again Janice checked her watch. She touched up her hair, and, at one point, while my back was turned, did her face. I heard the metallic snap of her compact. She'd make pretenses of fishing. Then, after getting her bearings, we'd be off again.

"Stop," she'd say.

I'd bring the boat around, the engine humming and rattling. Sun, low and bright in the water, jays calling from pines some distance away.

"No, not here."

It was warm, and she'd taken off her jacket. She rolled up her sleeves, thin, expensive watch and gold bracelets. Those slender hands.

"What time do you have?" she asked.

"A little after one," I told her.

She seemed not to be enjoying herself, was waiting for something. We were off again, now Janice pointing from the bow. I worried we'd have enough gas.

I wanted to get back in early, take another shot at finding Al at the Rambler's.

"There," she said, finally. "That island there."

I tied up, then put a shore lunch together. While I built a fire Janice told me stories about Len's business in Chicago, some kind of brokerage company. I remember thinking her stories held about as much water as mine had the evening earlier.

"He isn't in insurance, then?"

I'd worried he was with my insurance company; that would have explained those looks he was giving me at the dock. I'd lied about so many things to get coverage: the old wiring; the hail-damaged roofs of the cabins and lodge; the swimming area, not roped off, and certainly not supervised, and no tower for a guard.

(Gwen, swimming laps, every morning, across the bay and back.)

"No," she said.

There was the sound of an outboard. I tried not to look surprised, but I was. A woman in a denim shirt, her red hair in a bright knot at the back of her neck, skimmed around the island and docked.

An expensive, candy-apple-red boat.

Janice skipped down to the lake. The two women pecked each other's cheeks, gave touching little presses. All of it for me.

"Do you mind?" Janice shouted.

I waved them off.

>> ◇ <<

I rigged up a Hoola Popper and worked the lily pads off shore.

Cock the wrist, give a space of line, not more than a foot or so, and snap the bait out. I covered the shady areas to the east, then west, jigging the popper so its legs kicked.

A bass struck, explosion of water and tail thrashing, the fish, gaping, creamy-bellied and brilliant green, coming down big and heavy with a flat wet slap, my heart in my throat, the fish diving. I had the rod canted off to my right, then was working him, working him away from the rocks, this big old fish. He went down, and down, all weight and longing to live, and my line, I saw it, stretching.

That fish circled something on the bottom, and my line, singing, broke.

I stood there, thrilled.

Upshore, that red boat docked. Janice very nearly jumped out of it, but awkwardly, stumbling, the other woman making some gesture, an appeal. There was a whole world in that moment, the fish, Janice, the late-afternoon sun, the flat, gray water, a kind of final stillness.

Then the boat was gone, and Janice, gathering herself, smoothing down her hair and rolling up her sleeves, came up the path.

"You're late," I said.

"Am I?"

I thought of her husband, in the lodge, trying to eat dinner. What would he make of it? Would he sense it? And, too, it was as if loss had attached itself to me, again. It was nothing to me, this woman's trouble, I told myself.

"Do you have a cigarette?" she asked. "I'm a little shaky."

I offered her one.

I smoked, too, first in agitation, but for me that never lasts, and then there is the sadness. She didn't have to tell me what it was about.

"Well?" I said.

"Seems awfully bright out, doesn't it?"

"Yes," I told her.

Now it didn't matter that she had money and I didn't, that she'd graduated Vassar summa cum laude, or whatever. It didn't matter that she had a swank home in Minneapolis, or that she probably had chatty teas with friends on Fiftieth and France, at those fancy boutiques, ribbons and bows and cheerful hearts and Holly Hobby dolls. Or that her husband, of thick wrists and white bucks, was after something.

She cried a little. There was nothing I could say.

She wiped at her eyes. "All right," she said, a note of resignation in it. She squared her shoulders, then smiled a ten-thousand-dollar smile.

She looked like an aged model, which I'm sure was exactly right. She had the bones. It was a frightening transformation, as if she'd put a mask on, and only for a second there, getting into the boat, when her shoelace caught on a seat stay, and tripped her, did she curse, and let go a bit, sob, a deep-down choking.

>> ◇ <<

At dinner, Clark was in good spirits. He was overdressed, striped Oxford button-down and jacket, twill pants. There was an enthusiastic flush in his face, that overeagerness he was prone to.

"I've got an idea," he said, setting his elbows on the table.

"What?" I said.

I could hear Janice talking behind me. While Clark went on, outlining some way to give me the money, I pitched my ears back. "—that wasn't it at all, Len," Janice said, "really, you'll see. I'll be nice." I imagined, at that point, she took his hand in hers. "—make up for it, really I will. We'll stay up late, to make up for my being late. And I'll be nice to you."

All of that sank deep in me, their awful little drama, which was all too close now.

"You're not listening again," Clark said. "We're talking money here."

"Stop reminding me," I replied.

I sat glumly there for a second, wanting to put my head on the table. It seemed I was always being handed things I needed but couldn't use. I smiled, for Clark. The old owner, Frank, had taught me the ropes. Remember, he'd told me, what you've got here is a Theme Park. You're the happy native. Life is good and easy on the island. Got it? They talk politics, you talk trophy catches.

"I've got it under control," I said.

We both rocked back in our chairs, laughing. I lit a cigarette.

"Your eyelid is twitching, old Paul," Clark said, punching me in the shoulder.

"Is it really?" I said.

"Like a window shade."

"What did Gwen say to you?" I asked.

"The appliances are falling apart."

I shrugged.

"Well, are they?"

I felt caught in it. I could say no, but it would be an obvious lie. The place was going to hell around us, and all you had to do was look. Or I could say, yes, and he'd ask why I didn't do anything about it. Behind us, Janice was still talking, in that persistent, apologetic voice.

I wanted a drink. "Go away," I said.

"I won't until you give in."

"Really—"

That he'd known me as long as he had, and used those words, *give in,* surprised me. He'd almost had me. I was happy to be in the dining room. As long as there were others around us, things couldn't get too bad. The look Len was giving Janice now gave me the willies, and I shut out their voices, or tried to.

Mardine poured coffee. She chatted us up, Twins this and that, winked over Kirby Puckett's batting average, frowned at the weather, too hot. It was something she did when guests cornered me, which Clark had.

"Just drop it, Clark," I said when she'd gone.

"Gwen is right."

"About what?"

"You can't tell your friends from a fucking hole in the wall."

"Stop," I told him.

But he didn't, and I stood, pushing my chair in. I had things to do, I told him. Things that couldn't wait. Like what? And when I couldn't say exactly, I let him come along, knowing I shouldn't have, too tired to resist any more.

7

"Just like old times," Clark was saying, belly to the bar in the Rambler's.

I shook my head, taking it in. It looked like old times, all right. Maybe it was just a mood I was in; God knows, I got them.

I sat, listening, nursing a 7Up, trying to be virtuous. It was difficult, the taps to my right; behind the bar Absolut Citron, Seagram's, with a gold crown; off to the left, cheap Arrow Liqueurs and brandy. I spun around on my stool. There were Christmas decorations on the walls. Tinsel. Colored glass bulbs. An enormous, life-sized illuminated Santa standing in the corner. Near the ceiling was a pen, a good six feet long, a sign in bold letters under it: *If you can sign your check with this pen, we'll take it.* That had been my idea. A joke, but Al had gone and done it. He was always taking bad checks and then expecting me to bail him out.

I bought Clark another beer.

The place was packed, shoulder to shoulder, and we were jostled from behind.

Then Clark was telling me about some tangle with his law practice. He got one of those *I've-got-a-friend-who's-got-this-*

embarrassing-problem looks on his face, so I listened. He'd gotten stuck with an especially nasty divorce case, he said. The particulars were awful. This woman got around, but wanted to take everything if the client booted her out. I wanted to say, Your client isn't a lawyer, is he? but instead, told Clark,

"Enough."

We tried not to look at each other. But then Clark laughed, was telling me about this client who'd tried to trim a hedge by lifting a lawn mower level to it and had been rewarded with the amputation of most of the fingers on his left hand. He was suing Toro, the lawn mower company, for two and a half million dollars.

"Great," I said, not altogether amused.

The juke played Johnny Cash while Moses Debundunk, slope shouldered and barrel chested, cleaned glasses behind the bar with a towel. On the tube, back of Moses, the Twins were sinking themselves further in the American League. The door whomped open behind us, and I smelled lilacs.

"*Hey—*" a voice whispered in my ear, and then Gilby sat between Clark and myself. "I didn't think I'd see you in here again."

Christ, I thought—just what I didn't need. I let my head drop back. The ceiling was a carpet of dollar bills—slogans on them: *One for the old Gipper!* the nearest read—from the front door to the pool table in the rear. Money, just what I didn't want to think about.

One dollar bought one lottery ticket. Every couple months, on a slow night, Al put the tickets in a barrel, and when things heated up, pulled a winner, who played host for the night, had the dubious honor of tearing the bills from the ceiling to pay for drinks. That had been Al's idea, to give the winner something to do, something not quite nice, so there wouldn't be any resentment. See? he'd said. I'd just smiled.

But where was Al?

"Aren't you going to introduce me?" Gilby said, something lovely but cruel in her mouth.

"Clark, Gilby; Gilby, Clark," I said.

Now Gilby did not seem so wounded. No, in fact she seemed positively nasty. I broke out in a sweat. She knew things about me, things I didn't want Clark to know. He'd been away those years Gilby and I had tangled, and so had never met her.

"Gilby," I said.

"Yes?"

Only now she'd turned her back, was talking to Clark, tawny skin and those bumps in her spine. Her hands flew over her head, birds.

"You didn't tell me that, you old dog!" Clark said, craning his head around Gilby and slugging me in the shoulder.

"What?"

"Have a beer," Clark said, triumphant, and slid one down the bar. "Why don't you tell us these things?"

"What?" I said.

Gilby threw me a crooked smile. "I was telling him how you signed the deed for Frank's place, for the lodge, last fall."

I'd signed the deed the day after Bobby died. I'd just been going through the motions, was near comatose with grief. So I had told no one. Except Gwen, of course, and Gilby. Still, given the way the council worked—even though it was headquartered in Cass Lake, far south of the Northwest Angle—I'd assumed it'd gotten around.

"Don't listen to her," I said. "It's all bullshit. I just manage the place."

Gilby made a fanning motion. She'd done her hair in a thick braid, bound a strand of red cloth in it. It was beautiful, thick hair. She set a proprietary hand on Clark's forearm.

"Right," she said.

"*Gilby—*"

"Ask Moses," she said.

"I'll ask him something," I said. "Where's Al?"

Moses shrugged; he tossed that towel over his shoulder. "You know how he just disappears. Probably down in St. Paul."

"What makes you think that?"

"Him," Moses said, motioning with the towel. "Over there. He said so."

Len was seated in a corner, back of the pinball machines, talking to George. I hadn't seen him because the shuffleboard had been in the way. The skin at the back of my neck prickled.

"Hey," Clark said. He thrust two fingers in the air, a V, for victory, joking. "You got it!"

My stomach turned at that; my winning the resort didn't seem such a victory now. Maybe, I thought, my having tried to do it was the very thing that had started all that had gone wrong.

Moses poured drinks. His braids got in the way, and he tossed them over one shoulder. Gilby was all over Clark, her hand on his knee, laughing. She threw me a teasing glance. The bar got darker, so dark you could barely see, the music louder. She glanced back at me over her shoulder now and then, deciding something.

"So what did he say?" I said, nearly shouting, to Moses.

"About what?"

I was trying not to get angry. "That made you think Al was in the Twin Cities?"

"Oh, that," Moses said. "Len said Al'd get more for his boat down there."

"A Chris Craft."

"Yeah, it was a real beauty."

"So, Moses," I said, giving him a sober look, "you got something going with this... *Len?* You pals now or—"

Moses jammed a glass down so hard it broke.

"Get off it, Paul," he said. "He's just another asshole to me."

Clark went back to the Men's.

"Enjoying yourself?" Gilby asked, spinning around on her stool. Dimpled knees, those dark, dark eyes. But sad, I could see that.

"Don't mess Clark up," I said. "Okay?"

A fat guy and his equally fat wife were jitterbugging in a corner. They weren't half bad. Gilby bent closer, whispered in my ear.

"Do you still love me?"

I kept my eyes on the pen and sign over the bar. What could I say?

I glanced up from the pen, into the mirror, there in a sickening, tilted perspective, George and Len huddled over beers. Red plaid and work boots; expensive bomber jacket and tie, respectively. They had the look of conspirators.

I must have blinked at it, seeing them together.

"No?" Gilby said. "Don't you have anything to say? You had so much to say before. But now you don't say anything."

She reached into her purse, poked at her mouth, that voluble, ripe mouth, the lipstick so dark it was almost black. Checked it in the tiny mirror, pressed her lips together.

"Hey, it doesn't matter," she said.

At that moment, fresh from the head and whistling to himself, came Clark, threading through the crowd. He grinned a self-satisfied grin and put out his elbow, and Gilby took it. Snatching up her purse, she gave me a peck on the cheek. In my ear, she whispered,

"They mean to hurt you," then went out the door.

I froze there on my stool. Suddenly, I was getting ten hostile looks from ten directions.

I was talking to a dentist from St. Paul. I'd broken out in a cold sweat, kicked nervously at my chair. There was a packed-in, tight feeling, and I couldn't get out. I didn't want to push by George, who was standing with his back to the front door. I faked opening my mouth wide, as if drunken. With a pickle the dentist mimicked drilling. *Rrrrr, rrrrr.* I threw my arms and legs out, this way and that. The dentist's pal laughed behind him. The whole bar laughed. Even Len in the corner.

"What about that wild rice?" Moses said. (We'd been battling off-reserve production for thirty years.)

"What about it," I said.

"They're harvesting wild rice in California, you want to buy in?"

"No," I said. Did he want me to put my fist through his teeth?

Just then, Parker Keewatin, whose loan from the Tribal Office I'd refused, and Truman Wheeler, his old pal, short, and rough looking, pushed in through the front door, past George. To my right, they clowned it up, big as circus bears.

"Hey, Pardner," Parker said, slapping me on the back. "How's our college boy. Went to...what school was that out east?"

Truman, the friend, named the school.

"He's the real thing," Parker said. "The Gen-u-ine article!"

The jukebox mercilessly quit. The ball game was on the tube, ninth inning. Someone broke a rack on the table. We all knew each other in there. People were messing around, but listening, waiting for something to happen. George, hunkering over the pool table, was twisting a cue in his hands. I'd turned down a fair number of them for summer work and there'd been bad feelings. Very bad feelings.

The change in mood was palpable. A smell even, a hot, animal sweat.

"Hey," Parker said, grinning: capped teeth, toilet-porcelain white, tribal money. "Hey, hotshot," he joked, "how about buying the bar a round?"

There was a fit of applause. Laughter. Parker, his eyes glassy with fun, whooped.

"Come on," he said. "You're a rich man. A big tycoon. How else could you buy up half the north shore there, huh? What's a few beers? It's all in the family, right? Hey," he said, poking my shoulder hard enough that I slipped off my stool.

"Hey, whaddaya say, *Paul*?"

There was an ad on the tube for shampoo, a model making not so subtle overtures there, puckering her mouth. I kept my eyes on it. I was shaking something awful. I grit my teeth. Years back, I'd gotten a reputation for having a very short fuse. I'd deserved it.

My father, who'd come in when I wasn't paying attention, gave me a harsh look from down at the end of the bar, one I couldn't quite read, but I took to mean—don't. But *don't* what?

"All right," I said, quietly.

I rifled through my wallet. I wondered how Parker had set it up. After all, bad feelings between our families went way back. Or had it been Moses, just messing with me? I wondered if Gilby had helped. Or was it Len? Who had his back turned but was watching me in the mirror now, not so much as a hint of amusement on his face.

"Chump change," I said, and laid my last bills on the bar.

Hundreds, both of them.

When Moses closed, I went out with the dentist and his buddy, and we were good friends, all the way to the government docks, and north to Moose Lake, and the lodge, where I dropped them off.

8

Gwen was up when I returned, reading on the lodge porch. I came down the path, the gravel crunching under my feet. She'd wrapped her hair in a towel, a high cone of turquoise over her head, swung slowly on the love seat, the rope creaking dryly.

"Why the hat?" I said.

"I was swimming," she told me. She swung forward, caught herself with her heels, let go again.

"In the dark?"

"Yes, it does get dark at night, doesn't it."

I didn't know what to say. I felt sick at the thought of it.

"Please don't do that," I said. "Not at night."

"Why?"

"Because." I was thinking about what had just happened at the Rambler's. There'd been something in the making there, something I just couldn't figure.

"And what about you?"

I lit a cigarette. "Me?"

"I thought you were going to call," Gwen said, "this *next time.*"

"I did, too," I told her.

Gwen switched off the light. Spots of blue swam in the dark. The rope creaked.

"Clark called."

"Did he?"

"Yes." She yawned, caught herself again, swung back. It was not boredom, but exhaustion. "He seemed to think someone was going to try to... '*hurt you,*' was how he put it. He was pretty upset.

"So I went swimming."

I didn't want to get into it. Gwen did things like that. Once she'd joined the American Arbour Society, and had planted thousands of trees, Scottish pine, red pine, blue spruce, all sent to her as seedlings, in heavy cardboard boxes. I'd helped, a regular Johnny Appleseed. Even when it had snowed, that late May, we'd been out planting. Gwen had gotten sick. She was always overextending herself like that. Ricing in the fall, just to help out; in spring, berrying, with Mardine, for the Our Lady's benefit breakfasts; fall, in Red Lake, going door to door with old Alex Pukwan, with hot meals for the elderly.

And now this—she'd been swimming mornings all year, but never after dark.

"Where is he?"

She let out a sigh. "Oh, I don't know. I think he went to look for you."

"He'll be all right."

"You're going to just leave him out there? Is that what you're going to do? Drunk and out of his mind like that?"

The moment stretched unbearably. All I wanted to do now was keep things on the level. I got up slowly. I didn't want to go out.

"Paul," she said, setting her elbows on the arms of the chair.

"What?"

The moon had risen over the lake and her eyes shone in it. Big, glassy, porcelain blue. I'd kill for those eyes, is what I thought.

"I can't take much more of this," she said.

I had a lump in my throat, big as an apple.

"I know," I said.

> > ◇ < <

I circled the Rambler's. Then went down along the government docks. Pea-green fifty-gallon drums of fuel oil, silver cylinders of propane, battered boats, wood and fiberglass and aluminum, old and new, bumping against the docks, slap of water.

Clark was nowhere in it.

So I was off again, driving faster now. The moon hung quicksilver heavy on the horizon, tore through the treetops, flashing. Here would be yet another failing, not having looked out for Clark.

Murders are a dime a dozen up at Red Lake. Suicides are just as common.

Either can be made to look like an accident.

I was imagining the worst. A knifing, or a drowning, a car wreck. At the wheel I told myself I was being ridiculous. Yet, here was the moon, Trickster light on the horizon. Just thinking it sent a chill up my back. There was a flip side to this balancing act I was caught up in, a dark side that wanted it over. I saw myself swerving, sending the truck crashing end over end. Setting the lodge and cabins on fire, just a can of gasoline and a rag, a few matches, as easy as stepping off a bridge railing, the way you think of it, all rocks and water far below, your stomach pulling up sharply.

All such thin skin, safety. I opened a window and the night spilled in, cold.

Just north of Pine Point, I stopped by the old root beer stand, where 525 came in from Roseau. Clark sat under the front windows, the glass shooting up at a dizzying angle to intersect the roof, all around us pine, high, silent, dark.

"Hey," I said. "How ya doin'?"

I jumped out, ecstatic. It was the closest thing to happy I'd been in some time, finding him there. I nearly bubbled with it.

"I feel like shit," Clark said. He had a ruffled, unfocused look about him.

I laughed.

He dug for a stone in the sand, squinted across the highway, then gave a long-armed toss, the rock rattling into the weeds on the shoulder.

"Jesus. I *should* be angry," he said, glancing up at me. "I *am* angry. I mean, it isn't every day someone leads you on like that, then drops you off in the goddamn middle of nowhere when your back is turned. But I'm more...confused. I feel like...like I tolerate things. You know? Just *tolerate* things. We tolerate things, you and me."

I sat beside him. "So?" I said. It was quiet and dark.

"You could tell me what's going on once in a while, you know?"

I laughed again. I was more determined than ever not to get him involved now. I would sell a few boats, or the launch. That would do it, and in July, we'd catch up.

"Like what?" I asked.

"Just things. I mean, there were a bunch of people out here waiting for something. And it wasn't me."

"It's just turnover," I explained. It would all just take time, I said. It was an adjustment whenever property changed hands. Those people I couldn't hire on again were bound to be pissed.

A car came around the sharp sweep of highway, slowing to a near stop. The car's lights cut blindly up into the night sky; a moth fluttered wildly in them, just then bright and silver. There was a jumble of arms and legs inside. Someone climbed over the front seat, into the back.

"Is that them?" I asked.

Clark said it was. The window in back of the car came down with a well-oiled, electric whir. I stood and walked toward the car.

"What's up?" I said, real chipper.

I tried to look inside.

A head popped up in the window, a kid in his late teens I'd never seen before. Crew cut, almond eyes. He saw Clark there, then grinned at me, as if I'd won something, Pepsodent white teeth.

He poked what looked like a 30.06 out the window, and yelled,

"Boom!"

I laughed. It was a toy gun, wasn't it?

There was an explosion, flash of light, a *ter-waannng!* of metal. I felt the hump of it in my chest, the car pulling away, loud laughter, running after the car then, the pavement slapping up sharply under my feet, the car, rocketing away, oily exhaust and that crazy, intoxicated laughter. The license plate light was out, and I couldn't get it.

Clark dusted himself off, standing.

"You all right?"

"Fine," Clark said. "I think your truck might not be, though."

The bullet had struck the tailgate and gotten caught inside. I let down the tailgate and tried to shake the bullet out.

"You might need that," Clark said.

I was still breathing hard. Too many cigarettes, shore lunches. I'd set a record for the fifty-yard dash out east, way back when. I had to put my hands on my knees now.

I laughed, "Little snot-noses."

"Funny, huh?" Clark said. He tugged at that red hair of his. "It's a joke, right?"

"Get in the truck, Clark," I said.

I knew, given the way Bobby had died, Clark wouldn't argue now—and he wouldn't mention it to Gwen. Any talk about guns now, or accidents, or near accidents, would just bring that awfulness back.

I swung around and pulled on the lights. Turned onto old 525. "You know reserve humor," I said. "That's all it was.

"Don't tell me we didn't shoot up some stuff in our time."

Clark pulled a face, and we both laughed—the stupid things we'd done as kids!

"What a night!" I said, a new happiness bubbling up in me.

It was warm and close in the cab, and just then, it seemed we'd escaped it all.

9

Two weeks later, outside the Rambler's, I parked the truck waiting for Moses to open. It was Friday, and he was making slow work of it—in the grocery, circling the bait tanks, dusting the hardware hanging from the ceiling, arranging cans on the shelves, the sun catching, suddenly, in the big front window, dangling sausages, a ham in red mesh, letters in gold script, *Eagle's*.

I got a pencil from my pocket, sharpened it with my pen knife. I glanced in the mirror, then up the road, and to my right, nervous.

The Rambler's lot was quiet, just a broad stretch of rutted sand, bordered by timothy hay and nettles, a heat haze over it. Nothing unusual there; nor was the building itself anything in daylight. Peeling paint. Cockeyed star on the roof (those two bicycle frames wired together with coat hangers). Green glass on the stoop, bright as emeralds. Off in the pines, jays were calling to each other.

Still, watching Moses now, it hung there, big in my head like an echo: the rifle coming out the window. Heart freezing. Flash of blue light, the explosion, truck shuddering.

Kid stuff, I told myself, working the tip of the pencil to a point.

And all that in the Rambler's earlier? How Moses had seemed too familiar with this Len Barthelowe? And later, how Len had looked at me in the mirror? Not related, I told myself.

I gulped down a coffee. It tasted flat and bitter, an indication I'd already had more than I should. The early-morning sun shone through the windshield as if through a magnifying glass.

I added to the list Gwen had given me.

Juice, bananas, oats, five gals 2%, beans (pinto)
TP, must, tartar, six lemons, 10 lb oranges
6 med porter, 6 sir, 10 lb burg, 15 chick

I tried to make specific those things she'd wanted.

Cereals (your pick) 10 bxs, chili pdr
4 qt mayo, 10 cases soda, 8 cases br
Bread, aspirin, veg oil, cake mix, fruit

With the edge of my hand I wiped the sweat from my forehead. It was going to be another hot day. I felt a kind of reprieve in that. It had been hot, unseasonably so, and the fishing had tapered off. We'd had cancellations, ten of them, and I'd brought up a church group, Kumbayaing and all that, and now it didn't matter that I'd sold the launch and five of our best boats to make our June payment.

Our pontoon, old oversize wreck that it was, could pack twenty of those kinds of guests at a time, easy.

Sunscreen, I wrote. *#s 10-50*

Carton Cmls. Two Marls, case Evinrude Green
$50,000 in twenties
2 Tickets to Mazatlan

I glanced up the road and back again. One of the Yellowbird girls went wobbling by on a bicycle, knees scabbed, hair in knots. I wanted to get out of the truck and buy her something to eat, but her father, Carl, got angry when I did that.

There was the smell of bacon on the damp morning breeze. My mouth watered. I looked glumly at my middle. I'd been careful not to eat shore lunches, but in the last few weeks I'd started working on a bit of a tire. I pinched it.

Shit, I thought, chuckling. I'd float better that way.

I doodled on my pad: Boxes within boxes. A rough sketch of the lodge. A caricature of Clark, then myself—a clown with big feet and raccoon dark eyes—a boy

—my boy—*our* boy, and I remembered,

how he was raven-haired, and blue-eyed. Was standing when he was just months old. Was into everything. Was fascinated by ants, moths, fish, pebbles, dirt in general, all smells, liked light, laughed at ducks and chased them, hooted at owls, imitated the barking of dogs. He began speaking early, and picked up what Mardine and Gwen gibbered, and forced me into it.

Climbed trees, especially high ones, like the pine outside our cabin, and in the worst weather, even thunderstorms.

I squeezed my eyes closed; it came like that. As if out of nowhere, shook me.

Oda'minoh'win, Papa, he'd say. Come play with me, papa.

I would talk haltingly, in the old language.

My head ached with pulling all that from memory, and what it brought with it. What was the first thing I'd missed, that had brought on the end?

Bobby, when he was two, crawled under a log, and when I got him out, he was swollen, from a bee sting. The kid was too tough, otherwise, but there it was: we had to get antihistamines for him. It was nothing, the doctor told us. He'd probably grow out of it.

I grit my teeth, thinking how a bee sting, just that, could bring the world down on your head.

From the front window Moses gave me a suspicious, not altogether friendly, look. He pointed to the watch on his wrist, mouthed,

You're early.

I smiled, for Moses.

10

A car came crackling around the gravel drive from behind now. I looked into my mirror and slunk in my seat. Swell of dashboard at eye level, the glove compartment knob winking in complicity. I felt like the teenager I'd been as Charlie Groten, Pine Point's finest, pulled up alongside.

"Hey there," he said, coming around to my window.

"Cup of coffee?" I asked, holding up my thermos.

The wings of Charlie's nose flared in revulsion. "You mean that muck you're calling coffee?"

He was a man in a rumpled blue uniform, looking serious. He had a sizable gut on him, straining the buttons of his shirt, but his forearms were hard, his hands thick-fingered and powerful.

"Rough night?" I asked. He smelled of cheap cologne and beer.

"The usual."

Charlie had been sent up from St. Paul, back in the sixties, after an incident at the Little Earth Projects where a teenaged boy had been shot. Now he oversaw the station at Pine Point, a kind of punishment, we all thought.

He threw my door open, made a sweeping, imperious gesture.

"Well, old friend," he said.

I gave him the dullest look I could. "Cut the theatrics, Charlie. I've got things to do."

"Well, so have I."

We got into his cruiser. I'd been in it before. That same old Chrysler, olive green, black interior, gun on the dash—sawed-off twelve-gauge, which, as far as I knew, he'd never used.

"Smoke?" he offered.

"Quit," I said.

He guffawed, turning left, foot heavy on the gas. Glanced in my direction.

"You eat yet?"

At the Western, Charlie ordered two Number Sevens, hash browns, eggs, toast, slab of bacon and muffin, dropped down on a stool, back of the counter. The place was a crush of wool shirts, hard hats, steel-toed boots. Clatter of silverware on Buffalo China, waitresses in fawn skirts and beaded headbands, Hank Williams on the old red and chrome Wurlitzer in the corner.

Your cheatin' heart
will make youooo cry

"So, why so generous?" I asked, taking the seat beside him.

Charlie winked. "Condemned man's gotta have his last meal, doesn't he?"

"Oh, what a funny guy you are," I said.

I set my elbows on the counter, nodded to people I recognized. Charlie got up and bullied over to a table in the back, reconnoitering. There was the sharp ring of laughter. It was a fair mix of locals here, timber and resort people, Cree and Chippewa; and farmers, descendants of Swedes and Scots and Germans who'd homesteaded in the 1880s.

I was thinking about that, because three of them back there were council members: Walter Standing Strongly, Irma Kobeckaneck, and Samuel Running. Those very same who'd held things up with the lodge, had put the deed for sale in escrow all those years.

Every spring the council members had come up from Pine Point to find fault with something—submerged wreckage off shore, old batteries dumped in the deepest places, a dangerously shallow and unmarked length of channel. So I put buoys in the channels, dove for the batteries, raised that wreckage. Got another flight path for the DeHavillands, so as not to disturb the geese nesting in the Grassy Narrows.

I let my father buffalo his way onto my eighty-acre allotment outside Pine Point, out of guilt, or shame, or just plain old inertia. (I was furious about that at first, but then took a strange pleasure in his ruining the house and garage, the trees in the yard, ensuring I'd never return.)

The council let the lodge go after that. It was a loose form of reciprocity, a kind of benign extortion. My father had once been connected to everything up there: people still owed him, big time, and he'd needed a place to hang his hat, that simple.

Now Charlie, pointing with his chin, motioned me over. I froze on my stool. Was he crazy? Still, I had to do it, and cheerfully.

"Mornin'," I said, and we small-talked, the hot weather, the wild rice ripening too quickly. The Mystic Lake casino, down south. Walter's lip curled at the mention of it, a certain disgust there. Irma poked me affectionately. She and my mother had been good friends. Sam scratched his head. It was all friendly, as if they'd tried to do me some favor, the three of them, by holding things up.

Our waitress squeezed by, a pot of coffee held up like a torch.

"Your order's on, Chuck."

Charlie took me by the elbow, steering me back to the counter and our Number Seven plates. Charlie was eating, his eyes on the *Tribune,* open to the sports section.

"I could kill you for doing that."

"Eat," Charlie said.

>> ◇ <<

We were driving south to Bemidji, down a windy, narrow two-laner. The sun cut sharply through the windshield, the radio barking out dispatches. I got my cigarettes from my pocket and lit one. I complained that I had more important things to do than to drive down to Bemidji.

"Why didn't you take 71?"

Charlie's eyes wrinkled with mean humor. "Why didn't you report that shooting?"

"What shooting?"

I flicked cigarette ash out the window. The road was spinning by under us. Charlie glared. "Your friend there, Clark, said he saw the whole thing."

"Would've pegged me if they'd wanted to," I said. "Just more kid stuff."

"You think so?"

Charlie hit the gas, the cruiser surging forward. We passed a car, swerving into the oncoming lane to do it, engine roaring, the traffic coming on, so close the first car pulled off onto the shoulder.

"Don't rush on my account," I said.

The car seemed to float. One of the wheels was off balance and thrummed, making the whole cruiser shudder. Approaching a car from behind, Charlie used his light, then the siren.

"I got a suicide," he said, turning to look at me.

I wanted to grab the wheel. That car was wandering all over the highway. I'd gotten one hand under the seat and was hanging on.

"Suicide."

"Yeah," Charlie said. He fumbled with the lighter in the dash.

"You don't want another one of those," I said. "Coffin nails."

Charlie nodded, pleased. "It's that or cut the bacon mornings." He pulled his sunglasses from under the visor, put them on and smiled, bug-eyed.

"Speaking for myself, I'll take the smoke over bacon any day. How about you?"

The mile markers were flashing by even faster now. "Right," I said, nodding.

"But can't seem to forgo the ice cream." He patted his gut. "No, sir. Chocolate fudge. Butterscotch. Peanuts, too. Tin roof, that's the best. Chocolate cake. Vie's doughnuts on the corner there back of the Western. What do you say? Are they good or what?

"How about you? What do you go for?"

I rolled down my window. The car had filled with his smoke. A cold blast of air hit my forehead. I had a copper tang in my mouth.

"Steaks. Salty."

"Oh, you're a salty?" he said.

I glanced down at the speedometer. The red needle had stopped at the right. Charlie grinned, angry at what, I wasn't sure.

"Personally, I go for the sweets. But, then, you got your porterhouse, tater tots, mushrooms sautéed in butter, a bit—" he held up his hand, made a chopping motion "—just a bit of parsley, or thyme, and—" he brought his pinched fingers to his mouth and made a kissing.

"Voilà!"

He swerved around a cloverleaf onto a lower highway, tires protesting, then out on a straight stretch, wove back and forth, right lane, left lane, passing, using the lights, now siren, braking hard behind a semi, then swerving around it, accelerating hard, all the while, that wheel wobbling like crazy. I swallowed hard.

"Now, you take your other cuts," he said. "Your sirloin, flank, ribeye, and tenderloin. Those are good cuts, too. Especially if they're well marbled."

The radio squawked; he jerked the mike from the dashboard.

"Groten here."

There followed some garbled exchange. Charlie, fumbling, tried to find the catch for the mike. I took it from him, hung it from the dashboard. Glancing up, I knew I'd be sick if I didn't keep my eyes on the road.

Charlie gave a long, oblique look out his window.

"Where was I? Oh, yeah. Ribeye. No, prime rib. You marinate that in some red wine, it's gotta be dry, real dry, and as a secret ingredient, give it a squirt of lemon. Grind some peppercorns on there, and grill some baked potatoes."

I grit my teeth. I was breathing through my nose. Suddenly his cigarettes smelled worse than awful.

"Vegetables? Fuck 'em. Potatoes. Grilled, or baked, but never fried with steak. A nice Italian red goes with the meat. A side order of bread, with honey butter. Whipped. Coffee after, and a shot of brandy. Courvoisier. In a snifter. And across from you, some fine lady, wearing cobalt silk, and smelling of Chanel.

"Then, for dessert—"

"Shut up, Charlie," I said.

He grinned from ear to ear, all gone to gray, but a kid enjoying himself. But angry. There was something vindictive in it.

"Let's see. Crème caramel; or maybe, a little zabaglione, with strawberries in the bottom.

"But it's got to have enough rum in it, and plenty of egg yolks, you know?"

I said, "Marsala." I was sure I was going to be sick. Still, I wasn't going to give in.

"What?"

"Zabaglione should have *marsala* in it, *not rum.*"

Charlie glared. He sniffed, looking out the window.

"Smart-ass," he said.

>> ◇ <<

Now Bemidji was in sight. Sharp, shiny buildings, the lake, sparkle of sun on water. Redbrick banks, looking respectable. Post office. Everywhere elms, and on the south side, rolling hills and large, broad lawns and old Victorians. Charlie made a beeline for the Justice Center, a squat, glass building the shape of a hat, with flags out front.

"You know this place."

I said nothing. I'd been there a few times as a juvenile—Charlie'd taken me. We parked, I caught my breath beside the car, and we went in. Gray desks. Men and women in uniform. Efficient bustle everywhere. The fluorescent lights seemed to slide by overhead. My stomach was working like a pump. I looked for a rest room. We went down a long, asphalt-tiled hallway, stopped at two stainless-steel doors.

Charlie got his arm over my shoulders. "Whaddaya think?"

Beltrami County Morgue, the sign on the doors read. I threw Charlie's hand off.

"You'd better have a *goddamned* good reason for dragging me down here."

"Oh, I just might at that," he said.

Inside, there was a thin-faced doctor with a reflector light on his forehead. He gave me a quick, incurious look. A body lay on a table, a sheet over the legs. I turned away. Stainless steel everywhere.

"I got someone to identify that 0-9," Charlie said.

The doctor adjusted his glasses. Pulled out a drawer in the wall. Charlie clucked.

"Take a look-see over here, Paul."

As I bent down to look, and saw who it was, he gave me a shove. Shocked, I jumped back and banged my head on the stall door.

That I vomited on his pants, I told him later, was the result of his pushing me.

11

The full blast had caught Al at his chin, and from there on up, had peeled back the right side of his face—like a glove might look, if you cut the leather back from the lining. He was bloated something awful, his skin sallow and hardened, the color of corn, burial markings on his cheeks.

"See," Charlie explained, doing that angry blinking thing he did, "botched suicide. Look here." He put his index finger into the palm of Al's hand where the skin was nearly worn away.

"What does that mean to you?"

I felt sad, a weight in my stomach, looking; I started to hiccup and couldn't stop.

"He had a double-barreled Marlin with him," Charlie said, explaining. "Bird shot. Pulled the left, it did this." He touched Al's face. "The second—" Charlie lifted the green plastic bag away, yellow shirt, toucans, and palm trees, a fist-sized hole over his heart. "—the second he took right in the ticker," Charlie said.

"See here? How all this skin's worn away, on his hands? See how it'd even started to scab? Means he was alive a long, long time after that first shot. Real long. An hour, maybe. Maybe more. Means he was crawling. See how the pants are dirty on the knees?"

The pants were otherwise clean, newly pressed khaki, Al's usual, aside from two dark smudges down the thighs, also burial markings.

I said I saw it.

"Yup, looks like a botched suicide, all right. Put one shell in, and fires it. Gets this—" He pointed to Al's face. "Then he crawls back to his car, and has to get another. Fires that one, and—" he clapped his hands together, "finishes it.

"Left a note, too."

Charlie tugged it from his jacket. It was in a Baggie, with a zip lock. Graph paper, those lines running both directions. Al had always used graph paper. Makes it easy to write columns, he'd said.

Just couldn't take it anymore.
Put Moses in charge of things.
Register's picked up mornings.
No regrets.
Al

"That sound like him?" Charlie asked.

He was smoking again. I was afraid I might be sick a second time, so I plucked the cigarette from his mouth and crushed it under my heel. I had to tell him, yes. It did. Al had always spoken in that clipped way: Got to tell you something. Come on by. Looks good if things keep going right. And then it'll be clear sailing. Al had always believed the best would happen.

"I understand he owed you a fair piece of change."

I said that was true. I slapped my hands against my arms. That room had all the warmth of a freezer compartment. It was all pressing in on me, too close.

"So much, you were goin' under a little yourself."

"I don't want to talk about it," I said. "I don't think it has anything to do with this."

"Oughta ask the council for that money he owed you."

"Why?"

"They own the Rambler's now."

The thought of it shocked me. Al had always thought the council, or at least a fair number of its members, was corrupt. Both of us for that reason, when in trouble, had never considered help there. But why was Charlie telling me this now?

"We never had anything on paper," I said. "If that's what you're getting at. So there's nothing in it for me. You understand?"

The doctor, at the other table, lifted something up. I turned my back to it.

"Well, like I said," Charlie said. "It looks like a suicide. Pretty much everything goes together. The gun shots. The marks on his hands. The knees. These things here," Charlie said, pointing to Al's face, then his arms and legs, as if he didn't know what they were.

"Burial markings," I said.

Something like a light went on in Charlie's face.

"Ah," he said, grinning.

I gave Charlie a mean look. "You know, you're a lousy actor."

"Maybe I should take lessons? From you, huh? But what do you think?"

I bent over the body. The markings had been done painstakingly, and correctly, it seemed. But I had to be sure. I reached down, and with my index finger drew a line through the circle of brown on Al's left cheek, the flesh cold. I raised my finger to my nose. Sniffed. Fungus. Brown fungus. Just as it should be. And the red swatch? It had been painted above the circle, and back, ending just short of his ear. That was right, too, I thought.

Over the entire body was a fine, white dust, a last purification—I rubbed a bit of it between my fingers—white mugwort, or artemisia—but here, almost like salt and pepper, black bits in it.

Was that ash? Had Al smudged himself, too? Burned cedar around himself? Because it smelled like that, a bitter, pencil shavings smell. But it was mugwort, the white powder, and that was enough.

"They authentic?"

"I'd say so," I said.

"Well," Charlie said, grinning. "I guess that does it, doesn't it?" He was huffing there beside me. He pointed with his cigarette.

"But, you know, there's one thing still bugging me."

"Is there?" I said.

Charlie lit another cigarette. Clank of Zippo, dry rasp, smell of lighter fluid. He blew a plume of smoke at the ceiling, then pulled back the bag still covering Al's feet.

Al had on one boot, a lace-up, yellow rectangle of Vibram sole at the bottom. The other foot was bare, the skin worn off the ankle, toes meticulously clipped.

"How did he lose his boot? You know? How does a dead guy lose a boot?" Charlie made an airy clucking. "Could have just come off, crawling around out there like he did. He wasn't one to tie his laces."

"Right," I said.

It was true. Al had always been a study of something in the making. His clothes had always been too bright, tossed on for the day with abandon.

I got a pressure in my face. I remembered all kinds of things about Al just then. Most of all, how he'd throw his head back and laugh. Don't look so glum, Paul, it won't last forever! Right, I'd say.

"I looked all the hell and back for that boot," Charlie said, squinching his face up. "You know? It must have come off out there, and then I'd think some goddamned dog carried it away, or a raccoon or whatever, porcupine—you know how porcupines eat anything salty, even if it's a wooden toilet seat?

"But it was *nowhere.* Just, plain, nowhere. Not so much as a piece of it.

"And then, one day—you know how god-awful hot it's been—" he took a deep drag on his cigarette, eyeing me through the smoke "—I was walking to my car, gonna go out again, you know, have one last stab at it, and there was your truck.

"Walked right by it, thinking about old times, how you used to steal those cars and go by the station at about a hundred, honking the horn, and how I'd end up chasing you into the game reserve and all that. Getting stuck in the sand. You and your pals laughing out in the woods, yelling all sorts of things. *Chingus* and all that, as if I didn't know what you were saying.

"Al and Moses and you, just having a grand fuckin' old time."

He offered me another cigarette. It was like a tic. Or was he trying to get to me? Did he think I knew something I wasn't telling him?

"Well," he said, grinning, "I just thought I'd take another look at what that shot did to your truck. All outside, mind you. I didn't open the door or anything. I'd been told the bullet got stuck in the gate, between the inside and the outside skin there.

"So...I looked, and what was there?"

Charlie reached into a box on a table there, lifted out a large freezer bag. Blue-green ziplock, a fair amount of condensation in it, heavy as fog.

Something like electricity ran up my spine, sat on the top of my head.

"Ever see this?"

In it was a boot. That boot.

"Yes," I said. "I picked it up at Kennebeck Lake. Just back of the beach."

"All right," Charlie said, and ushered me out of the morgue and into the bright sunlight.

We marched, more than walked, up State Street. Broad avenue of elms. Painted curbs. By the Erickson Holiday Discount Store, hamburger places, Wal-Mart, in high red letters. Fire hydrants painted to look like trolls, in Swedish kitsch. Happy to be outside. Maples with heavy green whirligigs in them.

Charlie nodded at a driver at an intersection, ushered me across, against the red light. Here was the patrol car. Charlie got in. He didn't open the passenger door.

"Get in the back," he said.

He meant the wired-off section. I did, but grudgingly. I didn't trust him.

"Good," he said.

"Good what?"

"That's all done, then."

"What's done?" I was starting to be irritated. Even angry.

We were on the highway again, driving north, though now on the larger, broader 71. Open, green, undulating land, mostly farms.

"You're not going to tell me," I said.

I studied the side of Charlie's face. He had the face of a bulldog when he was set on something. Now he was set on not talking. The drive was interminable, one unbroken silence.

In Pine Point Charlie dropped me off.

"Have a nice day," he said, staring at me in those Ray-Bans.

"Oh, I'll just do that, Chuck," I replied.

He waved, a jolly, loose-wristed wave, then turned the corner and was gone. Standing in all that too-bright sunshine, right there, the truth of it sunk into me:

Someone had killed Al.

12

Back at the island the twenty or so kids in our latest church group, barely into their teens, in shorts and T-shirts, and smelling of coconut sun lotion, were laughing and carrying on, chasing each other through the lodge, two of them colliding with me and nearly knocking me over. The lodge was sweltering. It was a little after noon, and Gwen had set fans up back of the office that roared and shuddered. I stood in a funnel of air coming off the nearest.

"Where'd you get the fans?"

"Hugh brought them in," Gwen said. "Got them at the Rambler's grocery last week."

I went into the mess hall and ate but had no appetite at all. My head pounded something awful, a veritable drum. Our church group's pastor, Bud, big, squarish face, was relating some facile homily.

"Somebody shoot that son of a bitch," I said glumly to myself.

The kid at the end of the table, dark hair and silver-framed glasses, must have heard me.

"What are you looking at?"

"You got a real goose egg there," he replied. "How'd you get it?"

I'd gotten it knocking my head on the morgue door.

"I got it shaving," I said.

The kid stared. "No, you didn't."

I shrugged.

"Okay, have it your way, kid," I said.

I went back to my lunch. Tried to force it down. I felt nauseated, and when I stood, I was dizzy. Like that, I slid out the back.

I sat on shore, the sun high and bright over the lake.

"Hey, old man," Hugh, my summer kid, said, brushing by, a load of life preservers slung over his shoulders like orange wings. "If you can't take the heat, get out of the fire."

"Is something wrong?" I asked.

"Not that isn't wrong with you."

He went up the south dock, to the pontoon, where he swung back the gate, all the kids piling on, neon bright, so much nylon, kicking and pushing and pinching.

He started the boat and a cloud of oily exhaust drifted in.

I was sick back of cabin 3.

There was a slap of shoes, then a nervous shuffling of feet, as that boy who'd been sitting at the end of the table came down the path. Hugh was already out on the bay. It hurt just to look, the sun cutting up off the water.

"Should I bring it back in?" Hugh shouted.

I waved him off.

"Let's you and me go out," I told the boy. He had on a T-shirt that read *Are We Having Fun Yet?*, a peculiar clown beneath, sporting a five-o'clock shadow.

"I'll show you how to catch large mouth."

"I don't like fish," he said.

"Great," I said.

I couldn't think just then, and so resorted to another bribe, one not appropriate to the occasion. I asked him if he'd like to run the motor. The kid took notice at that. It was a whole new ball game. Gwen was watching us from the lodge porch. I squeezed the kid's shoulder.

"Really?"

"Sure," I said.

Exuberant, dizzying circles, the bow thumping down; wide, chuttering turns, slow spins. A fast start, motor pulling hard, the *chuf-chuf, chuf-chuf-chuf* of the boat planing, then pulling hard left, right, in a circle, trees in a blur. Exhaust. Spray. The kid enjoying himself, having an adventure.

I was barely hanging on, up there in the bow.

"Hey, Captain Bly," I said, "how about you slow down a little?"

He didn't. I was sick, over the side, pretending to check the water temperature.

"How cold is it?"

"Sixty-seven degrees," I told him, holding up the thermometer.

"That's too cold," he said. "My dad's pool is almost eighty degrees."

"Is it." I set my forearms on the bowplate. There was that fatherless anger in the kid. I couldn't help thinking of Bobby. I would just have to get through it.

"But he hasn't cleaned it out lately."

"When you've been there, you mean," I said.

The boy looked at me askance. What I'd said was too close for comfort, so he looked at his feet, then back at me, squinting.

"That lump on your forehead's gotten bigger."

We bobbed there back of an island. Touching my forehead, I swallowed hard. I thought I might be sick again. The kid rummaged in the bag he'd brought along.

"Here," he said.

It was one of those chemical cold packs, the kind you fold in half to start. I held it to the bruise, exquisite pain, and numbing chill.

"I suppose your mother sent you out with that."

He nodded. "You look like somebody just died." It was an attempt at a joke.

"Really." I worked on a smile.

"Well?"

"You ought to be a boy scout," I told him, a little meanly. "All that *reading trail signs* stuff."

"Can't," he said.

"Why?" I peered at him, from under that ice pack.

"—got epilepsy."

"So?"

The boy turned his back to me. Here was the whole lake again. I'm never any good at cutting myself off, and I felt his disappointment.

"Can we go up there?" he said, pointing, a boy's finger, an arrow.

"You can go anywhere you want," I said.

I got to bed late that night but couldn't sleep.

"What is it?" Gwen said.

"Money."

"Oh," she said. "Al?"

I wondered if she saw it in my face. I was afraid. My skin was clammy. I felt a worse than usual distance. Was *not* telling her a lie? I would take care of it. That was all there was to it.

I asked Gwen if she wanted me to brush her hair as I had done years before.

It had been one of our rituals. I held the hair tenderly now, brushing, green sparks in it. I loved that curve of neck into shoulder, and the hint of breasts, from the side, and the smell of her, rose and powder.

"Is your head all right?" she asked. I'd told her I'd hurt myself loading supplies, which was a half-truth, as I saw it.

"It's fine, really."

I brushed some more. The loons were calling across the lake.

"We could go back down to the Cities," I said, drawing the brush down her back.

Gwen shuddered. "No," she said.

I didn't ask why. She'd said, when we'd first come up in May, I want to get used to it, before we go anywhere else, I have to get over it. I have to go up where it happened.

Where it had happened was only miles away; I knew she hadn't been there. And getting over it? I didn't have the heart to tell her, you never get over it, you just go on as if you had. Every moment of your life playacting from there on in, or intentional distraction. After a while, you might come to believe it, on good days.

"Clark called," Gwen said.

"Did he," I replied, brushing.

I must have pulled too hard, because she turned to look at me. I tried to kiss her and just got her cheek. Down by the lake, the church group was singing. I bitterly imagined them doing rounds of "Michael Row the Boat," though really, I couldn't hear what it was.

"Gwen," I said.

"It's good news."

I stopped with the brush. I had it in mind to ask her if she was involved with him, with Clark, but decided against it. I had enough to deal with.

"I'll talk to him," I told her.

I kissed the crown of her head and began brushing again, long, slow strokes, the hair silky and thick and dark. There seemed to be purple in it, and now a number of white hairs. I imagined her hair gray, in a tight braid, her face weathered, her eyes still that sparkling blue. It was a picture I liked.

"Do you remember that time we hiked up the Hudson that fall?" Gwen asked. "And the sumac had turned red?"

I nodded.

"It was so quiet and dry." She laughed, her head tilted to one side, wistful. "There was that buoy out there, in the middle, and you were throwing rocks at it, and you wanted to hit it. You *had* to hit it."

"I didn't *have* to hit it."

"Oh, yes you did. You told me all those lies about—"

I nearly cringed at that. "They weren't lies."

"No, just *exaggerations.*" She laughed. "You and all your exaggerations. Those Christmas stories. All that baseball stuff. You were such a liar. All those impossible stories. You've never really been to Florida, have you? For training?"

I told her no. It had been a relative, one of the Finedays, who'd made it into Double A baseball. I'd been desperate to win her. It made me uncomfortable, remembering. How ridiculous I'd been! Brushing her hair now, it occurred to me I was still trying to win her, all over again.

"I thought you were crazy," Gwen said.

I shrugged. "I was."

"And do you remember," she said, "there were those swallows, they'd made their nests in the sandstone, and that one bird looked sick, on shore there, and you climbed up and put it in one of those holes and it just sat, looking out, and when it couldn't keep its head up—even though it was getting dark—you went up and put some grass under it.

"That's when I knew I loved you. Taking care of that bird."

I wanted to tell her, she was that bird.

Gwen tugged my arms around her. I didn't dare move. The night sounds came louder. Crickets. The soft slap of water down at the dock. Those loons, far distant now. I remembered:

Gwen running from the lodge, seeing the blood on my shirt, my leaden voice, calling, as if in a dream, but not a dream, He's dead, Gwen, and Gwen, swinging around, hitting me so hard I fell, rough dirt, wrestling her to the ground, her mouth open, a wail coming from it I couldn't bear,

God damn you, Paul! Oh, God damn you!

Gwen settled. I wanted to tell her about Al, but then thought that would be weak of me and would only make our life together harder. And, too, I thought there might be some connection between Al's death and Bobby's, and wanted to look into it, before I told her.

"Gwen," I said. "Gwen?"

But she was sleeping.

13

At breakfast, Mardine smiled from the kitchen, a certain hopeful suggestiveness in it. I wondered what *that* was all about. Ah, I thought. Must have seen the light on in the cabin. She took my disheveled look for something else—if only, I thought.

"Mind if I join you?" Bud, the pastor, said, pulling out a chair.

He sat, then made a display of placing his napkin on his lap. I didn't need this, I thought. Policemen and pastors, two things I can do without.

"I want to apologize for the commotion last night."

The kids had been chasing each other with bottle rockets, whooshings and sharp explosions and flashes of light. I'd gotten up to put an end to it, herding the kids back to the cabins.

I didn't tell him I hadn't been sleeping anyway, or that it had been an oddly welcome distraction.

Kid stuff.

"It's a little early for the Fourth," I said. "But it's all right."

Bud launched into a wandering narrative about state politics, environmental concerns, and was circling around to something else. Though he was wearing a sad, heavy face, I could see he loved politics. It didn't surprise me. Clerics love politics.

"So what is it?" I said.

He wanted to know how *we* felt about the whole land use issue. I glanced at the clock on the wall of the kitchen. 5:45. Not even six yet. I'd gotten a little over four hours of sleep.

"Land use?"

"Yes," he said, matter-of-factly.

"The only reason *I'm* here," I told him, grinning nastily, "is that the owner of this dump had to hand it over to an Indian since the government wouldn't renew his lease. They changed the reserve boundaries and bumped him out. Then some vigilante types with a hotshot lawyer from Duluth changed them back.

"I just happened to be around doing a little guiding when being Indian paid off. Lucky me.

"That do it?"

The pastor lit a cigarette. I was wishing he'd go away. He seemed to consider what I'd said with some seriousness.

"Aren't you a little nervous?" he said. "You don't think private interest is dangerous?"

I knew what he meant, but shrugged it off.

"The whole reserve is a tangle anyway," I said. "Half of us living up here want that happy shit—Wal-Mart, and all that—to lift the development restrictions; and half don't. One way or another, someone's always trying to twist your arm. I just try to stay out of it. It's a real pain in the ass."

"So it's like that," he said.

"How did you *think* I'd feel?"

"I'd be bitter," he said.

"Up here that's an occupational hazard." I picked up my plate. "But then again, if you don't talk about it, it doesn't exist, right?"

I was thinking of Father Prideaux, and what he'd said to me, *You don't have to do this. You can just go on as if it never happened. Can't you?*

I smiled a big Theme Park smile. Bud crushed his cigarette out, the ashtray rattling. He gave me a look I couldn't get around. It was a decisive moment.

"You don't believe that, do you?" he said. "Not really."

"No," I said, and excused myself.

Kids and more kids. Clambering in and out of boats. Lost lures. Lost token jewelry. Lost candy money. One anchor untied and dropped into the bay. Glass broken on the stone ledge outside the lodge. One kid cut his hand with a hatchet. Into town for stitches. Archery. I called Clark after breakfast, then again around lunch. Waiting, the afternoon reeling out. Hot, suffocatingly hot. Calling again. More kids. A greased-watermelon fight, all twenty or so of them, throwing up gouts of water and tugging at each other's hair and dunking the smallest and most vulnerable.

They wanted a campfire, Bud told me, of all things, an overnight. On an island, *out there.* I tried to convince him what a bad idea it was, outlined the potential there was for bad weather, a windstorm, or hail, or visits from bears. But he turned a deaf ear on it.

I wanted to get into town again, so as to pump Moses. He'd been out there, in the Nin'godonin'djigan, the day Bobby had died.

But I was caught up in it now and would have to put my trip to the Rambler's off a day or two. It made me a little edgy. Packing. Tent stakes and rope and cookware, sheets of Mylar in case it rained (our canvas tents always leaked). First-aid kits, splints, flares. A kitchen box and canned goods and coolers of perishables. Take it out, put it away elsewhere. Take it out, put it away elsewhere. This time in a number of canoes. By late afternoon we were ready. Hugh was flirting with the oldest of the girls, Anna. She was dark, and pretty, but more so, that thing girls can be—*charming*. I warned Hugh not to bother her.

"Got it?"

"Yeah, I got it," he said.

A big plane, orange and black and silver-winged, circled the bay, then slid low over the trees and, skimming down, cleared the dock by nothing, sending us scurrying—the kids, Bud, Hugh and me. The pilot taxied to the dock, engines roaring. Clark waved through the windshield. He tossed his duffel bag out and jumped down after it.

"Hey, you bum!" he shouted.

The pilot motioned us back. He throttled up, easing the plane around. In minutes he was in the air again, then gone. I grinned at Clark, but not for the reason he might have thought. Here was something better than talking with that lying Moses—

Clark, after all, had been there that afternoon.

"What's all this?" Clark asked, nudging one of the canoes with his boot.

I told him if he couldn't see for himself, I wasn't going to tell him. The kids were running up and down the length of the bank, playing tag or some other thing. I gave a sharp whistle.

"Let's go," I shouted.

I got them loading the last of it, and then, as if I'd forgotten something, ran to the lodge, and carrying what I hoped looked like more fishing gear, all wrapped in a jumble of blankets and whatnot, went down to our cabin.

I slid my Remington twelve-gauge under the bed, five shells in the pump, then checked, on my hands and knees, now under the bed what appeared to be just clothes and an old blue and white paisley quilt.

I didn't want Gwen to see the gun and ask what it was doing there.

I told myself it was—*just in case.*

Just a precaution, for when I came back.

> > ◇ < <

Canoes upside down, gray and broad-backed as hippos, the kids were playing submarine. Hugh headed up one bunch, that girl, Anna, the other. The canoes made a hollow, aluminum bumping. It was raining lightly.

Bud sat on shore, a broad-shouldered bulk of purple raincoat, playing lifeguard. It was pretty, the pines, the laughing kids, the way the rain dimpled the lake, making the slightest watery hush.

I offered Clark a cigarette. "Why do they bug me so much?" I said. "Clerics, I mean."

We were sitting on folding stools, upwind of the fire. The hood of my poncho made me feel as if I were in a cave. Every minute away from the lodge now was an exercise in self-control.

Clark laughed. "He isn't so bad."

I told him I supposed not.

"That girl," Clark said. "That one there. She looks a bit like Gwen."

I didn't want to think about it. The kids had tired of submarines and were at swamping each other, the whole mess of them, teetering, the canoes going over. Plash! Plash! The rubbery squeak of flesh on aluminum. Hollow, wet thud, and over a canoe would go again.

"Your eye is still doing that thing," Clark said. "Twitching."

"Is it?"

"You know it is," he said.

"Let's leave the subject of my facial tics, can we?" I asked.

Clark said he was separated. I told him I was sorry. I'd liked this latest one. Her high, good-natured laugh, her sharp sense of humor. Of course, she'd been pretty, too. Long, long legs, a lovely face and big eyes. They hadn't been together very often, Clark said—hadn't been lately, anyway.

"Wasn't it a lawyer friend of yours who was having this same sort of trouble?"

"Who?"

"Your client? The one you were telling me about at the Rambler's?"

Clark didn't respond to that.

"It just all gets so—*complicated*," he said.

"Yes, it does, doesn't it."

I watched the kids playing. They seemed remarkably free. When did all that hiding start? I thought. Trying to be people we never were, and weren't going to be?

"It's just..."

"What do you want, Clark?" I said. "Just now?"

But I knew exactly what he wanted. He wanted me to say, I forgive you. It's all right. So I couldn't ask him about any of it then, just couldn't, so I said,

"What do you *think* you want?"

"To be happy again."

"Ah, *happy*," I said. "That, old friend," I said, "is one tall order."

After dinner the rain stopped and there was a brilliant sunset, purple clouds bunched down low on the horizon, arrows of yellow and red shooting from behind. Bud scooted up a path that dead-ended in a bluff, ducked under it, and was gone.

Hugh and the kids were over at the point, had a fire going.

"What's Bud doing, playing pocket pool out there?" Clark joked.

"He's got a bottle," I said. "I suppose."

"*He's* getting happy."

I was scrubbing up the last of the sooty cookware. I'd soaped it, so it was easy cleaning. I glanced at Clark over my shoulder. Clark winked, took a bottle from his duffel bag.

"For old times."

"Give it here," I said. I put back a couple fingers, breaking my resolution of the November before. It burned. I felt a loosening in my middle.

"Here's to happy," I said.

"I'll give you happy," Clark shot back, taking the bottle.

We both sat glumly there, the kids carrying on over at the point. It looked like fun; even that kid with epilepsy was having a good time.

"So how're things at work?" I asked.

"Shitty."

"Oh, well," I said. "Things are wonderful here, of course."

We both laughed.

> > ◇ < <

I set another rig down, Day-Glo bobber just visible in the water off shore. We'd nearly polished off the bottle; after a fair number of close calls, we had come around to it again.

"It was an accident," Clark said. "The whole thing—do you see that now?"

He meant Bobby.

"Clark," I said. "*Stop.*"

But we had to talk about it. I had to. It was like a skip in an otherwise perfectly good record—or had been, before his mooning around Gwen—that rotten afternoon when everything had gone wrong and Bobby had died. And, too, I needed to pry into it now because of this business with Al, and how it made me see Moses in a different light. Maybe all that had happened the afternoon Bobby died wasn't an accident?

I had to make Clark give me the details now, all over again, which I knew would be unpleasant.

"I'm *not* blaming you, Clark," I said.

It was a mean thing to say. Yet I knew it would get a reaction out of him. After all, it wasn't the injury that had killed Bobby, but having bled so badly.

"Why should you?"

"I don't," I told him.

"But you do," he said. "*Don't tell me* you don't. I just heard you."

"I didn't say that," I said.

"Oh, yes you did too!"

He got to his feet, hands flying in all directions. That afternoon, Moses had come up the dirt road, said his car needed a jump. Didn't I remember that part? Didn't I? What should he have done? Just sat there, for Christ's sake? Said, No, I won't help you, Moses?

"I told you," I said, "under no circumstances move the truck. Remember? I wanted it there, if anything—but...Shit. You *did,* Clark."

"Jesus," he said, "how could I have known you'd come down with Bobby like that?"

"Whose jumper cables?"

"Mine. No, his," Clark said. "What difference does it make? What a *stupid* question! Why do you ask *stupid* questions like that, huh? *Jesus!*"

He was thinking I was going to bring up how he'd made a mess of Moses' car; and I was, only, I wanted to hear something else in it now.

"Of *course* he had cables. What difference does it make?"

"Tell me what he said again."

"Who?"

The moon came up through the trees, big as a spotlight.

"Moses," I said. "Who the hell else would I be talking about?"

Over on the point, the kids were singing.

"*Why* are you *blaming* me?"

"Jesus! I'm not," I told him.

"Well, goddammit, it sure feels like you are. Aren't you? Why don't you just say it!"

"Shut up," I told him, "they'll hear."

"I *don't care!*" he shouted.

"Well, you have to remember *something* of it, don't you? If it hadn't been for your fucking driving off with the truck, then—"

Saying it, I felt disgusted with myself.

"I mean, Christ!" Clark said, his eyes glassing up, "you talk like I did it on purpose or something, you know?

"I mean, shit! Moses said to do one thing or another and then it got all screwed up. *All right, all right!* God as my witness, *I screwed it all up!* I pulled the wrong fucking switch or something in the dark and wrecked his fucking battery. Okay?! *I did it. Okay?* So his car wouldn't start, and I had to drive him into town in the truck, and when you came down with Bobby—

"I *wasn't there.* It was *my* fault! That make you happy?!" He threw his hands up. "You just sit there like that!"

I was just sitting. Part of me was angry enough to want to kill him, for having driven off. Part of me wanted to forgive him.

But here it was, the thing I'd paid no attention before.

"*What* got screwed up?" I said.

"I just *told* you! I pulled the *wrong switch* or something. You know how Moses and I've never gotten along. What an *asshole!* It was like that. I was nervous. I did everything wrong. I pulled on the light switch, so I could see what the hell I was doing in there, and he jumped the fuck all over me.

"'You're ruining the battery,' he says, 'Shut it off!' all bent out of shape!"

I said, as calmly as I could,

"Did the lights come on when you did that? When you pulled on the switch?"

"Of *course* they did, *how else could I see?*"

"But the engine wouldn't turn over."

"No."

"Not at all."

"It was *dead.* I told you."

"It didn't make any noise at—"

"I just said—"

"All right," I said.

I picked up one of the rods. The moon shone in a broad yellow swatch across the lake.

I made pretenses of jigging the rod, then, cranking in the line, bore down so hard on the reel I broke the handle off it. So. That's how it was. It was a setup.

The engine should have at least turned over if the lights came on. And those hunters, who'd just happened to be there?

"Shit," I said.

Clark was watching me. "What?"

"Nothing."

"Nothing *what?*"

"Just *nothing,*" I lied.

A spark of hope there left Clark's face. I felt as if I'd killed him. I wanted to go to him, like in some sappy movie, absolve him of it, be a good guy.

"Listen," I said, "I *don't* blame you."

"I can help," he said. "Just let me. I want to *do* something."

"It's not your money I need."

"What is it, then?"

I looked away, across the lake, all darkness, diamond-sharp stars over it.

"I need you to stay away, can you do that?"

"Stay away," he said.

He got up, and a little unsteadily, went off toward the trees downshore. There was something awful in his shoulders, how his head hung down.

"What is it, Paul?" he asked. "What is it I've done to you?"

"It isn't that," I said. "It's going to get ugly up here."

"What is?"

"I can't say, exactly," I told him, and for once that was all there was to say.

BOOK II

14

I did not see Clark for some time after that.

It was midseason and I was worse than busy. When I had any time at all, I made repairs, to the dock, cabins, the lodge, until I caught up with all that. Through it all, I was biding my time, waiting, until early one evening I went into Pine Point for supplies.

I stopped at the Rambler's, filled the bed of the truck with groceries, and when I got to the turnoff to the docks and my boat, instead, drove north, up one of the roads that led to the Angle Inlet.

It was balmy, late June now, and I put my hand out the window, cupping the air, my hand rising and falling with it. Topping a rise, the Nin'godonin'djigan stretched as far as I could see, miles and miles of blue-green pine, and cutting through it, the inlet, sparkling silver.

The air was thick with the scent of dry grass, water, a baked, green-nettle smell. I loved that place, the clouds, flat-bottomed, scudding past overhead, high and white.

It was near here Clark and I had been hunting, here that Bobby had died.

I turned on the first spur east, and there, the road pitching—potholes big as wheelbarrows, washboards that made my teeth rattle—admitted to myself that I was not out for a joyride. I had all those sweets in the car. Twinkies, and candy, for kids. Hostess pies.

I veered right, up a winding, sandy road to Hulbert Morrison's place, a kind of dread settling in my stomach. Chippewa are for the most part private people, and I was trespassing. I stopped the truck back of Hulbert's cabin, a worn, grayed affair, rusted tin roof, aware that I was being watched.

But then, big gutted and slow moving, Hulbert came around the side.

"Don't tell me," he said. "I've won the Great Lakes Lottery!"

I tossed a pack of Twinkies to him. Hulbert loved sweets.

"So," he said, popping one into his mouth. "What brings you up here?"

"Hot, isn't it?" I said.

I got Hulbert talking about the recent, unseasonable weather and worked it around to predictions for fall, all typical talk, mentioning that last fall had been too rainy for much of anything, much less hunting.

"You were up here, weren't you?" I asked.

Hulbert's eyes took on a wary, heavy-lidded look. He sniffed at that second Twinkie, then popped it into his mouth, working his tongue around and over his front teeth, chewing.

"Yah," he said. He brushed yellow crumbs off his black shirt.

"See anybody out here? Anybody new? City guys, maybe?" The two men who'd filed the accident report had been from Chicago.

"I try not to pay it any attention," Hulbert said. "There's people passing through here all the time in deer season." He grinned. "I just sit down low," he said, ducking, "you know? In the house, so if a bullet goes through, I don't get hit."

"This would have been right around the first weekend in November."

"Enh?" Yes?

"Waiabiskiwedjig," I said. White guys.

Hulbert bit the last Twinkie in half, tossed part of it into the willows bordering the drive. He swallowed, sniffing again.

"Last November?" He brushed his hands clean on his pants, looked off over his shoulder, as if he were listening for something. "Shit, I can't remember what happened last week, much less the year before," he said, and winking—his way of saying the conversation was over—went into the cabin.

I lit a cigarette and leaned against my truck.

It was no different at Gladys Fisher's, or at her son's place, farther east, where three bowlegged kids stood behind their mother so quiet and well behaved it felt rehearsed. I got out packs of Twinkies, handed them to the oldest, a girl of five or so. She had the biggest, whitest teeth.

"What do you say," the girl's father said.

"Thank you," she said. She bit her lip, looked between me and her father; the kids were all watching, staring, hungry, but didn't eat.

"Well?" Eugene said.

I knew Eugene from school. He'd put on some weight, and now those pearl buttons of his paisley shirt were strained over his belly.

"Just wanted to ask you a few things."

Sophia, Eugene's wife, ushered the children away with a smile. Eugene's face drew in, as if he might cough, and then he grinned, as always, implacably friendly, eyes wrinkled in good humor. We did all that with the weather, the gill netting debate. I asked about last November, the deer hunters who'd gone through.

"Can't help you there," Eugene said.

"So, nothing unusual?"

"How's fishing?" Eugene said.

It was awful, and he knew it. He also knew, I wouldn't say that.

"Great," I said.

>> ◇ <<

Driving south into Pine Point I put the visor down. I'd talked to fifteen or so people, and not one of them had offered up so much as a maybe, but I got the feeling there was something they weren't telling me, and whatever it was had scared them.

The sun hung fat and hot on the rim of the horizon; fireflies danced green along the road behind me and in the ditches. I stopped at the Rambler's, twilight coming on, cool now, the elms leafy and full, the ground dappled in shadow.

In the last of the evening light, kids were playing stickball. Cheerful shouts and teasing. "Toby's got a wooden leg," one of the Yellowfeather kids chanted. "Better to kick you with," the boy said.

There was the smell of fry bread, a rich, oily bread smell, parents calling their children—*Darian! Clarence! Delia! You come now!*—the restless sound of roller skates on hardwood rising from the south end windows.

On the stoop, I paused, my hand on the door. I meant to go in and talk to Moses.

Standing there, I recalled my uncle, Niskigwun, my mother and father, and my sister, years earlier, before all the bad things happened, sitting for hours, right here, cool cement steps, taking turns playing stickball. My uncle, usually so quiet and still, with a whoop, would jump up, dancing, spinning, twirling, dodging, spinning that ball out in front of him, and my father, too, would jump up, stealing the ball, the men tussling, laughing, and the women coming up then.

Twenty, thirty people. Right here in the Rambler's lot, all that time ago. Gingham dresses, the men in corduroy. Laughter, the women making a kind of ululating cry, charging, also great stick handlers. Now most of them were inside, or had passed away.

I watched the kids play. I knew all their families, the Yellowfeathers, the Finedays, the Morrisons and Strong Rock families.

"Weasel," a small boy shouted, charging.

I felt my legs go tense with his rushing the end of the lot where they'd knocked down the nettles to make a goal. I drew the Rambler's door back, intending to go in again, then skipped down the steps, a kind of release in it.

I snatched a stick from a kid sitting on the side, skittered across the lot.

"Hey!" I shouted.

I caught the ball, and spitting it out to the Yellowfeather kid, we charged, passing it back and forth, elastic catch, and flicking out again, the others ducking, poking for the ball.

The Yellowfeather kid snapped it in from the side, scored.

They came at us, the Morrisons and Strong Rocks, passing back and forth. Smell of dust, nettles, the lake, a motorboat, distant, that sputtering, water-muffled chatter, pulling away from shore, night coming on, the sky a cap of bright rose, wood smoke.

I stopped to listen. I got that feeling I was being watched again. Or was it just that it was getting dark? I was distracted and they scored.

"*Mi'nawina,*" the Yellowfeather boy said. What is it?

"Nothing," I said, and ducking in, got the ball, and we started it up all over.

15

Monday morning, new guests. In the eighties, and not yet noon. I'd double booked and had to make more frequent trips into Pine Point. I had planned on a few no-shows, due to the heat, but hadn't gotten them, so I had to put people up at a motel in town.

A week swam by, Monday afternoon, smiling, always the investment in what Frank, the old owner, had called first impression equity. Fishing, deep bays and bobbers. Tuesday, tours around the lake in that infuriatingly slow pontoon, a ride into town, a hike up Snowbank Island. Wednesday, middle of the week, dazed with it all, boats in and out, minor injuries, cuts, bruises. Thursday, trolling for northern, shore lunch, Friday, wrapping it up, the end in sight.

Usually, Gwen and I would have two days to ourselves then. Two long, quiet days. Saturday and Sunday. But now I'd booked the weekend with fly-ins.

So the weekend went by in a rush of activity, and then it was Monday, and new guests, always wanting something, special breakfasts, a night on one of the outlying islands, a tour of the bay.

Ora Shoenfeld, big on legs like inverted bowling pins, sunglasses, was waiting for just that now. She squeezed by me, saying "Excuse me," in a musical voice. She went up the dock and with an "umpf!" let herself down into a boat.

"Oh, taxi!" she said, joking.

Hugh put on a ten-kilowatt smile. He slapped me and, winking, said,

"All yours."

Slumming, on an island, I listened to myself chatter:

...tamaracks are really larches. See the cones? The boughs hang scraggly like that. Deciduous needles. Larix laricina. But the name tamarack is an Algonquin one, picked up by the Hudson's Bay people. The name is really hackmatac.

From wherever I was, I watched the lodge dock, the boats going in and out.

...this stone? Granite. It's igneous. You can see how it was rolled and flattened by the glacier that left these moraines, that's what made these lakes. The glacier melted. Granite comes from the word grain. If you look close, you'll see quartz, that's this crystalline part, the rose part is microcline and mica.

From the bay, I could get to the lodge in minutes, but that was not good enough.

Day after day, I ran supplies out from Pine Point, repaired appliances, fixed up trouble. One afternoon, a kid went for a joyride in one of our boats and put a jagged hole in the bottom, which took a welder to fix. Someone stole the wheels from my truck at the government docks. We had a chimney fire in the kitchen.

Up at five, in bed at ten. Eyes in the back of my head. Starting at loud noises. For the Fourth, I rented a school bus and drove our latest group into Baudette for fireworks. Colored daisies of blue and yellow and white bursting overhead, one kid got lost chasing a glow-in-the-dark Frisbee through the crowd. Another got sick, eating too many corndogs. A third was disturbed in some way and kept hitting the others no matter what I did.

Usually I enjoyed the fireworks, but now I looked through the crowd, for what I wasn't sure.

"What are you starin' at?" Emil Debundunk said.

"Your tie," I said.

Emil wasn't wearing a tie. I just wanted to get back to the lodge, where Gwen would be irritated with my "mooning around," as she put it.

16

In our cabin later that evening, I brushed Gwen's hair again. Had anyone heard from Al? she asked. I worked the brush down to a knot, started again, lower, trying to steady my hands. I didn't answer.

"What are you thinking?" she said.

I was thinking I had to run into Pine Point in the morning, was thinking of boxes of Hostess pies, glazed in sugar; of hot dogs, and steaks, and bread, and paper towels; of motor oil and gear case lubricants.

And I was thinking, it's coming at us, what had come at Al.

"Supplies," I said, to turn her from Al.

"Oh, that."

"What about you?"

"I don't know," she said. She let go a deep breath. "I guess I'm not thinking much of anything right now. None of it seems to make any difference."

"What?" I said.

She picked up the clock on the nightstand, set the alarm.

"It's late, Paul."

She kissed my cheek, turned on her side, and pulled the covers up over her shoulder.

"Go to sleep," she said.

> > ◇ < <

I got out of bed later, dressed, and went down to the boathouse. I rigged up one of the outboards, and in the dark wove through the buoys, the buoys looming high, phosphorus blue-white, counting them off, six, seven, eight, until there was open water, the stars overhead. I followed the arm of the Big Dipper—or the Fisher Stars, Ojeeg Anung, as my people call them—turning around Snowbank Island, then Kettle.

I was rushing then, up Bull Rushes Narrows. It had occurred to me, lying in bed, that I should press Gerry. The thought had come out of nowhere, with the force of revelation.

He was the only other person who could have known I was going hunting that afternoon, through Larissa. Larissa, whom I'd called to share the good news with, that I was going to sign the deed on the resort, the day after.

Coming into the government docks, I hunched down in the back of the boat, so no one could see me, could tip Gerry off.

> > ◇ < <

I narrowed my steps, climbing, pines now, inscrutable, high, whooshing in the late-night breeze, came at the cabin up Jacobson's Hill. The lights were on in the cabin and my father's truck was gone. I had hoped it would be, not wanting him involved. Gerry's truck was parked up alongside the house. Going by, I gave it a look-see, walked a circle around it, putting off going inside. On the front were mismatched tires—one radial, one bias-ply; on the rear, weird off-market, nearly bald retreads.

But what of it? Half the vehicles up on the reserve have mismatched tires.

I knocked twice at the stoop. "Hey, you decent?" I said.

There was the sound of scuffling inside, and then Gerry called out, through the screen door,

"That you, Paul?"

"No, it's Kaiser Wilhelm," I said. "Bring out the military band."

Larissa swung the door out, jeans, an old maroon University of Minnesota T-shirt, high-top Keds. She made fists, pressed them into her eyes, yawning.

"Is something wrong?" she said.

"No," I told her, going in. I knew I was abusing an old tradition.

"Beer?" Gerry said, holding out a can.

I took the beer and sat across from him, taking it all in. The lamp beside him was cockeyed like he was. On the lampshade was a children's cowboy chasing an Indian. Gerry collected things like that—Gene Autry junk, Indian memorabilia in bad taste. It was all over the place now, on the walls, in the kitchen.

How had Larissa let him do that to the house?

Gerry'd had a few but was trying to focus. He crossed his legs one way, then the other, uncomfortable. Larissa, in the kitchen, was making something to eat.

I felt the run of it, a kind of luck; Gerry wouldn't look at me.

When Larissa had the fridge door open, and I knew she wouldn't hear, I smiled at Gerry and said,

"I think you had something to do with Al getting killed."

I'd wanted to shock him, catch him off guard, and I did. Gerry's eyes came open, as if something were falling on him. Then he blinked, sleepy-eyed again.

"Did not," he said, sullenly, and crossed his legs, sinking into the couch.

"So, how do you know he's dead?" I asked.

"I didn't say that. I meant that he was *missing*."

"No, I heard you say, 'Did not.'"

"Oh, stuff it."

"Do you want mustard on your sandwich?" Larissa called from the kitchen.

"You got onion?"

She said she did, but they were in the cellar. I knew that. After all, it was my house, or had been, anyway. There was the clunking of her feet on the steps, the flap of the wooden door into the root cellar.

"Ah, hell. Everybody around here knows Al shot himself," Gerry said, "and anyway, I was down to the Twin Cities that weekend. You check it out if you want. Talk to Moses."

"Moses," I said.

Gerry was looking into the kitchen, hoping to see Larissa pop up.

"Which weekend was that? When were you down in the Cities?"

"The last weekend in May."

"So how are you so sure that was the weekend Al was killed?"

Gerry rolled his eyes, brought his hands down on his thighs with a slap.

"Why do you keep saying that?! He wasn't killed; he shot himself."

"And *when* was that?"

"How the hell would I know when he shot himself? The last I saw of him he was up here messing around, behind the cabin, with that boat. Then Moses came by, and we went down to St. Paul, over there at Little Earth.

"You can ask Moses—we weren't anywhere near here."

I said, "I saw the body. Had burial markings all over it."

Gerry drank his beer. He was staring morosely down into his lap. For a second, I thought, maybe that's all there is to it. A suicide.

"I heard about that."

"You did," I said. "How? You seem to know an awful lot for somebody who wasn't even—"

"Shit! All kinds of people know about it, how he painted himself up and all that. You aren't the only one. I mean, it wasn't Charlie that found him. It was one of the Finedays down there. A kid. Vincent, who just had to tell everybody."

Having said it, Gerry stared down into his lap; now he'd gone and done it.

"Down *where?*"

"Rice Lake! Where have you been, Paul?"

Rice Lake? Rice Lake was a good hundred, hundred fifty miles south, on the White Earth reserve. There was something I wasn't getting. Why hadn't Charlie told me? I'd wondered why they'd taken the body to the Beltrami County morgue. And then it came to me—it was all in that boot.

That's what Charlie had wanted to know, where I'd picked up that boot.

Where Al had probably been killed. Something went off in my head like a burst of light.

"I saw your tire tracks up at Kennebeck," I said, just like that, pushing it now. "You were up there when he got rid of my boat, weren't you."

Gerry laughed; it was a forced, frightened laugh.

"You're funny!"

"Hey?" I said, throwing my hands up. "Who else has tires mismatched like yours? I'll bet those prints are still there. Hasn't rained all month. Firestone on the right, Goodyear on the left, those two hashed-out Kellys on the rear.

"Maybe I'll go up and take a few pictures."

Gerry came off the couch, his face swelling, his mouth working—

"You stay the fuck away from there!"

"Why? What's it to you?"

Gerry's face turned ashen. He looked positively furious.

"That wouldn't prove anything!"

"Why *should it,* Gerry?"

"Now you just *get the fuck outta here!*" he shouted.

Larissa was coming out of the kitchen with the sandwich.

"What is it?" she said.

"It's nothing," I told her.

Gerry was stomping across the living room, then back again. "This is *not* your house anymore," he shouted. "You just Get—The Fuck—*Out!*"

Larissa tried to take Gerry's arm, and he yanked it away.

"Gerry," Larissa said.

He swung at me and hit that cockeyed cowboy lamp and it tumbled to the floor and went out with a blue flash. I came at him, and ducking, jabbed him once in the stomach. It knocked the wind out of him and he dropped to his knees, whooping.

"Great," Larissa said. "Just great." Her eyes shone in the near dark.

"Why do you do this to me?" she said, and then she was crying, and I pulled her outside.

>>◇<<

At the Makogan Bay Motel I puffed up a pillow, then looked out the windows.

I could see the Rambler's star through the trees, winking blue and red and yellow. Farther off was the red Pegasus at the corner Skelly.

"What's with the house?" I said.

"Gerry said if he's going to be living there he should have some say in what's in it."

Her eyes sidled away from mine, hiding something. I crossed the room to her and threw my arms over her shoulders, gave her a brotherly squeeze.

"Is he in trouble?"

"No," she said. "I mean, I don't think so. You know Gerry." She picked at a stray thread in her jeans. "But I don't know what he does most days. He's been real crazy lately."

"All right," I said. "Why don't you get some sleep. I'll call you in the morning."

"What's it all about?" Larissa asked.

"Nothing," I said.

17

From somewhere, water was dripping on my face. The roof was leaking again, I thought. I was looking for a Folgers can to catch the water, was hearing that tin can plunk, plunk, plunk.

I felt a hand on my shoulder and bolted up.

"Hey!" I said, rubbing my eyes.

Bright room, sun streaming in. Gwen stood back of the bed, laughing. It was a good kind of laughter, silver. She was in her suit, a black one-piece, shapely, a lime-green towel draped over her shoulders.

She dried her hair, thick, black, sleek, her eyes blue with flecks of white.

"Where'd you go last night?"

I rolled onto my side, pulled the pillow over my head. Gwen peered in at me.

"Where?"

"I went into Pine Point, got into a muckraker with that jerk, Gerry, over at the house."

"Get up," she said.

And like that—I could see she was making a real effort—I got up, and we had breakfast together; there at the table, the guests around us, Gwen beautiful in blue, graceful, and we talked about nothing, and it was lovely; it almost seemed like it had been.

That evening, a warm listless breeze blew up from the south. It was Friday, the last of it for this group, the Hendersons and Binghams, Rosenbergs and their children, Roths, Kleins, all up from Cleveland, the Mitchells, who'd been coming up since I could remember. We had a big, sit-down dinner, steak and potatoes, corn on the cob, all grilled, which everyone happily ate, and after, sat up high on the spine of the island, the kids blowing bubbles.

I made rings out of coat hangers, filled empty soup cans with soapy water. The breeze carried the bubbles shimmering and wobbling big as dreams over the bay where they sparkled rainbow colors and disappeared in a flash. If you watched closely, you could see a drop fall, a circle in the lake.

The water was that still.

Later, the breeze shifted, came out of the northwest, a strong, cool breeze smelling of rain. The twenty, twenty-five of us, smoking, a cooler of beer, wine, the sun shooting out fingers of orange and yellow, kids playing, tugged jackets around our shoulders, chilled.

A half moon hung over the lake; rippling back from it was a bolt of pale cream.

I made small talk but couldn't get over an uneasy, anxious feeling that something was wrong. The woman to my right, Donna, in her forties, her hair a no-nonsense helmet of red hair shot with gray, related how the Day Kennedy Died smelled of chalk dust to her.

Her teacher, she said, who was going to write something on the board, had just stood there banging an eraser on the chalk tray.

"It was like being in a cloud," she said, "but it made my eyes sting and we were coughing."

I had my own memories of that day, and they were not nearly so pleasant. I had pocketed a box of paper clips at the Ben Franklin, in Pine Point, where I'd gone with my father. While he'd dug through drawers of washers and sheet metal screws, I spied the paper clips on the counter, had palmed them, moving toward the door.

I'd wanted to make figures out of the wire. It was popular at school then.

Outside my father asked me what I had there. I told him, Nothing. For lying, my father had crushed the box of paper clips in my hand, had taken me up and down Main Street, showing everyone what I'd stolen.

"Lookit what Petey's got here," he'd said. That he used my nickname made it worse.

Nita, my grandfather, had called me that. He'd made a toolbox for me, had put my initials in maroon paint on the front. "P-Tee-P," he'd said, winking. "Sounds like Petey. Old St. Peter. The rock. Nina'pomigwun, huh? That's you," he said, "huh?"

And like that, I'd become, for a time, Pete. Or, as Nita called me, *Nawaji*, Little Rock.

So I was watching this woman, talking at me, remembering all that, and how Eugenia Morreaseau (how beautiful! those dark, pupilless eyes, a mouth, like some ripe, smooth-skinned fruit; I wanted to just touch her face, with an outstretched finger, I was so in love with her!) began to cry, when my father held out my grubby hand.

"Do you remember any of that?" Donna said.

I told her, "No, not really."

I was aware of pine scent, body odor, cologne, and cutting through it all, a faint smell of gasoline. I sat up, wondering where it came from.

The kids, seven of them, were chasing each other, bright colors, some still blowing bubbles. I drank a soda, watched the bubbles floating out over the bay.

I was about to get up, when there was the mechanical whir, whir, whir of a starter, a boat out on the lake, and I thought—that's it—a powerboat, that's what the gas smell was coming from—stalled.

I heard an airy *whoooffff!* like a burner makes in a furnace, coming on.

A fireball boiled up, over the dock, orange and blue flame, and we all got to our feet, startled, one kid shouting,

"What is it?"

The wind carried the hot, oily smoke at us through the trees and then we were running all directions, crazy, and I tried to keep people back from the ledge without being pushed over it myself. It was a long drop down, fifty or so feet, to the jagged shoreline below.

"Hey!" I shouted, trying to get them moving in one direction, sick fear in my stomach.

"Get-over-here!" I shouted, jerking people into place, trying to keep them moving, down the narrow, steep path to the lake. Everyone crowded onto the path, kicking and pushing and shouting,

"What about my things? *Mark?* Where's *Mark?* What are you going to do if it comes up the ridge?"

"If it comes over the ridge, we'll go into the water," I said.

The smoke was heavy and greasy, choking. Everyone was shoving now, blinded.

"*Stop!*" I shouted.

They were nearly pushing me off the ledge, Elaine Mitchell, half-crippled with arthritis, hobbling, farther down, Judy Bingham trying to get around her, hysterical, crying and tearing at herself in frustration. They pressed in harder. I was being shoved back, barely able to keep my balance, behind me just open space, and that drop to the rocks, so I pushed back at them. There was not much to stand on and I was about ready to punch at Norman Mitchell, when Gwen swept up the smallest boy, who was screaming, and slapped his brother, who'd knocked down Elaine.

"*You!*" Gwen said, and got the boy moving, carrying, as much as leading, Elaine.

"But what about my things?!" Norman was shouting. "What about—"

"You shut up," Gwen said.

The smoke came down over us, pitch heavy and blinding. Gwen kept them moving, where all I'd done was work up people's panic; it amazed me, but then, she'd always been like that.

I passed the kids to Gwen, hands clutching at me, shoes skidding on that steep path, hollow shuck of soles on sand, fingernails, scratching.

We got them all down, and I ran up the path to the lodge, over the ridge, my shirt off, breathing through it, everything lit violent orange, the clouds, overhead, dark, and promising rain, illuminated, on my hands and knees at times, the path flinty, cutting my palms. Smoke so heavy breathing it stung.

The boathouse was in flames, the pines upshore catching like torches, the hillside black with ash, and when the wind changed, again, the flames came down, burning, licked the lodge roof.

Flames everywhere.

Mardine was slamming all the lodge windows shut, so the curtains wouldn't start up.

I got blankets in the lodge laundry room and ran outside. Hugh was there now, staring, his hands at his sides.

"Don't just stand there," I shouted.

I tried the spigot.

Nothing. The electric pump wasn't working, wouldn't work.

The wind shifted, driving the flames out onto the water, the water orange with it. High, billowing flames. Hugh and I ran the blankets to the lake, where we dunked them, just as the wind shifted back up the hill, the flames rolling up and over the dock and coming at us, a wall of yellow-red. We slung the wet blankets over our backs and went up, spreading them on the lodge roof. Sopping wet and heavy and steaming. Mardine brought more from in back. Hugh was sick, on his hands and knees. We went down to the lake again, and coming up, Hugh fell.

"It's too hot!" he shouted.

"What?!" I said.

The flame came at us again, a wash of it. I had my head in fire—my hair crackled on my head, burning, fierce heat. I had my eyes closed, and when I opened them, here came Mardine down the path, big as a bear, shouting,

"Get outta there, you stupid sons of bitches!"

She grabbed Hugh by his braids, dragging him up the hill, and he came up with her, stumbling, "Goddammit, Mardine!" then he was on his hands and knees, and when he tried to swat Mardine away, she whacked him on the side of the head.

"Get up there!" she shouted, but he fell again, and I got his shirt, and we dragged him, now half running, half stumbling, up back of the lodge.

Steam lifted from the roof and into the trees. The three cabins down near the water caught fire, and there was that awful *pock-chink!* of shattering glass.

I got a sick, rending feeling; those were the oldest cabins, the first ones.

I ran down to the cabin farthest west, and got inside, the room lit with fire, tucked the old Edison spool player from the mantel under my arm, heavy as cinder blocks, my grandfather's pride and joy—the first on the lake—, crazed, tried to get my mother's beadings off the walls, tore at them, beautiful floral-pattern leggings, in seed beads and porcupine quill.

The seed beads spilled everywhere, were glassy under my feet, I was sliding on them. I got on my hands and knees, chased them across the floor. Shoved them in my mouth.

The ceiling fell in, knocking me across the room, burning my neck, smoke black as ink. I caught a lungful of pine smoke and charged outside, and sucking in big ragged breaths, I swallowed all those beads.

>> ◇ <<

I charged up the spine of the island, legs rubbery under me. Lungs like pincushions. The guests were huddled down on the west shore, a knot of odd color there, wet khaki, coral, dull lemon, some of them in the water.

"Gwen!" I shouted.

I turned around there, full circle, my legs nearly giving way under me.

It was all burning. The cabins, the boathouse, the trees there. Blue-red flames so high they seemed to lick at the clouds, the clouds flashing as if exploding from inside, colors like a furnace.

The shore was engulfed in flames.

It had been so shady and lovely. There'd been a rope swing, and on hot days, we'd swung from it out over the water, dropping into the deep green lake with abandon.

Gwen came up the path from the lake, came at me so purposefully, I couldn't move. Face sooty, her blue shirt torn. She put her arm though mine.

"Don't move," she said, pinning me there.

"I've got to *do* something," I said.

"There's nothing to do right now," she said, her voice quiet. "You've burned yourself."

"Oh, hell," I said.

That night it rained. In the morning it was still raining, a light, quiet rain, clouds bunched down low on the horizon. I ferried guests to the government docks on the pontoon. They got off hurriedly, the older regulars stopping to shake my hand and say how sorry they were. All of that went on as if in a dream, the day unseasonably cool, damp, and green.

"I hope it works out," that woman, Donna, said.

"Thanks," I told her.

My face burned something awful, but I paid it no attention.

The rain came down and didn't stop.

The ruins of the boathouse and cabins smoldered for the better part of a week. The police came out, black slickers and rubber boots; poked through the wreckage. I helped, digging with a shovel. Mardine called us in for lunch.

At the stoop, I tried to wipe the soot from my boots, but only made them worse. I was impatient—soot was everywhere, in everything—so I wiped my hands down the length of my pants, then over the sleeves of my shirt, until my hands were clean.

Mardine, seeing me through the kitchen doorway, looked stricken.

"What is it?" I said.

She motioned for me to go out, to go away. I went into the hall and looked at myself in the mirror. A black stripe up each leg, over each arm, my boots black with soot. I laughed to myself. I looked like someone prepared for burial; all I needed were the round spots of brown fungus on my cheeks, the horizontal lines of vermilion.

Mardine rushed out with a wet towel. She dabbed at my legs and arms.

"You don't want to attract things," she told me.

I laughed. "As if I haven't already."

The fish were biting, and while the police poked in the ruins, I angled from the point.

Gwen, I was surprised to see, was still making her swim across the bay and back. A little over a mile, all in all, and getting longer.

"She do that every morning?" one of the officers asked. He was trim and dark and efficient looking in his outfit and badge.

I told him she did.

"Boy, that lady can swim," he said, and went back to digging at the foundation of the boathouse. "Sure is pretty, too."

"She's my wife," I said, in a deadpan voice.

The officer laughed. I laughed too, then looked him face on.

"It's not a joke," I said.

It was a mean little trick, and I felt ugly after.

In the end, arson was thought not to be the cause, no matter how much I tried to convince the police, or the private investigator the insurance company sent up, otherwise.

The cause was electrical, they claimed.

"See?" the investigator said. He was a thin man in gray slacks. He lifted the remains of the wire that had carried 110 to the boathouse. The cotton insulation was burned as far back as the lodge.

"Simple," he said. He was nearly bald, and the breeze off the lake tossed back the hair on the crown of his head. "Resistance," and when he began to explain, I said, "I know. Opposition to electric current characteristic of medium, substance, or circuit element—here, a direct loop, a short, and so—heat. Lots of it."

"So, you're an engineer, are you?"

I shrugged. "Why down on shore?"

The investigator nodded in the direction of what remained of the boathouse, a pathetic square of charred timber and blackened cinder block. We walked down. With the toe of his shoe, he turned over a lump of something in the ashes. It was the size of a casting reel, but much heavier, at the end of it what looked like a chrome nipple.

"What is it?"

"Fan," he said. "Somebody left this fan on. Bearing probably seized, it's an old fan, right? Those crappy brass bearings. Then you got direct resistance. That's all she took."

For a second, I thought he was going to say, You're lucky it didn't start in the lodge. He must have seen the old fans there, too. And when he didn't, I felt a new measure of respect.

"I think that does it," he said.

I didn't explain that I had never had a fan in the boathouse, and for that very reason—fire hazard. But, after all, he was right about that, the fan, and who'd put it there was my problem.

"You going to take it?" I said.

"No," the inspector said, "we've got photos. It's all yours."

The third day after, Charlie came out. He stood on shore, dumpy discount-store golf jacket, the sleeves worn thin at the elbows, laces shoddily tied on his muddy boots, not minding the light rain, his hand in a bag of powdered sugar donuts. There was powdered sugar in his mustache. He clucked his tongue.

"Anything?" he asked.

"No," I told him. We stood in the light rain. "Anything with you?"

"Same old, same old." He was making those eager swallowing sounds, had his hand in the bag again. "Any idea who did it?"

I kicked at a loose board. Cool, pinprick of rain, Charlie, eating those donuts, his eager chewing. I was going to say, Haven't got the foggiest, when I felt my face heat—

I was staring at my boot, soot blackened, on the white dock.

"You think of something, you call me," Charlie said. "Okay?"

He poked a donut at me. Powdered sugar, nasty granular lemon sugar-creme filling. It was familiar, and almost good.

"Will ya do that?" he said.

Mardine called from the lodge stoop. The washer had broken again.

"So?" Charlie said.

"It's a deal," I told him, and headed back up the hill and into the lodge.

I got down to that washer and, my hands busy, put my mind to it.

There is an old belief among us Chippewa, that the northern lights are the ghosts of the deceased, dancing, all dressed up, warriors in their beaded leggings, the brightest turquoise and lavender and blue, women in flowing robes of red and yellow and green.

You had to be prepared to join them, though, had to be marked for their company when you died: brown spots on the cheeks, the line of vermilion. All the rest of it.

That's how the story went.

On the other side, the deceased, recognized by friends and family and loved ones, rose up and danced.

I thought about that, head under the washer, hands sure, putting things together. Needle-nosed pliers, cir-clips, neoprene bushings. Bright, chemical smell of soap, a stray kernel of popcorn poking into my back.

You had to be recognized, all that had to be done the proper way, I remembered. It was the obligation of friends (or the suicide) to paint the cheeks brown, apply the vermilion stripes over, draw them back to the ears. Set aside trinkets and articles, a gun, beading. (Or now, other articles: Once, I'd seen a tennis racquet, a basketball, an old radio.) You had to put aside a kettle, a dish, and a spoon, for the journey. (I'd seen a McDonald's hamburger, once.)

All that I knew. Had known. About the face, the trinkets, the vermilion stripes, the fungus paint. But I'd forgotten the feet. In the Medicine Society burial, the last thing said was,

You journey now on the road of souls.

Always, the deceased, man or woman, the traditional, would be buried with his feet painted in that brown fungus, the body set with the feet facing west. My mother had been buried like that.

I remembered the look of it, her too-narrow shoes, those bunions, her feet, painted, looking for all the world like dark, lumpy potatoes, just worn out with it all and heartbroken, and me, glum at graveside, clutching her spirit bundle, too sad to cry.

I hadn't thought about it since. It was the last traditional burial I'd been to.

On my back, looking up into the maw of that washer, I thought, Al would have prepared himself. Suicide, among our people, is just a passing. Al would have done it right. Would have painted his cheeks, put on the vermilion. Would have run a stripe down each leg, down each arm. But last, he would have painted his shoes.

And had anyone Chippewa killed him—then, too, surely, with someone like Al, one of the Eagles, they would have followed the proper rites. Or made pretenses of it. Al, for all his outward clownishness, had been a *dja'sakid,* a sorcerer; you didn't mess with people like that, not without taking precautions.

Whoever had killed him, had to have known all that. But there were others, too.

One had to be an outsider, pushing things, so that whoever had done the markings had either not gotten to Al's feet or had forgotten them.

I could just imagine the panic when, seeing how things had been done wrong, one of them, a traditional, had yanked that boot from Al's body, had thrown it as far as possible, so that the spirit, hobbled, would walk in circles. That's how Al's boot had come to be there in the weeds.

So Al's shadow wouldn't come looking for them.

Under the washer, turning a wrench, I chuckled. All of that was superstition:

That the dead talk. That the spirit, distressed, hovered near the body, and caused mischief, even accidents, sometimes fatal. That those not at rest called out. That the spirit, ill-prepared, and unrecognized, caught on the near side, watching those dancers in the above world, would look for a way to get across.

That the dead, ill at ease, would come looking to settle things with those who'd done them wrong, and, too, for someone to help do it.

I cut my hand on something in that washer. Cursed. Right then, I knew who that person was.

18

The rain kept on, a day or two more, into August, but it was a different rain. I lay nights on my back, staring into the dark, trying to make all that I knew fit together, but it wouldn't. Nights, too, there was that smell. A sharp, burned pine smell that permeated everything. Bacon. You couldn't escape it.

"What is it?" Gwen would ask.

"Just everything," I said.

I had barely saved enough over the month to make our last payment, and we were stone broke. We had eleven cabins, empty. Three burned. No boathouse, a number of ruined outboards and boats. We'd lost our August first-week guests, and maybe our second, and now, in the rain, the fish were biting wonderfully.

It was a disaster, but we weren't saying that.

From what remained of the dock, I caught a twelve-pound walleye, a record in anybody's book, but did not so much as bring it into the government docks to register the catch.

I wet my hand, and feeling that walleye's water-cool,

silver-green-lovely, muscular body, tinfoil eye staring in its socket, released him.

>> ◇ <<

I left the light on those nights, sitting up, pretending to read, while trying to think my way through it. Gwen, her back turned to me, her blue-black hair shiny on the white linens, slept fitfully.

There were all kinds of things not right, and it wasn't just the boot, but Al's face, too. Al's face, which I pictured nightly, something in how those red swatches had been painted too high. But how would someone know to do so much right, and miss the rest? And Charlie poking around, after the fire. What was it to him? What could he want from me? Charlie, who was now even friendly?

And there was this: my insurance, I'd discovered, was woefully inadequate, yet I had to get things up and running. I was at the end of it, my resources.

Lying there nights, I was tormented at the thought of asking for help; I broke out in sweats, felt ill, fevers passed through me. Who would have anything to do with me now? I was finally, and unarguably, *de'wene,* touched by that which brings sickness and death.

It was in my fingers, my hands, my feet. It was working inside me, was there in my face, my uneasy smile. I'd seen it in others and knew what it looked like. I'd avoided those people myself.

Tchibai. A walking shadow, that's what I'd become.

"Go talk to someone, get help," Gwen said finally. "Anyone."

"I can't ask," I said.

"Why not?"

"Why can't you tell me what happened to you?" I said, raised on my elbow. It was a bad kind of dodge.

Gwen did that thing with her hair. She wrapped it around her finger.

"We're not talking about that."

"But don't you see my point?"

"What point?"

"Why I can't ask?" I told her. "For help, I mean?"

"It's different," Gwen said. Gwen, at times, had black moods. They had nothing to do with me, she said, but wouldn't say what caused them.

"How?" I asked.

"It would attach to us then, and I'd never be free of it," Gwen said. "And besides, you know well enough anyway. Why make it real, why bring it back?"

Once, Gwen had told me, If I tell you, you'll do something. I know you. You say you won't, but you'll go after him. *Him,* that was her only concession. And she was right, I would have.

"See?" I said. "Now do you see? I've got to do it myself."

"No," she said. "I don't at all."

We lay there, saying nothing. The clock on the mantel made a hollow, irritating *cluck-tick, cluck-tick.* I tried to think how to put it. How to explain my position. Why, even after all that had happened, I couldn't so much as consider outside help.

Years ago, all my early years, really, those last few awful years of the fifties, my father had made it a point of showing me how I was responsible for things. How asking for help, or even looking like you needed help, put you in a condition of obligation.

"Get one thing from 'em, they'll come back asking for ten," he said.

Somehow, it always came down to tribal politics, the BIA orbiting dangerously like some dark moon behind those offers of loans, or material things we needed. Any good deed up there was suspect.

That's what my father said.

"Don't take any handouts, 'cause they're not. Believe you me, buddy boy."

I listened. It explained my father's behavior, at least some of it. By then my father was drinking, and prone to fits of violence, and he showed me in no uncertain terms how I was responsible for the car's crumpled fender, because I'd asked him to drive me into Pine Point. Or how, when he hadn't gotten a buck, hunting, it was because I'd asked him not to walk so fast, had held him back by being slow and selfish and stupid.

Asking for things got you in trouble.

It was my fault that Larissa was having trouble at school, because, if it were so easy for me, why did she have to struggle? It was my fault the cabin was a mess, that the stoop settled to one side, that a tire on our car got a nail in it. The bruises on my face were my fault, too.

All that time my mother was silent. But when my father would leave, she'd say, "He means well." And I would hear her version of that old story again.

I had heard it, by then, a hundred times, how my father, after returning from the war, all hope, and know-how, and goodwill, had gotten in the middle of a long, bitter struggle with the BIA. There was a paper plant to be built to the south. The Au-au-wak, the Giwadiswin, and Pillager Clans were opposed to it. But the Noka, and a few others, were needing jobs. The plant would use methyl mercury in its processing, would dump the water off Wheeler's Point.

I remember my mother dressing my father before he took the Burlington Northern down to the Twin Cities:

Blue, double-breasted navy uniform, epaulettes, like fancy gold wings on his shoulders, shoes so shiny you could see your face in them.

He'd ruffled the hair on my head, squeezed my sister until she giggled.

That was the last good time. My mother smudged him with sweetgrass and cedar. Sprinkled artemisia on him, then, laughing, a bright, sunlight laughter, sprinkled it on Larissa and me.

"Well?" my father had said.

My mother kissed him on the cheek. Then they were gone, my father and two other men, and when they came back from St. Paul it was no good.

Samuel Fisher died in a timber accident, the other man drowned late one night, fishing. The paper plant went in, and my father never said what happened down there.

But I felt it:

I remember bringing the wrong rice sacks, one fall, in our canoe, the big ones, and so had ruined our profit, my father said. The sacks had holes in them, my father said at the weighing. Why had I brought the wrong sacks?

Those sacks had holes in them all right, one big hole, which was my father's soul, which he poured all that liquor into.

That afternoon, he'd fallen asleep in our canoe, leaving me to do all the work. Desperate, coming in just after dark, I'd thought partially filled bags would look better than one full one, so I carefully poured the grain from one sack into the other five.

So, six, barely filled, lumpy sacks.

I stood back of the grain agent, exhausted. It didn't matter that every other canoe had had two people in it. Or some of them three. Had filled eight, or ten, hundred-pound burlap sacks, each fat to bursting.

I'd expected to make grade anyway.

And when the grain agent put our pitiful bags on the scale, that merciless, bare bulb hanging over it, my father said, in the old language: "Pah, what a worthless boy, see? That's the reason we got so little rice. He's why we don't get ahead here, see? Lazy! Sleeping all afternoon in the boat, and holes in the bags!" he said.

He lifted one of the bags and the grain funneled out, through a hole near the bottom.

I didn't see him do it, but I knew that hole had been made with a knife.

"See?" he said, lifting the bag.

I remember feeling as if my feet had taken root. All those people watching, the Finedays, the Morrisons, the Streaked Cloud family. The Strong Rocks, the Debikamigs, the McClouds. The disgusted looks on their faces; I thought all that was for me.

I didn't forget things like that, not for a moment. I'd be on my own, if I wanted my life to come to anything other than humiliation.

And so, at the end of that October, when the priest, at the parochial school, Our Lady of the Pines, Father Prideaux, was pestering Larissa, and she told me, in the utmost confidence, how he had violated her, time and again—and how he had said he would kill her, if she were to tell—I took care of that myself.

I didn't ask for help.

And that started a whole new life. But I didn't do well with it.

I had no idea how hard it would get, how certain a habit secrecy would become, how awful would be the weight of what I'd done.

A month later, the end of November, I chased a bottle of Seconal I'd stolen from the Pine Point Pharmacy with a quart of turpentine, thinking to fix that. But I'd vomited, and ended up at the hospital in Baudette.

That's when I met Dr. Piper. Hunting jacket, a funny hat on, red flannel with earflaps.

We did not talk about why I'd done it. We talked about birds. I made bird calls, and he laughed. I told him about turtles and how they hibernated in the mud, winters. He'd liked that, too. We talked about respiration, and blood cells. Phagocytosis. The limbic system. Osteocytes.

"Where'd you learn all that?" Dr. Piper asked, as if joking.

"I don't know," I said. "I like to read."

"I'm going to get you out of here," he told me one evening, pressing my arm.

And that's just what he did.

> > ◇ < <

"So," Gwen said, peering up at me, her eyes sleepy. "You aren't going to tell me?"

She sat up. She lifted the clock; it was just after four. She got out of bed, snapped on the light, began opening the dresser drawers, tossing out clothing. Pants, socks, her best blue silk blouse.

"I'm leaving for a few days, maybe as long as a week or more," she said.

I set my book down. I had long ago decided the best policy in matters of love is to give people what they want. It was a fine and good policy when you lived in your head, but the rest of it was awful.

"Why?" I said, barely able to speak.

"You don't need me around right now."

I took that as an accusation, trying to be reasonable. "What do you mean?"

"You know what I mean."

"I'm not like that anymore," I said.

Gwen laughed. I had told her about things I'd done in the past. The worst things I had not told her, not about Father Prideaux, or how Al and I had made money stealing things, as kids. After I'd gotten beyond the little stuff, she told me to stop.

"Aren't I right?" she said.

"No," I said. "It's not that simple."

"Well," she said, turning from her suitcase, "I'm going to make it that simple. You take care of this however you want. I would've thought you'd have somebody looking into all this by now, and you know what I mean. Charlie's willing to help you, I think. But I'm not going to tell you how to do things."

"Gwen," I said. "You don't know Charlie."

From the dresser, Gwen threw me a pitying glance. "You can either tell me right now, right here, what's going on, or I'm leaving, and you can take care of it yourself."

"It's not what you think it is," I said.

Gwen punched the clothing in the suitcase down. She laughed again, a bitter, short laugh. I felt, just then, a kind of despair. I thought, *Say something*. But what?

"I'll fix it," I said.

"Don't insult me."

"It isn't anything," I told her.

"You should just be damn glad nobody got hurt. What if that fire had started after dark?"

I sat at the desk, overlooking the lake. It was getting light out. Everything had greened in the rain, and there was that morning hush over the place.

"God," Gwen said, turning away. "That's it, then. Isn't it?"

>> ◇ <<

Later, I stood on what remained of the dock, burned log footings, paint yellowed and blistered, my hand cupped over my eyes, a visor. The boat cut a deep V across the bay, now a flat stretch of gray-green water, then turned up the channel, and passing the high, tossing buoys, motored out onto the lake toward town.

Gulls lifted, pinwheeling white in all that blue sky.

I waved from the dock, the imprint of Gwen's kiss on my cheek.

The hull flashed red in the morning sun, and she was gone.

19

Pine Point, late afternoon, I was driving a circuit of construction sites, meandering sandy roads, scraggly cedars, looking for George Stronghold. George, who'd been implicated in a long-past murder, an especially grisly one involving a BIA functionary, which he'd been acquitted of on a technicality.

Six-six, two hundred and sixty pounds, he was one of my father's people, of the Au-au-wak Clan, those who'd been against the paper plant. He was a cousin, and a not too distant one.

That I was looking for him should have made me nervous, but here I was humming some Buddy Holly tune,

Every day, gets a little closer
goin' faster like a roller coaster

I was crazy. I was out of my mind. I was happy. All that darkness with Gwen was gone for the moment. I had taken the plunge: I was driving out from the Ten Chiefs Tribal Office, where Parker Keewatin had approved me for a loan I knew I would not get. I had all the papers on the seat beside me, yellow sheets fluttering crisply, outlining what I needed, and what the council had allotted, all signed by Parker in a long, pompous flourish.

I'd called Weyerhaeuser in Baudette, arranged for the supplies to be sent up. Everything I needed to build three cabins and a boathouse.

The cost made my head spin. If I thought about it, I felt a certain panic. It was tricky what I was doing. Parker wasn't about to give me that money, not in a million years.

But I knew that.

Gwen gone, I was going to mess with them, if even indirectly, make them come after me, and take care of the lodge at the same time. All I needed now was some muscle—some especially nasty muscle.

So I was looking for George. At a site now. Someone in overalls cutting high, leafy poplars with a chain saw, oily exhaust and that irritating roar. Lumpy-looking Ford ¾-ton trucks. *Thonk, thonk* of hammers. Had one of these men killed Al?

"Is George around?" I said.

"No. Hear you got work out there?"

"No," I told them.

Worn leather tool belts, suspicious glances, shoulders rucked with labor. Walter Davis, Roy Waseya, Bill Neyadi. Suspicious looks, hands rolling cigarettes. "Hey, sorry to hear about the fire," Walter said, and meant it. Some, as I walked back to the truck, mouthed epithets and threats.

"*Gi'winewa,*" one said. The proud fall.

Still, I was happy. I whistled that tune, lilting and cheerful. My luck was going to change. I just knew it. I had to put the lodge in order, and then I would clean up the rest of it.

It was a plan, and I smiled at the thought of it, the neatness of it, the simplicity, how Parker's intention to do harm would come back at him.

It would be my little piece of magic.

>> ◇ <<

To my right, a house was going up, newly framed; the foundation still gave off that damp, green cement smell. Shiny Tyvec foil insulation. Galvanized tin chimney, speckled particleboard.

I'd been to ten or so sites, but this one had George written all over it.

Old pines, lovely and high, lilacs, a row of them, a hundred years old, or older, lavender flowers, thick green leaves, and farther out, on high ground, broad-limbed oaks gnarly as time.

George came around the corner of the house, twill pants, plaid shirt, carpenter's belt, big as a bear, and as mean looking.

I eased up the driveway, tires crackling.

"Hey! White Man's Dog!" he said. "We were just talking about you."

He scuffled down to the truck, put his big hand on the roof, shoved the other in his pocket.

"Is that so," I said.

George chuckled, his face a copper moon of pocked skin, eyes ill-meaning raisins, crow's-feet at the corners, from squinting.

"Yup. Hear you got a real problem there. Burned all to hell. We all were betting on what you'd do. Cry for momma—" he screwed his face up "—or maybe you'd hang yourself," he made a cheerful choking sound, "or just maybe, just *maybe,* you'd call in some of your *own people,* hey?" He gave me a friendly wink.

"I said you'd hang yourself first."

"Really?" I said. I squinted up at him, the sun bright over his head.

"I know you're on a short rope there, Paul."

"How do you know that?"

"You know how it is around here. Can't take a piss without somebody knowing about it."

"Personally, I'd go for poison," I told him. "I don't like the idea of messing up such a beautiful face."

I smiled, showing my teeth. It was too hot.

Heat haze shimmered off that house, all silver insulation. George slapped the roof of the truck; it made a hollow, metal thunk.

"Well?"

"I need a good carpenter," I said.

George laughed. "You need more than that."

I poured myself a cup of coffee from the thermos on the seat. George was walking away, that thick neck and immense, heavy chest and shoulders. I wanted to know what he meant. Did he know something I didn't?

"I'll pay Union wage," I said. "Double time over sixty hours."

George stopped. "Who else? Some of your other apple assholes?"

"No."

"Like hell."

"You pick 'em," I said. "How about that?"

Ugly boats. Castoffs. Coral pink, with tall chrome-tipped fins. A V-hull Glasstron, once red, faded to the color of butterscotch. One that was sort of broken looking in the middle, as if some kid had made it out of clay, pressed down just back of the windshield to see what would happen. The boats bobbed at the dock. I swung around wide, to come into shore, and waiting for me on the bank was Clark. He looked like a kid sitting there, hair flattened, his clothes rumpled.

We shook hands, Clark turning one way, then the other, taking it all in, boyish.

"So how's it going?" he said.

I laughed at that. "Oh, just fine," I said. "Just terrific. We're in the middle of some remodeling. Black's the fashion color here, you know?"

George lumbered down the path, his belt on, hammer slapping his leg. He tossed back a bottle of beer. Pointed behind him with his chin.

"Simon and Terry are on the cabins."

Simon and Terry were George's brothers, two stick-together rough types.

"Wonderful," I said.

Clark, watching George go back up, registered a certain surprise. He knew George disliked me; and, too, George had never been fond of Clark, "that spoiled rich kid," he'd always called him years back.

"Don't ask," I said.

"Jesus." Clark gave me an almost astonished, but wary look. "It's like an accident just waiting to happen. I mean, of all the people you could bring up...."

I had to turn away so he didn't see me grinning.

We dragged the wreckage down to the point and burned the lot of it, and what wouldn't burn we dumped in the deepest place. Roofing. Trees. Furniture: tables, chairs, bookcases; melted glass; commodes that had burst in the heat into a hundred jagged pieces of white china; a guitar; an old Franklin stove.

All that took days, and we worked in the heat and smoke, a constant cloud over everything. We were head to toe covered with soot, so badly, one day I lay down on my bed before dinner, and when I got up, there on the covers, in black, was the imprint of my body.

It startled me.

20

I was drinking along with George and his brothers now. My head hammered at it; Clark, thinking it was all in fun, drank, too. I wanted to bring on the inevitable, before it got too big to handle. An argument, a parting of ways—hopefully, one that didn't involve a rearrangement of my face by George, who seemed, already, close to obliging me that. It was why I'd hired George and his brothers in the first place, only, soon enough, I'd have to redirect things for it to work.

And now, too, while I waited for the inevitable explosion, or impasse, Clark was telling me how things had gone bad in the Cities. We were down by the remains of the dock.

"I thought it was a separation?" I asked.

"It is. Sort of."

"What do you mean sort of?"

"She's making all kinds of threats."

"I thought that was your lawyer friend's problem?"

"Oh—give it a rest already."

"No connection there?"

Clark rolled his eyes, grimaced. He'd said a lot to me that night in the bar, a bit loosened up.

"So tell me."

He gave me a warning look. It was too much for daylight.

"But we're here, aren't we?" he said. "Aren't we, old friend?"

I was a little drunk, and melancholy, and what the hell—I told him, yes, we were. He set his beer down and stood. A few charred trees remained to be felled, but otherwise, things looked better. But god, was it ever bright. We both looked back at the lodge, just now not so high and proud amid the remains.

Clark grinned. "You've got yourself a medium rare here, Paul."

"I'd say 'well done.' An A-1 barbecue."

Clark lifted his bottle. "Here's to good barbecue!"

"Here's to us," I said. Just then I didn't care.

George came down the hill, dragging a burned four-by-six, a section of roof nailed to it. It was the last of the third cabin.

"I was just saying we got a barbecue here," Clark joked.

"Yeah," George said. "Paul here is fried."

George stopped on the path. The section of roof looked like wings, the four-by-six over his shoulder, and the roof burned blue black and shiny. He looked like an angel, of a kind you wouldn't want to meet, ever.

"And all these years I thought you were an asshole," he said.

I laughed, tossed back my beer. I knew what was coming.

"Well, Paul, I was right," he added, and dragged the wood around to the point.

"He doesn't like you," Clark said.

"Well, I don't like him much either," I said, and we both laughed.

We'd been drinking all afternoon, yet the work was going fine. We were in that happy near-drunk stupor, heat and beer and sweat, where work is work, even abrasive people can seem endearing, and time passes pleasantly.

It was odd that now, when I needed trouble, and of a kind I could have predicted, I wasn't getting it. Everything had gone like clockwork. We'd taken down those burned trees, variegated blackened bark, soot now on everything, hands, face, shirts. Dull hump of labor. Lifting, carrying, cutting. Burning.

Drinking, hot sun, sweat. Raw, chafing rubbage to carry, and burn again.

We took down the last burned pine. Roar of chain saw, oily exhaust, sweat. George and I stood back of it, one of the oldest; the tree gave a groaning, splitting great *crack!* and splashed into the lake.

I told myself that the view of the bay was better, there was more light, it was more inviting and open, when here came Gilby up the path from the dock, hair braided and tied back, smiling, long-limbed, breasts drawn up in a halter top, shorts, and those red socks and heavy hiking boots she wore.

"Hello," she said, a silky hook in her voice.

Clark was one big smile. "Hey, Gilby."

"We've got work to do," I told him, yanking him back.

I saw in her long-legged, butter-smooth, hip-swaying walk a kind of disaster, exactly the kind I did not want, and had worried over, from the first.

"You going to say hello, too, Paul? Or you just going to stand there?" she said.

We ate dinner, packed in at the table, Mardine in the kitchen baking for the morning. Clatter of pans, smell of cinnamon, bread, apple pie. A breeze blew in through the windows, that burned pine in it.

"We'll have the dogs following us around in Pine Point thinking we're sausages," Terry joked.

"So who do you think started the fire?" Gilby said.

"It was an accident," I told her.

George laughed. "And I'm Mother Teresa."

"Shut up and eat," I said.

Sooty, exhausted from the heat, and cockeyed with drink, we shoveled it in. More pike, corn, potatoes. Mardine's three-bean salad. We dug in. We chowed. We were ravenous, exhausted, stopped now and then to hack up clots of black phlegm into napkins.

Eating, and coughing. Drinking beers. The loons calling out on the lake.

Gilby was sitting beside me, and I threw my arm over the back of her chair. George's mouth drew into a flat, angry line.

I wanted to get it over, and now. I was almost enjoying myself. I was a little drunk. George was staring. After dinner, outside, I would make a pass at Gilby, George would take a few swings at me, and that would be that.

How much could that hurt?

I put my face in Gilby's hair. A perfume that made me think of gardenias.

"What is that?" I said.

Gilby blushed. Mardine waved me into the kitchen. I took a few plates with me. Mardine slapped one of them down in the sink, breaking it.

"I *don't* have to like it," she said. "And you know why."

"What else could I do?" I said. "And anyway, he won't be here much longer."

"It's not George," Mardine said.

"If you want to help," I said, in a measured, quiet voice, "you'll tolerate it. Just now."

She turned on the water, filling the sink. Bubbles frothing up. The clasp in her hair was hanging askew, and I set it right, with some real affection.

"You get outta here," she said. "I don't know what you're up to, but I'm *disgusted* with you right now."

. . .

Teasing Clark, and George, Gilby let her head drop back, laughing, her tongue dancing in her mouth, as if it were a thing alive. A fish. Her breasts shook, low neck, I tried not to notice. Lovely.

I sat again, put my arm over Gilby's shoulders, squeezed her. It was getting dark, and the birds were calling.

"Not really!" Gilby said, her mouth twisting, teasing.

"What did I miss?" I said.

"It is, though," George shot back.

They were talking about the powwow in Big Grassy. It was just twenty minutes east, on Falcon Island. All sorts of people would be there.

Gilby pushed her chair back, picking my arm off, as if it were something clinging she didn't like. But not exactly.

"So, why not?" She stood, all excitement, a hothouse flower.

I saw something pass between George and Gilby. All she'd done was nod, pucker her mouth, just the slightest, and George's black mood changed like that.

"Hey, Gilby—whatever," he said. "Why not?"

They went out the door, Gilby in front, hips swinging, George and his brothers behind, laughing, waving me and Clark on.

"Well?" Clark chided.

I had no intention of going into Pine Point after dark, much less Falcon Island.

"Come on," Clark said. "Don't just stand there looking like that. It'll be fun."

And like that, I went with them.

We came into the Narrows, just as it was getting dark, drumming, and that high, ululating singing. On shore, boys, seven, eight, nine years old, laughed and chased girls, all dressed in traditional garb—beaded moccasins, drop shirts, pants with floral embroidery on dark blue or black background. Lovely, all of it.

I felt a kind of bittersweet, almost sick nostalgia, and an almost equally repellent fear. There was safety in numbers, but not when you've set yourself against your own people.

But for now, we came through as a group, George in front, immense, and smiling, then Gilby, in tow, drawing sidelong glances, her walk a kind of oily honey, then Clark, George's brothers, ratty and loping, and tying up the rear, me, sharp looks for everyone.

All around was the familiar and beautiful: jingle dresses, fancy dancer's bells ringing, smell of saddle soap, and cedar. Bright, embroidered costumes.

I'd broken out in a cold sweat. They were here, I thought. Yet what I saw, I was defenseless against: smiles, a slap on the back, old, familiar faces.

I passed old Henry Selkirk, whom I'd studied with as a boy. Shook his hand now.

"*Booshoo,* Henry," I said, as if in a dream.

On one end of the field there was a platform with a roof over it, where the officers of the powwow stood; farther down, on both sides, were green bleachers, between them, the bower-covered drummers' clutch, the drummers there bent down, pounding out a rhythm that got into you and made you move with it.

Everything moved with it now, the drumming, that ululating singing, the cars and trucks coming in, down the hill, lights swaying, left, right, left, right. The fire, on the south side, blazing up, orange. Strings of lights winking red and yellow and blue. There was the smell of wild rice. Patchouli, lily, bluebell, rose. There must have been two, two hundred fifty people there.

"Jesus," Clark said, looking around like a kid.

Gilby was smiling. Some of the younger men winked at her as she went by, in tow.

I got stuck to one side of the bleachers talking to the Yellowfeather boys about the fire. Off to my left were Clark and

George and Gilby. George's brothers had gone off somewhere. I anxiously poked at the grass under my feet, dried stiff and crunchy with the heat.

Overhead the night was a bowl of inviting darkness, but I didn't let it be that.

I got separated, carried off in a river of dancing, hot happy bodies, jostling. The chanting went on, so that when I walked, I walked on the balls of my feet, to the beat, moving with it, going toward the stand, where Henry, now in black hat with silver dollars around the brim, in that clipped, nasal voice, said—

"*Come on down now and dance, all you people from Ponsford, you Au-au-waks and Noka people. You Highclouds and Morrisons and McClouds. We got the Superior singers, The Wind People, givin' us their best and we need some ladies here. We need a few partners for these braves here, so come on down. You people from the Cities, or wherever, we invite you to dance.*"

The dancers, all men, went around the circle, half-stepping, then with partners, women in black and blue and red and yellow jingle dresses, the singers' voices rising and falling, the jingles sounding like soft, insistent rain.

Clark had found me.

"Have a beer," he said, and thrust a cold bottle into my hand.

A Crazy Dog went by us, walking backward, twill pants and cleanly pressed shirt, feeling behind himself with an elaborately carved stick, the shaft a serpent, the head a grinning canine.

"What's he doing?" Clark said.

Gilby slid in around us, her breasts soft on my arm. Something burst in my stomach. All that history with Gilby went off like an explosion in my head, but it was no good.

"You mean, what *has* he done." Gilby laughed. "You ought to join him, Paul," she said, motioning toward the Crazy Dog.

I gave her a sidelong, warning look. I didn't like to be so rude, but I had to be, around her, or all that would get started up again.

I thought, just then, I saw Moses, out behind the bleachers.

I spun around to face him. But it was just George, coming out of nowhere and slapping me on the back of the head.

"Don't look so serious!"

"I'm not."

"Well, fuck ya, then!"

Clark was grinning, that beer in his hand; he bumped suggestively up against Gilby.

"Ooops," Clark said, and did it again, George giving him a positively warning look.

I pulled Clark around and behind the bleachers to the fry bread stand. I bought two, raisins in them, a dusting of powdered sugar, in white napkins. A handful of kids were playing stickball under the light. The ball shot by my head and I caught it, tossed it back, and the boys scrambled, in T-shirts, out-of-date logos, *Elton John, Ford Truck Tough, Anthrax,* in lurid spray paint, odd-looking with those embroidered pants.

I nodded in the direction of the boat.

"Let's go," I said.

"Where's Gilby?"

I was saying, "Don't mess with her—" when Gilby, her face shiny with sweat, came out of nowhere, dark hair purple in that light, and grinning, pulled Clark onto the field, half-stepping in that honeyed way of hers.

"See?" he called back over his shoulder.

They made a circuit around the dance circle. Henry in his black hat, at the microphone, made a joke about the city dancer with the big feet. George, on the side watching, got a sullen look about him. Clark and Gilby went around again, half-stepping, the jingle dresses making that wonderful rain sound, the drums throbbing.

I was half-stepping myself, gritting my teeth, when something jabbed me in the back and I jumped.

A boy of about eight stood behind me, with a cloth bag of wild rice.

"Five bucks a pound," he said.

I gave the kid a five and handed the bag to a woman beside me.

>> ◇ <<

Just after midnight they shot off the fireworks. The wind blew so that the ashes came down on us, everyone laughing when someone dodged an ember, in the wash of air, the ember seeming to chase. Clark and Gilby and I watched with the rest of them.

There were more bursts of color, and then a flash of hard, white light, and following it, a slap of sound that made you blink.

Each explosion made me jump. I caught sight of Moses again, orbiting. Farther back, a stocky guy, glint of light on balding pate that could have been Len.

My back crawled; I couldn't stand, like the others, facing one direction.

When the crowd pressed together, making that *ohhhhhh* and *ahhhhh* at the colors overhead, Clark took Gilby's hand. Just then she was more than lovely, a blush in her face from dancing, her temples damp with sweat. I told myself it didn't bother me, not a little, the two of them.

From around the bleachers, George came at us. I wanted to say, *Clark*—but didn't. A rocket went off, chrome-yellow tail, then bursting, left a light hanging from a red parachute. George spun Gilby around.

"For Christ's sake, George, leave me alone," she said, jerking her arm free.

For a second George looked confused, then his face squeezed into a hard knot.

"You heard her," Clark said.

Everything changed in that moment. All that had been motion, dancing, music, came up against want, against possession.

"Let's do this later," I said, startled at how ugly it looked.

"Who's he to be up here, anyway?" George said.

It struck me as odd, how he'd put us together, against Clark. It confused me.

"He's my friend," I said.

George swung on Clark and knocked him down. Clark shook himself, and I got a sick feeling, when he managed to stand. He was no fighter and stood stupidly with his fists up like some old-time boxer, and George hauled off and hit him again and Clark went down, his nose bleeding in the yellow grass, coughing and spitting.

Gilby kneeled beside him. Behind us another rocket went up—there was that hot whoosh, then *pop!* and another burst of yellow light, the crowd making that *ahhhhh.*

"I think you've broken his nose!" Gilby said.

"Don't get up," I said, putting my hand on Clark's shoulder.

But Clark got up, and George came at him. I caught George by the back of his shirt as he went by, tripping him, and as he was trying to right himself—taking long, loping steps—I ran him headfirst into the bleachers.

He hit a support pole there, and it made a hollow, metal *pong!* There was blood everywhere, yet he managed to give me a good jab, his fist as hard as brick, and Gilby, screaming and tugging at us—

"*Stop it! Stop it! Goddamn you, Paul!*"

But George stumbled to his feet, then came at me again, bleeding, and I sidestepped, swung him around, tripping him, and like that, ran him into the bleachers a second time, though now he didn't get up.

We stood there, Gilby, Clark, and me, breathing hard, back of those bleachers, like people who'd been in a car wreck.

George sat crumpled, that pole behind him. "You just don't get it, Paul," he said. "Do you?"

"No," I said. "What am I supposed to get?"

"You just get the hell out of here now," he said. "Go on you. Git."

21

Clark, reaching over the side, splashed water in his face. We'd stopped in a small bay, cut the engine, and were drifting, quietly.

"He's going to come after you, you know?" Clark said.

His right eye had nearly swollen shut, and his nose was swollen, but not broken.

"Thanks to you," I said.

"Very funny." He touched his face. "But you know, it doesn't hurt."

Clark, in his clothes, dropped over the side. I went in, too.

The water was warm up on top, and when you dove down, went through the first thermocline, which is at about fifteen feet, the water became frigid, and you shuddered with it, suddenly very awake, and drunk and in some other world.

If you looked up, you could see the bottom of the boat, in silhouette, a black arrowhead, the moon wavering in the water, off to the side, big and blue white.

It was quiet down there, and I dove, time and again, until I was clearheaded, then I lay on my back, islands on all sides, the stars overhead.

"So, you going to tell me?" Clark said, after a time.

"Tell you what?"

"Where's Gwen?"

I said, a little meanly, "I thought *you* might know."

"Wrong," he said.

All that crowded in—what I stood to lose, but hadn't, until just now, let myself think about.

"What's going on between you two?"

"Nothing," I joked. Which, of course, had me thinking, everything.

>> ◇ <<

One evening, at the director's home at that school out east, all those years ago, outside, under pines, on grass, a beer in my hand, and trying to hide my lack of social grace, I saw a girl come down the back porch steps, blue-eyed, pitch-black hair tossing behind her, so lovely I was stunned.

I'd been eyeing the back gate, thinking to go out, relieve myself of the torment I'd surely face later. That girl came over as if floating, across that trim, flat-as-a-crew-cut lawn.

"Hello," she said.

The others were going in, were smiling those prizewinning smiles where they counted. Senators' daughters and sons.

"You'll probably be wanting to go," I said, nodding in the direction of the others.

A skimmer, neon blue, its wings flashing, lit on my shoulder.

"Dragonfly," the girl said.

"No," I said. "Skimmer. See how slender it is, and how the wings fold together?"

I told her how there were four hundred species. How the name for the thing in Latin, Odonata, meant tooth. That they didn't bite, or sting.

I couldn't stop it.

"Are they always like this? This shape?" she asked.

She had the biggest, bluest eyes. I got a sad, faraway feeling looking at them, the way you do when you see something truly beautiful, and want it, and you know it will never be yours. I didn't want her to go.

And all the while I was talking.

I told her that when the damselflies were young, they lived in the water and looked like six-legged spiders. People used to call them devil's darning needles, or mosquito hawks. I was getting that sick feeling again, rambling on, had started sweating. I did that a lot out there, out east. Always out of place, saying the wrong thing, looking the wrong way. She must have seen it, and put her hand on my forearm.

"My mother always thought they were magic," I said. "They kinda show change is coming. That's what they used to say, anyway."

I got the thing to climb onto my finger. I blew on it, as if for luck, and it was gone.

"Who *they*?" Gwen asked.

"People," I said.

I'd see her around town, dark hair tossing behind her, moving with some purpose or another, eyes bright; we were friends. I was a friend.

Her family, I was happy to discover, though wealthy now, came from steelworkers, immigrants, Irish. I was not so strange to her.

I told her about my family, a scaled-down, cleaned-up version. Wanderers, until the BIA had tried to make farmers out of them, which had proved impossible, and bloody, and in the end killed my grandfather, Nita.

I'd been ashamed of all that. They'd made me feel ashamed, the nuns at the off-reserve school, Sister Seraphim and Sister Marita Christine.

Gwen had a beautiful smile; she listened to me. I could never get over that. No one had ever listened to me, not even my mother.

>> ◇ <<

Gwen had long, slender fingers. I wanted to kiss them. She had a lovely, slightly cockeyed mouth, which gave her a certain wry expression. And those eyes! Big, swoopy, blue eyes. Always those eyes.

I was madly, madly in love with her, but couldn't be.

September, October, November of that year went by, and then came the holidays.

I did not have the money to get home, nor could I afford a hotel, and I would not ask anyone to put me up. I hadn't known I'd be put out of my room, and would not ask anyone for favors. And there was this, too, what extra money I'd been given, I'd sent to Al, who was trying to resurrect a place for people to meet in Pine Point, now that the shootings—we thought BIA-inspired—had let up. How could I have refused?

I'd given him everything.

So, on December 18, I stood with my suitcase outside Pioneer Hall, pretending I was waiting for my ride. I had twenty-five dollars. The last boy left, waving cheerfully from his father's black Lincoln, and I walked to the train station, where I'd come in. After a time, I crossed the tracks, smell of diesel and oil, and hot machines. I walked in circles, my toes burning in my too-small shoes. I had twenty-one days to kill, no money, nowhere to stay, not a friend to call on.

Outside the YMCA, traffic rushed by, the light changing. Green, yellow, red. Green, yellow, red. I went inside. Torn wallpaper, warped bunk beds. Smell of urine and disinfectant. Dirty-faced men lounged in the bunks, eyeing me, there in my navy jacket, chinos, and tie. Polished black shoes.

"Mess with me, I'll kill you," I said to the biggest, showing him my knife.

At the corner store, I bought a loaf of day-old bread (it must have been a week old, it was so dry) and washed it down with a pint of milk. I watched the street life through the window—pedestrians, a tie-and-coat crowd, rushing every which direction, the street damp, traffic sizzling by—until the woman at the register, hair pinned up so tight she squinted, began to stare.

I went out. Across the street a grizzled-looking man had a hot dog cart, a tin awning over it painted carnival orange, green, and yellow. He was wearing a blue smock with the words MIDTOWN BURGERS 'N' BRATS in white across the chest. He'd mime people, make them laugh: A woman in a business suit in tennis shoes. A jogger, with a whistle around her neck. A businessman swinging an oversize briefcase.

They'd turn, and I could see that even if they didn't like the idea of the brats, or a greasy, bad burger, they liked his attention.

They liked him.

"Heya, youngblood," he said.

He looked rough, close up: the collar of his shirt was worn and his face was dark with five-o'clock shadow; he had a nose that would shame a good-sized kosher pickle.

He put a patty down. It sizzled. I smelled hamburger. I hadn't really eaten anything since early that morning. He got a bun out of a cellophane bag, brown, sesame seeds, put catchup and mustard and pickle on it. My mouth watered. He put the patty on the bun, set onions, lettuce, a tomato slice, on that, then held it out.

"Don't tell me you're not hungry. I know hungry when I see it."

A man in a gray wool cap rushed by, tan raincoat, shiny black shoes.

"I see ya there, Clarence. You haven't gotten by me like that. Fatso."

The man threw his hand up, two fingers.

"Asshole," the vendor said.

The hot dogs smelled spicy, and hot. There were those black lines on them. Mustard. Relish. My mouth was watering.

"You want one of those, too?"

We stood not saying anything while I ate, the traffic rushing by.

"So, what gives?" the vendor said finally. "You're not from around here, that's for sure."

"St. Paul," I said.

"I'd say you were off a reservation somewhere. You got that other body language."

He mimed me for a second. He had me down, the catfooted walk, too much on the balls of my feet for concrete.

"You're a runner, aren'tcha?"

"Yes," I told him

He sized me up again. "All right," he said. "But I'll only pay minimum, and you got to work it. You can't just stand here and look glum, you won't sell like that.

"Can you do that?"

There were at that stand lottery tickets, racing forms, scorecards, and dirty magazines of all kinds. There were cigars and cigarettes. "No dope here, you understand," he said. "No dope. One hint of that and you're history, pal. Do you get me?" I told him I did.

I didn't have much success with George's lip, so came up with one of my own. "Fresh Poodle on a Stick, Fresh Poodle on a Stick," or "Sir, could I interest you in a night of adventure? Ma'm, Diet Dogs on Wheat or White. Diet Dogs, get 'em right here!"

They were anything but diet hot dogs. But our customers knew that.

. . .

One afternoon, toward the end of my shift, I saw someone peering at me from across the street. I felt suddenly conscious of the smock I was wearing. Felt the mustard stain revolting, the dirty white collar shameful, the lettering I'd had emblazoned across the chest at a T-shirt shop not to be endured—*Chief's.*

From under an awning, out came a kid from school, Jeremy, that jaunty, signature self-congratulatory step, headed in my direction.

"Hello, Jeremy," I said.

He smiled. "Where's Ratso?"

"Up to mischief somewhere."

He was wearing a rumpled green felt cap with a feather in it. He took his hands out of his pockets, shoved them back in again, fidgeting, leaned against the cart, nodding to himself like a duck.

"What have you got there?"

He lifted the cloth from the compartments, as if lifting the lid of something he expected to smell bad.

"Ah, I should have thought so," he said. "Dirty books, gambling, red dye number four weenies in Quaker State Thirty Weight. Enough sodium to salt the Jersey Turnpike when it snows."

A car pulled up to the curb, a distinguished-looking man driving, fifties, heavyset, brown tweed coat. Jeremy gave me a curt nod, as if we'd just finished some business transaction, then skipped lightly across the street and got into the car.

Back at school, Jeremy and I exchanged glances. I wasn't about to tell.

I thought we were clear on that.

At a diner, downtown, I made up a story about how I'd gone home for Christmas. In it were snowmobiles, and venison, and a bunch of people singing songs. There were my uncles and aunts, all very colorful, some of them with names like Tall Leader, Walking Woman, and Stony Ground. Some of it was true.

We'd had a tree in my story, and lights, and all kinds of goofy gifts, things made out of birch bark, BIA stuff, hawk feathers and all that. I had a number of friends I went drinking with, and they'd gotten into Dunwoody, in the Twin Cities, were apprenticing electricians now. My dad had sold some useless land to the state for an exorbitant amount, I said, and out of it I'd gotten the promise of a car to use over the summer.

The others got up and went outside, where they argued over what movie they wanted to see. From across the table, Gwen looked at me very sadly.

"Why are you looking at me like that?" I asked.

Later, when Gwen and I were alone in my room, I worked up my Christmas all the more: fancy dishes, names of movies I'd seen, details about my nieces, all of it jigsaw puzzle sure. Gwen's face got longer, and sadder, and just when I thought she might cry, she laid her head on my shoulder and laughed.

"Paul," she said.

"What?" I asked.

Gwen hugged me. I felt warm and in love and angry. I hugged her back.

"Chief's?" she asked. "Did Jeremy make that up? Or was he just being mean?"

My scalp crawled. "Oh, well," I said.

We became lovers that night. Paul, of Chief's, and this smart girl, Gwen.

In March, Al Eagle visited, like a storm visits, lots of rain and wind. At a small Chinese place, low ceiling, waitresses in red silk dresses dodging between tables, spicy smells, Al filled us in on what we'd missed up at Red Lake.

His voice was like some kind of drug. He made you woozy, jabbering, running on in those strung-together telegraph sentences.

Hey, you know, those Nokas now, they're talking casinos, pull tabs, lotteries, all that kind of nonsense, they got some New Jersey guys comin' in, take a look-see, how they'd set it up, just to give their expert opinion, you know, out of the kindness of their hearts, as if we haven't heard that before—

A member of the Medicine Society, Al was a politico, a stirrer-upper, was throwing his weight around in Red Lake politics. He had a lot to throw. A bullet head, chest as big as a garbage can, legs like stumps.

He was jabbering on about that gambling nonsense, when I said,

"Al—"

"What?" He winked at Gwen and gave her an avuncular squeeze.

"Gwen doesn't want to hear this."

"Don't tell me what I don't want to hear," Gwen said.

"Fine," I said.

Al threw his arm around Gwen and squeezed her again. "Jeez, she's pretty," he said. "What'd you do to come up with one like this?"

Gwen blushed. I felt a big, uneasy grin creeping up my face.

"So you'll do it?"

"Do what?"

"Throw your vote in. We need you up there."

"Right," I said.

"Come on," Al said, poking me.

"I'm an agnostic," I told him, "I don't believe in that post-apocalyptic resurrection ghost-shirt stuff."

"Yes or no," Al said. "Why is for excuses."

I was beginning to get irritated. Politics were nothing but trouble.

A waitress stopped at our table, pointed to our eyes. Al's and mine.

"Chinese?" she said.

"Chippewa," Al said, nodding smartly. "Indian. Powwow. Wagon trains. Arrows." He winked, drawing his arm back, letting an arrow fly.

"Ah! You oh-reeginal wahns here!" She smiled, and we all laughed.

Then she was back with the check. Al and I took hold of it, tugging from opposite sides of the table. Just when I was going to say, *Mine,* Al bent down and kissed the back of my hand. *"Awesin nikan,"* he said, in a low, fierce voice—mine, brother.

I let go, Al snatching the check away, laughing.

"Will you look at him?" he said, nudging Gwen. I must have looked shocked.

"Now, I ask you—Have you ever seen an Indian blush?"

Gwen said she hadn't. Al tucked the check into his breast pocket and, sliding from the table, said,

"So, you'll write in?"

"All right," I said.

"All right what?"

"Yes—dammit! I'll write in," I said. I threw my coat on, exasperated, drawn into it. "And I'll call people, too! Fuck those assholes. That's what I think. Are you happy now?"

Outside, walking, Al expanded. He threw his arms out. Now the tall, dark buildings were stands of pine, the sidewalks rivers. The wind blew down, melting snow in it, the promise of rain. Al was thinking of expanding his business, he said.

It was all nonsense, this dreaming. But—God, how I loved him for it! Listening, I was happy. Truly!

"A place for the weary wanderer," Al said in a mock serious voice.

Al winked at Gwen.

"That's what I'm calling my new place—" he held up his hands and made a distant, dreamy face, part in jest, "—*Rambler's Inn.*

"What do you think?" Al said, turning to Gwen.

The wind caught that dark hair of hers, tumbling it around her face, framing it. She tossed her head back, drawn into it, too, Al's dream.

I was not about to explain to Gwen, that as recently as a few years back, opponents of development bills were found dead—off reserve.

That my father's friends had died that way.

"Why, I think it's *wonderful!*" Gwen said.

>> ◇ <<

I packed up my things at the end of that week, just ten credits short of graduating, and near the top of my class (but not the top, as that would have been too visible) and left there.

Just like that. I'd made those calls. Had written letters, in which I excoriated those pushing this latest development scheme.

I didn't want to explain to Gwen why I bolted awake some nights now, in a cold sweat; or why, some nights, I did not sleep at all.

>> ◇ <<

I got a job at Frank's resort and was guiding. It felt familiar, but was more difficult. I was the college boy, and the other guides teased me. What do you know, college boy? And you didn't even graduate! And in what? Philosophy, what's that good for? I didn't tell them I'd double majored, in chemistry—and could make a pretty nice poison that didn't leave any traces.

I became the brunt of bad jokes. Of tricks. Of gags. I took one party after another out, drunkenness, fishing, a near drowning, Chief jokes, farting, girl chasing by married men and single alike, just as it always had been.

But now, I didn't think I could bear it, not as a seasonal grunt.

>>◇<<

I got a phone call late one night.

I was at the lodge and cleaning fish. I came through the kitchen, blood on my hands. Scales. I stunk. It was hot. But it was familiar to me, home. White walls, that green flooring, the window in back overlooking the point. I was beginning to think I was all right with it, or maybe I was just beginning not to think, period.

"Hello?" I said.

"What are you doing?" Gwen said.

I stood there blinking. I could hear the lights buzzing overhead.

"You'd better say something."

"Gwen?"

"You think," she said, "just because you're...you're some *fucking... outsider* or something, that you can do this to me? You disappear, have me running all over the *goddamn place* trying to find you. And all the while you've just ducked out. Is that the way you are? You don't even say good-bye?

"You owe me that. *Say it,* Paul. I want to hear it *right now.*

"It's taken me a month to get this number. Do you know what I've gone through? I could just—I mean, you didn't even tell me you were leaving. Did you? Are you that afraid?"

Afraid? I thought. After all, I'd been trying to protect her.

"Do you always just throw away what you want?"

"Gwen," I said. It was hopeless.

"Who do you think I am?"

"I don't know."

"So say it."

"Say *what,* Gwen?"

"Say you don't love me."

Mardine came in from the kitchen. I turned my back to her. She was straightening up the dining room. I was afraid it would show on my face. My eyes had glassed up, I could barely breathe.

"I want you to say: *I don't love you, good-bye, it's over.*

"Say it."

I laid my head on the cutting board.

"But I do love you," I said.

"Well, then why don't you *show it?*"

"Do you want me to?" I said.

I meant for her to understand, there were things she might not like, at all.

"Yes," she said.

"Then," I said, a conviction like stone setting in me, "I will."

She liked to make things, plump bluebirds out of paper cups and colored felt. Soap bubbles for guests' children (that had been Gwen's idea, long before it had been mine). Kites, of all kinds, elaborately done up in colored tissue paper, flaming orange tigers or lumbering gray elephants, rust-brown, writhing pythons.

She collected cobalt glass, and electrical insulators, some the color of the ocean, or green, like a block of lime, nearly opaque, some heavy, some translucent. She would catch me up and squeeze me.

"Too serious!" she'd say. Her long, dark hair bobbed behind her. Bright, hand-printed skirts, airy blouses. One day, red tennis shoes, the next, knee-length boots. She loved music and sang beautifully. She made friends of the women in town.

Attended sessions of the Church, came home, big-eyed and mystical with peyote.

Did I mind? *Did I mind?*

She'd sing one of the old songs, in a lilting, clear voice. Mardine taught her those things. All of that came back with her. With Gwen, I could be myself.

Tell me a story, she'd say.

And I would. I'd tell her about Nanabozo and the old Djasakid, or about Noko and the Twin Sisters, or how Round as a Ball Boy tricked the Windigos out of their hearts. It was safe to know all that again.

And winters, in the Twin Cities, she opened doors. At first it made me angry, how easily Gwen could sway opinions. Elicit smiles, where I'd gotten a curt no.

I told myself it was race, or gender, or beauty, and it was all that, but even more so, it was a certain gentleness in the way she accommodated people. Her eyes shone; she laughed easily, drew people out. There was some of Dr. Piper in her, that dreaming yourself into life. She swam mornings, was off early to a small music school. The pay was lousy. I was irritated by it all. Winters I did carpentry.

"We're broke," I'd say, and she would laugh. "You're rich, Paul."

And like that, my mood would shift. If she thought so, well, then it was so.

All she wanted, she said, was a life. This she never explained. (Much in the way I never explained those things I had to just live with, and had, over time, finally come to forgive in myself, and in other people.)

And she was impossible, too: stubborn, angry, vindictive, even wrathful. At the resort, I'd find Gwen in the kitchen, cutting carrots, with an angry, quick chopping. Pointing a just and accusing finger, she'd say, "Your home is *here,* Paul." Which at times was a relief. "Who's in charge here?" she'd say. "You're letting those guests run all over you."

Moody, narcissistic at times, a lover of birds and clouds and water.

She was prone to explosions. They seemingly came out of nowhere. Or at the slightest provocation. Then she tore through the house or cabin, raging. One afternoon I found her breaking our china in the bathtub.

"What are you doing?" I asked.

"Breaking our china," she replied, lifting another plate over her head and hurling it down, so that it broke with an awful glass clatter.

"You think you're the only one with things you have to live with?" she said, crying. "Do you really think it was all so easy for me?!"

She sometimes cut me to the heart, made me so angry I could barely contain it—just that. And at other times, thrilled, assuaged, even comforted me to the point of oblivion.

Love, that's what it came to.

It was love between us, and everything I'd come to think of as my life.

"So, are you going to tell me where she is, or do I have to guess?" Clark said.

I'd been way down inside myself, turning there in the water, sick with the thought of loss. "She's at her parents'," I said. I was feeling worse than lousy.

"That can't be good."

"No," I said, "it isn't."

"I thought we were having a nice time and now everything's shot again," Clark said.

"It doesn't matter," I told him.

And, after all, I'd gotten what I'd wanted out of the night, a parting of ways with George and his brothers, and it could have been much worse.

Motoring slowly up one dark stretch of water after another on the way back, taking our time, I taught Clark an old 49'er. A 49'er is a song sung after powwow. Then there is courtship, and those that aren't courting are singing, crazy, lovesick, mad-at-it-all and still laughing singing.

This is the song I taught Clark:

One of these days,
Sweetheart,
I'm gonna take you home
in my one-eyed Ford

There are many ways you can sing that song, and I think we did them all.

22

The plane woke us early. Echoing batter of engines, then circling, the sun catching on its wings, gold. I had breakfast with the pilot while Clark got his gear together. I went down to the dock to see them off, this pilot, Ray, and my old friend.

Roar of engines, prop wash, rough water.

Then it was still and quiet, the plane gone; I worked down on shore, moving the last of the wreckage. The slightest sound made me jump. A jay in a tree. Thud of a boat coming up the channel.

Still, no George or his brothers.

When it was time, I gassed up one of the boats and went into Pine Point.

Crossing the Tribal Office parking lot I looked both ways, as if someone were there to run me over. Just a blue Cadillac, set at an angle to the small redbrick building, Parker's, and beside it, a red Dodge sedan on flat tires. The office window threw back a fistful of sun.

I took a deep breath and went inside, rapped my fingers on the plexiglass top of Parker's desk.

"Morning," I said, cheerfully.

"Well, if it isn't our man on the go," Parker said. He kicked back in his chair, knotting his fingers behind his head.

He had on a bolo tie with a heavy turquoise clasp, and it was pinching that extra pound of flesh over his collar; he smelled of Vitalis. Parker had married into Weyerhaeuser lumber, and it gave him a certain imperious air. How he'd won his seat on the council I didn't know, but he'd gone after it with an unmatched fervor.

Still, there was something positively greasy about him, a kind of slide out of a skillet egg sort of thing.

"Well?" he said.

"My carpenters up and quit," I told him. "Flat out. I've gotta have the money now."

I laid out the whole plan. What I needed in addition to what I'd already asked for. New motors, money for roofing, new washer, maybe a new generator.

"You'll probably need more insurance coverage, too," he said.

"I need the whole shebang," I said.

He got out some papers, doodled. Sharpened his pencil, absentmindedly lifted the lid of a jar, reading copies of the papers he'd signed earlier, turning the pencil in the sharpener, the scrapings falling into the jar. In the jar were finely ground leaves, sage, or artemisia, which he'd sprinkle on himself, I was sure, after I'd gone—to purify himself.

My mother had had just such a jar by the door.

Parker looked up from the papers, and seeing he'd used the wrong jar, slapped the lid on with a tin clank, lifting the lid of another—one filled nearly to the top with pencil shavings—and continued his scraping.

The irony of his purifying himself wasn't lost on me. After all, who was more into dirty politics than Parker? But then, what of it?

Sitting back, I could barely see over all that was on his desk: more jars, in them, snakeroot, for safe travel and health; muhl (wild pea), for safety and success. Perched on a Bible, a bright red velvet bag, bordered with iridescent beads, in it, Mackenzie seed, I was sure, which was said to be "magnetic" and drew money to the possessor. Antlers, a bowl of tobacco, a braid of sweetgrass, the end burned.

I glanced around the office. Cheap wood paneling, another desk, yellow papers stacked on it, framed pictures of earlier council presidents, Chief Hole-in-the-Day, lousy curtains that looked like they'd been made out of dish towels from the Ben Franklin.

Now Parker was at his calculator for effect, clackety clackety.

I got out a cigarette. Lit it. Blew smoke rings. Did some doodling of my own. On my pad, drew the lodge roof with skylights, a second fireplace, a playroom with windows, for tots.

Now and then Parker and I glanced at each other, smiled.

Our enmity was old stuff, Pine Point history everybody knew. Parker hated me because my father had gone up against him all those years back over that paper plant. And he hated me, too, for an even older injury. I was a reminder to him that he was an outsider. My mother and Parker had courted during the war. Parker had been 4F and stayed behind. It had been touch and go there, my mother, a traditional, and a member of the Medicine Society, almost crossing over. The problem was with Parker being Potawatomi—but after all, what was the big deal? Same language, our traditions nearly identical. But only that.

Nearly. How that must have hurt him! *Nearly.*

And just when he'd made headway, my mother agreeing to come to powwow with him, which was tantamount to an engagement, then, just then, the war ended, and my father in uniform came home, on the Monday of the week of powwow, all good intentions, tall, handsome, and decorated.

How could a narrow-eyed 4F Potawatomi compete with that? My father blew him out of the water.

All that was coming across the desk, flared nostrils, Parker enjoying himself immensely, grinning. We both chuckled. He'd waited for decades for this. To finish off my father.

"All right," Parker said finally. "Let's get serious here."

He put his hands in his lap. It was something, how he sat as if he were at some fancy dinner. A banquet in honor of my humiliation.

"Remortgage, is that what you want?" he said.

But there was real excitement in his voice now, of a breathy, dangerous, hungry sort, something not part of this pathetic little scene we were playing out. I recalled how he'd been at the Rambler's that night Len was up. But then, George had been there, too.

Now Parker's swollen face seemed to recede to the end of some invisible pipe.

"Well?"

I thought, he almost seemed—*turned,* was the expression we used. He was after something, all right.

"What about those papers you signed?" I said. "For my loan?"

Parker finished scratching on his pad, spun it around on the desktop. There was a figure with a dollar sign out front of it. I had to stop myself from staring.

"You know as well as I do what that paper's worth," he said, leaning toward me across that cluttered desk.

"Do I?" I said.

"You put your mortgage down as collateral," Parker said, setting his hands flat on the desk, brutal now, "and we'll talk business."

The room darkened. I turned to see if someone wasn't standing at the door. But it was just a cloud passing over the sun. Parker rapped his pen on the desk. I didn't want to believe what I'd just felt.

He could mess with me all he wanted, right from behind his desk.

"You going to bring in your deed?"

"How about the money?"

Parker smiled. "Cold day in hell."

"Fine," I said.

23

Back of my truck, where George and his brothers were waiting for me, I explained why I didn't have the money now, miserably trying to keep my voice from shaking, and why I wouldn't have it later. The sun came down bright, hot, unforgiving. It sat on us like some immense, crushing weight, baking us.

They were enormous, George and Terry and Simon, had been drinking since the powwow. Torn and dirty denim, ruined plaid shirts, they smelled of smoke and stale beer and sweat. George's face was a mess, crust of dried blood on his forehead, his nose swollen. He picked gingerly at the scab with those big hands, almost delicately.

"Parker," he spat.

I had to control an impulse to laugh. It was all too much. George bent over the forms Parker had signed, upper arms as big around as my thighs, and tanned, a peppermint rattling in his mouth.

"And he said this isn't worth shit," George said.

"That's the gist of it."

George puckered his mouth, made a smacking noise and spit in front of my boots. Simon and Terry looked off up Main Street, as if bored with it all, rangy as strays and as mean looking.

"Why don't you go get yourself something to eat," George said.

I ordered a hot beef sandwich at the Western—mound of fresh mashed potatoes over slabs of thick, salty beef, on homemade bread—and a piece of cherry pie with a softball-sized lump of vanilla ice cream. Air-conditioned, cool, the glare outside distant. Quiet clatter of the after-lunch crowd. Minty green upholstery.

Sadie Debundunk topped up my coffee, said, "Good to see you around again."

I said it was nice to be back, as if I'd been away. I supposed I had. I picked at my food, stomach turning. I couldn't eat, old Emil Odinigun hunched in one of the booths, humming to himself, walking-stick thin. I brought my plate over.

"It's on the house," I told him, "Sadie had me bring it over," and he lit up for Sadie.

I checked my watch. I gave it another twenty minutes. I tried to read the *Pioneer Press,* aircraft disasters and some trouble in Pakistan, but could think only of Parker, at his desk, now across it George and Terry and Simon, George picking at that scab on his forehead, blood oozing.

I sipped at my coffee, picturing it, how George wouldn't care how well connected Parker was, and hating him, for that paper plant business, and his Weyerhaeuser lumber connections, George hulking, that bruised nose and mean, raisin eyes, over Parker.

Oh, Parker! I thought, chuckling to myself. Did you really think I'd be that stupid?

A short while later, Parker, his face lit up with rage, marched over from the office, a brown suit in fast forward. I saw him coming, a ways off, through the green-tinted window. He threw the door open, face livid, dropped down beside me, breathing in short, quick tugs.

"You'll see *just how funny this is,* Paul," he said, shoving those papers at me.

I got the money that afternoon, wired up from someplace in St. Paul. I paid George and his brothers, even threw in a bonus. Back of the truck, George eyed me slyly.

"Even?" I said, putting out my hand.

George laughed. He had a handshake that damn near broke my fingers.

24

Then, seven endless days. How, otherwise, can I describe them? At the lodge, the Highclouds, all business, Warren, and his brothers, ran here and there, blue overalls, tool belts, pencils behind their ears, levels. We put down cinderblock and stone foundations, raised log walls. Mortared between logs. Roofing, green joists, steel beam supports. Smell of green cement. Buzz of saw. Asphalt shingles. Pneumatic guns, putting down nails—*ka-thack! Ka-thack!*—the generator, back of the lodge, roaring to power all those tools.

Day and night. Bright carbon arc lamps, bugs, after midnight, flying like snow around them, smoking pack after pack of cigarettes, bottomless pot of coffee, Mardine making sandwiches.

Warren, three days into it, held my hand down back of a circular saw, drawing my fingers on the plywood there.

"What's that?" I said.

"It's how you're gonna remember your hand looked if you're not more careful," he told me.

"Phone," Mardine called down, Friday evening.

I started up from the bench, in the new boathouse, sprawl of tools, circular saw, drill, a level, and chalk tape. Then, into the kitchen, where I'd had that other, significant talk, so long ago.

"Paul?" The connection was not a good one. It was Gwen.

"Are you there?" I said.

"Is something wrong?"

"No, we're just busy. Why?"

It was not the way I'd wanted to start this conversation. In the dining room behind me, Mardine was talking with Warren. *It's been hard for them,* she was saying, *you don't know how.* I pulled on the phone cord, going farther into the kitchen.

"How are you?" I said.

"It's been raining here."

"It's hot here." There was a long silence.

"What's wrong?" Gwen asked.

"Nothing's wrong. Is something wrong there?"

Gwen cleared her throat. "Just the usual hassle with my folks. I'm going to stay with a friend for a few days, travel up to Bar Harbor. Is that all right? I should be back on Saturday.

"Is it all right?"

"Sure it's all right, why wouldn't it be?" I said, perplexed at it.

"I just wanted you to know where I was." There was that radio hum on the line, like radiation. "You sound disappointed. You aren't mad, are you?"

"Mad?"

"Yes, you sound mad now."

I was sick to my stomach, my legs leaden. I wanted to sit down.

"No," I told her, "I'm not mad." I felt my head racing. What was it? "I'm just... *disappointed,*" I said.

"You are?"

"Well, sure."

"Paul?"

And right there, I did something that surprised even me. I said,

"It's just that, well, I *need* you up here." Why did I always choose such bad times to say things like that? "I got you something," I told her, trying to sidestep what I'd just said.

It was a lie, and I think she sensed that. Why did I say it? I thought I'd learned not to do that—but then, the first time I'd told her I loved her had been after I'd made a fool of myself over Christmas.

There was a muffled crying on the other end.

"You didn't have to do that."

"I know," I said. I was trying to think of something to say.

"Are you all right?" she said.

"You'll see," I told her. "I'm fine," I said.

I said I missed her, and we were cut off. She'd been at a pay phone, I told myself. That was it.

I went listlessly up and down the aisles in the Rambler's grocery, hours later. Buzz of fluorescent lights. Fans, turning the stultifyingly hot air, fans that made me wonder—but none like the one that had been in the boathouse—the last of the sun breaking through the front windows. Canned soup, or boxed soup? Lipton, or Campbell's? Or Progresso? Or skip the soup? I couldn't seem to decide anything. It was early evening, and I hadn't eaten since noon. Canned goods, in red and blue labels, shouting out the contents—stew, peas, beets, incentives to buy—*Save 50 Cents!*—bread of too many kinds, budget soda, and brand name. I couldn't think what to get, even though I had Mardine's list.

20 lbs. Meat, 8 cases Soda, Sweets.

"Why don't you just ask if you can't find it?" Moses said, in an anxious voice. He stood at the register, watching a portable TV, tearing at his fingernails.

"Don't know what I want," I replied cheerfully, just to devil him.

I snatched things off the shelves, out of the cooler, from the snack racks, filled the cart with nonperishables, tea, and coffee, and cookies in cellophane wrappers. I tore a package open at the register, stuffing the dry, crunchy lemon cremes into my mouth, couldn't swallow, and choking, washed it down with an orange soda.

"Hungry?" Moses said, grinning.

Moses made change. I pocketed the quarters and went outside, to the phone on the corner.

Phone clamped between my shoulder and ear, I pumped the machine. Mechanical, *pa-chink* of coins, long-distance hum. The other end rang, seven, eight, nine times.

I was going to hang up when an answering machine kicked in.

"You have reached the law office of Stricklin, Meyers, and Todd. For those of you trying to reach Mr. Todd, he can be contacted at 617-773-4097."

I scrambled through my pockets. I had my pad, but nothing to write with. 617, where was that? Something moved behind me and I dropped the phone and spun around, the phone clattering against the booth. Just a big orange tabby, bumping up against my legs.

"Hey, kitty," I said, and bent to pick her up.

I scratched under her chin. She was purring, smelled of perfume. I held her against my chest, just then, almost too sad to bear it. The cat did that.

High and up Elm Street, just past the Rambler's, was a car parked facing the wrong direction, an avocado-green Buick sedan, wraparound windshield, wing windows, clothes hanger antenna.

A fifty-three, I was thinking, Al's brother's car. Napoleon's car.

Something popped up just below the rim of the steering wheel. Napoleon's head, I thought. He was just fifteen, had gotten his driver's permit, and he was crazy, in the way boys could be crazy up there, looking for something to do. It was a dare, I thought, and not an unusual one. I'd done it myself, to Charlie.

"I see you there, Napoleon!" I shouted from the booth, chuckling, the cat in my arms.

The car dipped, coming down the hill. I scratched behind the cat's ears, the cat purring, butting its face into mine. I was not going to jump from the booth, or put on a clownish, startled face.

So the car came on, me grinning.

Flash of bumper in that evening light, polished chrome, grille like big smiling teeth, wheel spinners glinting, turning faster, the muffler banging down at the bottom of the hill with a rusty *crunch!* a rush and rattle of bad springs, it would swerve anytime now, yet loomed up, with a whoosh and clank, me holding that cat, grinning, groceries at my feet, waiting, waiting for Napoleon to swerve—

bright flash, my head, like a basketball, knocking off the glass, and back again, then sliding, caught inside that booth, end over end over end, rough, clunking tumbling, and stopping finally, a horn blaring.

I sat up. I had a lapful of glass, shiny as diamonds. I reached out and touched the grille of Napoleon's Buick, big chrome bars like teeth.

Moses bolted from the Rambler's. He looked around excitedly, but not altogether surprised.

"Jesus Christ! What happened?" he said. "Are you all right?"

"I don't know," I said.

I had blood in my eyes, a cut on my forehead. That horn was still blaring. I stepped from what remained of the booth, got the Buick's hood up and jerked a cable from the battery. I stood with it in my hand, and Moses turned away, taking in the rest of it, as if he cared. Hood buckled up and back, glass everywhere. No driver anywhere to be seen. The twisted frame of the phone booth.

"Jesus! God, you're lucky," Moses said. "You could have really got hurt."

The cat was cowering behind the stoop, watching us. It bolted out across the lot, so quickly its hind legs almost overtook its front.

"You gonna be okay?" Moses asked.

"Nothing I can't handle," I said, and, stooping, picked up my groceries and walked with them back to my truck.

"Who's gonna clean this mess up?" Moses yelled.

"You are," I called back.

25

Day after day, at the lodge, the August sun beat down like a torch.

August 7. New boatloads.

I took guests out for early-morning forays to shady inlets where the walleye were still biting, relieved to be busy. Took others deep fishing, bobbers, braided line, fathead minnows, late-morning lassitude. Lunch. A hike up Snowbank Island, hunting for glass; berrying, gooseberries now, sour, translucent, green. Tin buckets.

Always with guests now, never alone.

Afternoons, when I was not busy with carpentry, I took people into Pine Point, and at the Rambler's, while they nursed beers and took in the local color, I pried at the boozers swapping gossip and old lies.

"Same old, same old," they said, always with that sly, happy indifference. No one would tell me anything—but still, it was there.

Now, I never went into Pine Point after dark. Not for any reason. Not groceries, even when we needed them.

"I'm not going to explain," I told Mardine.

. . .

Friday. August 16. Beat down, dragged-out tired. A V of sticky sweat over my shoulder blades, understaffed badly without Gwen. Hair greasy. Hands smelling of fish. Gasoline on my boots. Two-day shadow. Kids spun off the dock in big, black donuts of inner tubes, splashing each other. Zinc oxide. Sunburns. I wore my darkest sunglasses, the swelling in my face nearly gone.

The dishwasher died again. I hired another girl and left her with Mardine. "You tell her what's up," I said. Kids, spearfishing, with homemade spears, welding rod they'd lifted from the boathouse. All illegal. I didn't see it now, didn't care.

I just wanted to finish. Just that.

> > ◇ < <

Gwen wrote me a postcard. On the front was a picture of Rodin's *The Thinker,* only some cartoonist had put a headdress on him. On the back side, it read, in her tiny, precise longhand,

I'll be back before Labor Day.
Gwen

I'd tried to call Clark at work a number of times, just to talk. He wasn't there, his secretary told me. He would be gone for the week. Did I want to leave a message?

Anywhere I could contact him?

No, she said.

26

Monday afternoon, August 26. A dry, bright sun cut down out of a cloudless sky. At the dock, impatient, sweating, I cut my hand, splicing a rope. I hurled the knife and rope out into the lake, cursing. New dock. New cabins to my right. New boathouse.

I'd done it all. I'd lasted the summer—almost.

"Hey, TP," Hugh said. He was trying to get by me. We had to pick up a boatload from the Twin Cities, and later, another from Chicago. The air was thick with August heat, and I stood as if stunned in it, heat shimmer everywhere.

"Coming?"

I had my hopes set on Gwen being there at the government docks, but was afraid.

"Wouldn't miss it," I said.

Later, I took the new guests to their cabins, got them put away, as if not a thing in the world bothered me. After I'd cleaned the boathouse and checked on Mardine in the kitchen, I sat on the porch with them, our new guests. They were not new at all to me, this bunch of upper-crust folks, our high-season people, big-city folks, from Chicago, and New York, Detroit, D.C., who always booked this last week in August.

Some of them I'd known the better part of fifteen, even twenty years.

Usually I found them a happy relief from our sanctimonious church groups, dour ministers, bottom pinchers, and the like, and enjoyed taking it slow, a few boat rides, a guide or two here and there.

These people came up because the lake was beautiful; I liked that.

These people were real estate, business, ad agencies (no one could bother them up at the lodge), old money, new money, but lots either way. I usually liked to sit and listen. They had a language all their own. Cambridge bookstores, Central Park, the Green Mountains, Bar Harbor, Filene's Bargain Basement, the Blue Note, the upper 70s, Washington Square. I'd seen some of that in my years out east, at that school they surely would have approved of, but never once mentioned it.

But now, listening to all that, I found it grating, instead of a pleasure, and wanted to stand. Generally, when I am gripped by melancholy, I work. I repair the motors, or wiring, plumbing, a roof. I repair something, anything—and there is never a lack of things to repair at a resort, especially one as thinly staffed as ours.

But I didn't do that. I sat, and sunk deeper into my mood.

My guests' nit-picking depressed and angered me now. But I wanted to feel full of it, to get to the end of it, and so sitting there, obliged myself, brought it on.

I keened to it. Gwen had not been at the docks. And here was my big reward, to cater to these people, tough-looking men in their middle fifties, and their wives, now much less attractive, who, even with all the heavy jewelry and mascara and facepaint, couldn't hold back time.

Drinks held in just slightly shaking hands. The once jaunty cigarette killing the smoker, that not-at-all-attractive phlegmy cough and rattle in the chest. A prosthetic breast. Three lines across the neck of an otherwise flawless woman, and the way she held her hand there, to hide it.

Which just made you look all the more.

Liver spots. Tendons. A vein in a forehead, thudding. Hypertension. Cool beads of sweat on forehead. Bulges, tics, a pill tossed back nonchalantly, Valium? heart stuff? lithium? I was looking at the middle myself, just three years off now, the lodge a mess, and Gwen gone, with nothing to show for it.

I tried to make it sit in my stomach. *Everything* had come to nothing.

"You know," a balding, heavyset man chuckled, "I don't know whether things are going faster now or they just seem that way."

"They're faster, no two ways about it," his friend, a contractor, said. "I can't keep up with all the goddamn permits and crap now. You can hardly build a shithouse without some inspector coming over and poking around."

And a third.

"It's both."

And all three laughing, tinkle of ice in glass, wind off the lake, subtle light and shadows, back of the table, the wives, talking in low voices.

"You know, I was a child model when I was little," one of them said. "I wonder where that would have gone if my mother hadn't stopped it. The photographer was splashing water on me and trying to get me to laugh, and all I'd do was cry."

To her right, a woman in hennaed hair, once a beauty, no doubt, fingered her diet soda.

"Did you get that outfit at Burmeisters?"

"Charlie's, at the Galleria."

"It's nice."

"Oh," the third said, "It's *dar*ling. Just darling. It makes your eyes look *so* much bigger."

"And more... *dramatic,*" added the first, in a voice positively nasty.

The woman with the outfit pointed to her husband behind her with her thumb.

"As if he'd ever notice." She put up her index finger, arching it, perky, and in just the right measure then, crooked it, until it was bent double, frowning.

"Judith, *really.*"

"They're all like that—" The three laughed, bitter, brown laughter.

Eddie Frobisher, one of those men, leaning back from his table, craning his head around, giving me a big, well-intended smile, asked,

"Where's ladybird?"

I took a sip of water from the glass in front of me and, swallowing the wrong way, choked. The conversation went on around me and I felt my heart pounding. I was trying to catch my breath, but only a wheezing came out.

"Are you choking?" Eddie asked, alarmed.

I shook my head.

"He *is too* choking!" the woman who'd crooked her finger said.

They were all out of their chairs, and over me, and their concerned faces just made it worse. Vein pulsing in forehead, twitching eye, reddish foundation, cloying perfume. I couldn't breathe. My heart jumped like a fish in my chest. Ed got me in his arms and, turning me around, jerked up on my stomach.

I was laughing, or was it *crying?*

"*Stop,*" I was trying to say, "*Stop, please. Please just stop!*" but all that came out of me was that whooping, and in the end, in great embarrassment, and trying to control what had gotten hold of me, choking it all back, I ran from the porch.

>> ◇ <<

The sun caught the coin going up, flash of silver, and I said, "Tails."

Hugh laughed. "You lose." Heads.

He would bring in the boatload from Chicago while I was out with the heir to the Old Dutch potato chips fortune, Owen Harnac, and his buddy, Edmund—Eddie—who thought, now, that he'd saved me at my table.

"Hope you have a good time with those two sons of bitches," Hugh said, then loped down the bank to the dock, positively gleeful.

"Right," I said.

>> ◇ <<

I had fallen back on old methods, out of necessity, had begun well enough with #5, humor, and wearing that out, tried #4, no opinions and general ignorance, only to find myself at #3, the truth as I knew it, then passed that in a nanosecond, to #2, which I thought of as taking action, and sailed right by to #1, give back what's coming at you.

It was bad timing. I lit a cigarette, my hands shaking. Owen was like sodium in water; he burned, and now, so did I.

I had listened to my fill of it in the two hours we'd been out in the boat:

Open up all and any federal lands to "development"; end welfare; prevent "communist" medicine; remove the trade and labor restrictions that were suffocating business, and by that they meant AMERICA; send the "darkies" back home, of which I counted myself one—and given they were up on the lake, on *our* aboreal lands, Edmund and Owen's arguments in that vein were somewhat preposterous, even funny; make cars like they used to (Cadillacs, three tons and nearly thirty feet long); end the Arab "oil nonsense"; put a man like Reagan back in office.

"Hell, why not Hitler," I said. "Let's not bother with any of that in-between shit."

Owen glared. Owen with his pencil-thin mustache, natty clothes (creased gray double-knit slacks, canary-yellow shirt), stainless-steel cigarette case (monogrammed ODH, in art deco script)—even opening his matchbook and lighting a match, always a complex one-handed operation.

"They should have given *all* those draft dodgers the chair," Owen said now. "Goldwater was right."

"Nuke 'em," I said. "Fly the flag!"

"They should have shot them all at Kent State. That's where everything went wrong."

"Hell, why there? When those Wobblies got started they should have brought back public hangings, don't you think? Make some money off concessions that way."

"You two, cut it out," Edmund said.

We were in a small bay of yellow and white lilies, ringed by waist-high bulrushes, and on shore, brilliantly white and black birch, silver poplar, high, old-growth pine back of it, the sun slanting down through the trees.

"It's in the Constitution," Owen said.

"What is?"

"Obligations as a citizen."

"You mean rights," I said.

I snagged a bass and had it in the boat, and Owen looked at me sourly. I handed him my rig and told him where to go with it, which wasn't where I was thinking. There was a run of bass, all smallmouth, not much over the minimum size.

"So you're telling me you would have dodged?"

"I didn't say that," I said.

"But you implied it."

"I'm a Quaker," I joked, lighting a cigarette. I wanted out of *that* boat; my hands were all over the place, with no end in sight.

Owen cast out. Now he was angry, too. "But you're not."

"How do you know that?"

"You Chippewa up here are all Catholics, or Presbyterians."

"You mean dutiful killers, right?" I said. "Like Luther advised, all that kowtowing to the state. Duty. Or like the Catholics in Nazi Germany. Just goin' along with it all."

I was beginning to sound ridiculous to myself. Owen brought out the worst in me.

Owen spit into the water. I could see I'd gotten to him. Ed wasn't too happy with me, either. It was not good for business, pissing off the guests, especially the regulars.

Never politics or religion, Frank, the old owner, had told me. Never. Still, I was enjoying myself now, though something in me watched, shocked.

I'd burn the whole goddamned place down myself, rather than let people like Owen put his mark on it, that's what I felt like.

"Let's get out of here," I said, and started the engine.

Night was coming on. We would have to go in soon.

Owen took in another bass under the legal limit. He'd taken in five under the legal limit in the last hour. I pointed this out to him, and he told me to mind my own business.

I told him, "This is my business."

"The smaller fish taste better," he said.

"I'm going to dump the whole bunch if the warden comes along, so don't be surprised."

"Over my dead body," Owen said.

He was a big man, and bent over me, to emphasize what he'd said. I did not move. The anchor was there at my feet. Eight pounds of cast iron. I imagined putting it, jagged tines and all, through his forehead.

I think Owen saw that.

He sat down again, but then, after a few minutes of silence, launched into a diatribe about what it meant to be an American. Ed gave me a friendly, warning look, but I ignored it.

"You know, Owen," I said, "you're as full of shit as a Christmas turkey. Did anyone ever tell you that? That you are completely and totally out of touch? That you are the most ignorant, presupposing, self-satisfied son of a bitch that ever lived?"

> > ◇ < <

Owen was lecturing at me over the engine. Something about the *Indian Problem,* and how I was an example. I was bent down, trying to ignore him, that Nazi. He said in a loud voice that the United Townships Association and PARR (Protect American Rights and Resources) were going to fix the bunch of us assholes.

"I'm all for it!" he yelled, poking me.

I throttled by a number of islands, basalt nearly a shade of purple down at the waterline and high, dark tamarack. We sluiced over shallow rock ledges, and coming up the channel, rather than slowing, I swerved roughly around the buoys I'd been forced to put in, bright white, each as big as an early-model Cadillac.

I swung the boat around at the dock, nearly highsiding, water splashing everywhere, a bit of showmanship—boathandling. Kid stuff, but a distraction.

I threw a rope over the bow cleat, pulled the boat up to the rubber bumpers.

Owen climbed out of the boat, onto the dock.

There were ten or fifteen guests watching from the porch. We must have caught something, coming in like that, they thought, and one of them called out,

"What do you got?"

"You," Owen said, glaring down from the dock, "bring my things." He clutched his tackle box under his arm, marched up the dock.

"Owen!" I said.

He waved his hand over his head, dismissing me.

"Hey," I shouted. "Did you hear me? Hey! *I'm talkin' to you.*"

"You tell 'im!" one of the guests shouted, then saw it wasn't funny.

"Ah, *fuck yourself,*" Owen said.

I came out of the boat like a shot, Eddie reaching for me and missing. I meant to hurt Owen. I was going to do it, was going to give him that whole goddamned ugly summer and then some. I wouldn't stop at hurt.

Hugh came charging up the dock and around Owen. I swung at him and he ducked. He put his face in mine, clowning, eyes wide, grinning.

"Hey, Paul— Hey! It's me. Hey—it's Hugh," he said. "Hey, you there? Remember me?"

I wanted to hit something. I swung at him again.

"Hey, Paul. Hey! Chill out, buddy," Hugh said. He pulled me close, said, gripping my arm, "Come on, you *gotta* do it. Just now—okay? Okay? Can you just let it go for now?

"Come on," he said. "You *have* to."

He let go, then stepped around and behind me.

27

Gwen came up the dock, darkly beautiful, cobalt muslin billowing around her legs, smiling a smile that was all kinds of things; then, her face bunched up, she was in my arms, and crying.

Rose and talcum, bright, almost violet blue eyes. I couldn't let her go.

"Hey," she said.

>> ◇ <<

Down at the cabin, we were together, the night birds calling out on the lake. Open windows, the curtains luffing, distant sound of voices. One moment, everything was as it had been, familiar yet new, and the next, she was far, far away, and crying. I stroked her hair, silky, heavy hair.

"You don't hate me, do you?" she said.

"No," I said. "Why would I hate you?"

She lay on her back, staring at nothing, blue sheets pulled up over her breasts. There was something defensive, but hurt, in the set of her shoulders. She would seem about to say something, and would catch herself.

"What?" I said.

I wanted it to be all right, but it wasn't.

"What are we doing?" she said. "I mean, no matter what you do, it's all the same."

"But it *isn't* the same," I said. "Just think about—*tomorrow.* It'll be bright, and warm, and there'll be that morning whooshing in the pines and—"

She looked over at me. Her eyes were big, dark; I wanted her again.

"But there's a kind of awfulness."

"But it goes away."

"Not really."

I got out of bed. Stood naked at the windows overlooking the lake. The moon hung over the trees on the far shore, fat with it all.

"Come back," she said.

I sat beside her, touched her cheek.

"Remember when I asked you if we could ever be ourselves again?" she said.

I told her I did.

"Well, we're not."

"No, I know that," I said, hurt. "But we are, too. Just different."

"I don't know if I'm anything anymore." She looked off, as if just maybe, if she tried hard enough, it would come back to her, this thing she'd lost. "I feel dead, mostly." She set her hand on my shoulder. "Oh, I don't mean that. But the rest of it. It isn't supposed to be so hard, is it?"

I laughed. Oh, Lord.

"It's not funny," Gwen said, and she was crying, and I held her. All that got started again.

Before it was light, she got on her suit and quietly went out. I went up to the kitchen and ate, watching her cross the bay. Black one-piece, crawl and sidestroke; one small, then smaller figure in all that water.

I sipped at my coffee, put my feet up, and lit a cigarette.

I got out my notepad and began jotting down things to do. What I needed was ritual, familiar work. The odd and unusual would take care of themselves. I wrote, *groceries,* and when I couldn't think of anything, scrawled,

He who feasts on hope
is rewarded with
a bellyful of madness

It was something my grandfather, Nita, had said. I'd been disappointed at losing a lottery for a snowmobile at a hockey game in Duluth, when I was just ten, one I'd convinced myself I'd win. Thinking about him, I got a thick knot in my throat: I remembered how he'd died, and not wanting to dwell on that, took up my pen.

Soap, I wrote, but I was thinking of Nita.

>> ◇ <<

He told me this story:

He'd said, Listen, Nawaji, because I want you to remember.

Back then, he told me, they were camped on the shores of Mille Lacs. The thousand-mile lake. It wasn't a thousand miles, but close enough, he said. The deer had moved off, and the fishing had gone bad. They had nothing to eat, and day after day they circled the woods on shore. It was Boba'kwudadime'gizis, the broken snowshoe month. You couldn't get anywhere in that waist-deep snow. The wolves howled at night, hungry too. Day by day they were weaker. What the men had to do was circle both shores, driving the deer north, to the mouth of an inlet.

The problem was, no one had the strength for it.

So they were all miserable and gave everything to eat to the children, but they couldn't hunt.

It looked like the end there. And then, an old woman, the oldest of the clan, called the fathers into her tent, one morning before sunrise. They were all dying. She'd made a fire, and over it was an iron pot. Something was boiling in there, knocking around on the sides. They'd all thought it was bones she'd been hiding, and they'd hated her for that, keeping the bones when they could have been used for feeding the children.

She stirred what was in there. She set out bowls, had them, the six of them, sit three on each side, across from each other. They were all trying to be good-natured about it. The soup steamed, and steamed, and she threw in herbs, chanting. She was praying for a good hunt, she was praying for health.

And, she was praying all kinds of things, but, finally, for the weakest to let another take his bowl.

They were going to eat that soup, the old lady told them, not give it to their wives and children.

Nita's stomach had twisted into a hard fist. And then, the old lady said, to honor her, they would have to close their eyes. They did that. She threw the flaps down and it was almost pitch dark in there. She poured out the soup. There was the clunk, clunk of those bones in their bowls. Nita drank his soup right down, to get to that bone and the marrow in it. But it wasn't a bone, or marrow, at all.

It was a stone. A fire-blackened, pitted stone.

Nita told me, "I was furious then, because now, my brother, Tci'anung, was making happy eating sounds. I had gotten the stone, the others meat."

But Nita couldn't say that, and so he made those sounds too, furious at having been deemed worthless, and by a toothless old woman at that! By then, even with his eyes closed, he could sense light, and with that, the old lady, suddenly screaming, rushed them from the tent.

What are you waiting for?! she screamed. I gave you all I had!

It was bitter cold, and the wind was blowing snow as fine as dust. The others charged in front of Nita. He caught up to the one in back and knocked him down, plunging through the waist-deep snow.

He had his rifle, and even hours later, eating the leather in his coat, and running in that snow, the others knocking him down, too, he saw the first deer. The deer was as surprised as if a bear had been coming at him in that deep snow, and so it froze, and without stopping, plunging along, and the last of him in it, Nita stretched his rifle out and shot that deer dead.

A child, I wanted to know the end of it. I wanted my suspicions confirmed.

"So, did everyone get a stone?" I asked, stupidly.

My grandfather laughed. He ruffled up my hair, and laughed some more.

"Did they? Didn't they say?"

He quieted, and I could see it, that old life in him, and what it had come to. He held me by the shoulders, and I was afraid of him. His eyes were all blinded up with milky cataracts big as dimes. He said in the old language,

"But don't you see? Not one of us got a stone."

Nita, in 1963, had unsuccessfully tried to revive the Anishinabe Akeeng, a land reclamation group.

He'd fallen on the Burlington Northern tracks one November night, and had been cut in half. Drunken, the coroner said, though Nita had never been a drinker, nor could even someone as constitutionally fierce as Nita have walked to those tracks with a blood alcohol level of .25.

I was the one who'd found him.

Janice Barthelowe stepped down into the porch, green cotton shirt, black slacks, fawn hiking boots. There was a kind of grace in the way she pulled a chair out at the table and sat. I was surprised to see her.

"You come out with the others last night?"

"Yes," she said, glancing over her shoulder.

Mardine brought out a coffee and Janice thanked her. We had both turned to the lake; the sun was coming up over Snowbank to the east. The water was cast in pink and orange, and in it was Gwen, across the bay. Behind us was the hiss of the grill, the smell of bacon. Hugh talking at Mardine, about a boat he wanted to buy. The thumping rattle of the bread slicer; down by the shore, a longish, springy twanging—one of the cabin screen doors—and a final, flattish wooden slap.

The island was coming awake.

Gwen was throwing herself into the last of the distance that separated her from the boathouse. She was out half a mile or more.

"You really love her, don't you," Janice said. She was smiling, a certain melancholy in it.

"Yes," I said.

She sipped at her coffee. We were both watching Gwen now, arm over arm, feet kicking up diamonds of water, the lake dark around her.

"We don't have much time," Janice said, "so I'm going to be direct about this." She glanced in my direction, raised her mug to her mouth. She blew the steam off it, so the steam lifted, carried through the screen, her eyes averted.

"And then I'm leaving. Could Hugh take me back in?"

I told her I'd arrange it. There was the splash of someone diving into the lake. Shocked-at-how-cold-the-water-was quick breathing.

Typical.

"You're in the way," Janice said. "There's some kind of bond for development up, and you've got land they want. I'm not sure who all is pushing it. One of your own people is in it, someone in your tribal council."

"Who?"

"I don't know. But Len thinks he has him 'wrapped around his little finger,' or so he says. Whoever it is, they've got all kinds of land."

I nodded. "But Len—"

"He's a—" She tossed her head, undid the turquoise cloth around it. "—'*Businessman who takes care of the business,*' that's how he puts it. I don't know what all it comes to, but I know some investors out in New Jersey want to build a casino. It'd make a lot of money. Len'll make a lot of money."

I remembered that petition Al had given me, all those years ago, against letting exactly these people in. I'd signed it.

"But this is a small scale—"

Janice shook her head. "Something like they have at Mystic Lake. Or the Grand Casino Mille Lacs. You know, all those lovely cinder-block buildings, Seven-Elevens, KFC, airstrip, yellow lights.

"They're even talking about some boats, riverboat-type things, so they could move around, dock north up at Kenora, or down at Baudette.

"I heard him talking about it one night. If Len can 'move things' with the property, he'll get a percentage of their annual revenue.

"All that wonderful activity, more tourists, jet boats, plane rides. An airstrip right outside the reserve border, just land now."

"In Pine Point."

"Yes."

"And the rest of it?"

"They want to go as far north as a place I can't even pronounce."

I named the One Swallow Land, the Nin'godonin'djigan.

"Yes," she said. "That's it."

I wasn't surprised, exactly, though I still felt as if something large and threatening had loomed up.

"Do you know where Len was the first week of November last year?"

She had to think about that.

"Why?"

I lit a cigarette; my hands were shaking.

"Can you remember?"

"He travels a lot. We—" She was going to say, We didn't live together, you know, but nodded. "—he was away. Does that mean anything?"

"Do you know where?"

On that she was certain. "No," she said, "things weren't like that between us."

"And earlier this summer?"

"We were over at Barney's Ball Lake. Len was off fishing all the time—left me at the cabin. That's why I wanted to go out by myself—well, that and..."

Gwen came on across the bay, one last burst, long, fluid strokes.

"She swims beautifully, don't you think?" Janice said.

I told her I thought so.

"Why are you telling me all this?" I asked. "Why'd you come all the way up here?"

She touched her hair, her fingers, sadly expressive, even tender.

"I thought you'd want to know," she said.

I must have looked at her strangely, this shared thing between us. After all, what did she think I'd do? Janice tossed her head back, laughing. Thick, honey-dyed hair, deep-set eyes, that sharp profile. Still, I got it, something dark.

"Did I surprise you?"

"Why are you with him?"

"I'm not," she said. "Not anymore."

We sat, me smoking, Janice drinking her coffee, watching Gwen coming across the bay. Janice stood, pushing the chair into the table. Rasp of legs on floor.

"Thanks," she said, touching my shoulder, lightly, before she went out.

"What for?" I asked.

"That afternoon, when things—you know. If you hadn't been there—"

"It wasn't anything."

She stood between the porch and lodge dining room. She thought for a second, arms crossed as if wondering herself, then gave me a penetrating, sure look.

"No," she said. "You're a survivor, and not a bitter one. I needed to see that."

> > ◇ < <

At the dock I squatted beside Gwen. I handed her a towel. White dock, freshly painted, cool water, slap of waves on shore, that brown foam.

"What service," she said.

"I aim to please," I quipped. "A little rough out?"

Gwen threw her hair around to one side, twisting it, so the water ran down her shoulders, quicksilver, and over her breasts—a spatter of freckles there—the black suit giving off a rainbow sheen.

She was tan now, very tan. "It was fine," she said.

There was a far-off hammering of air, then engine clatter, and that big black, orange, and silver DeHavilland circled the bay, its shadow, just for a second, racing along the trees, then over us in a flash.

"I'm cold," Gwen said. "I'm going."

She went up the hill and into the lodge, long, powerful legs, that sinewy cast of her shoulders, shock of black hair down her spine.

The plane taxied to the dock, the oval door in the side thumped open, and Clark jumped down, his red hair tossing, as if his head were on fire.

"Hey, you bum!" he shouted.

I blinked at that, his jaunty appearance. We eased the plane away from the dock, cold, painted metal skin, then the engine coughed. The pilot circled once, dipped his wings, left right, a kind of wave.

"Well?" Clark said.

"You eat yet?"

In the lodge dining room, the others all up and around us, the Pilchers, our Aetna Insurance people, and ten or so others, Clark fit spoons into his eyes, holding them there by squinting. He looked ridiculous, the handles of the spoons sticking out like long, chrome antennae.

"The money's in the bank," he said, joking.

I laughed. "Right."

"I'm not kidding."

"Yes, you are," I said.

Everyone was watching us, the sun coming in off the lake, the ceiling bright with it.

"Cut it out," I said, "it isn't funny."

"Well, I'm not meaning to be funny."

"Jesus." I could see myself in those spoons, two bug-nosed twins, pointing fingers. I'd have yanked those spoons out of his eyes, but I was afraid I'd hurt him. "Just cut it out."

"Say you will."

"I can't," I said.

"That's no answer."

"Just shut up," I said.

He cocked his head, side to side, grinning. "But I don't *want* to shut up."

"You look—" I had to catch myself. "You look ridiculous!"

I was too aware of the guests who'd turned to watch.

Gwen came into the room, a number of plates balanced across her forearm. She saw us in the corner. A kind of shock registered on her face. Had I blinked, I would have missed it.

It was the kind of shock that throws the whole body back on itself.

"Hey, what is it?" Clark said. He set those spoons down, rubbed his eyes.

Gwen was dodging between tables, blue apron, taking orders. Our guests, decked out in clothes bright as confetti, laughed, talking over old times, making plans, all in a clatter of china and hiss of griddle.

"I just remembered something," I said, and rushed from the table.

I strode toward the point, and passing the last cabin, climbed the ridge from the side, steep, bare granite, kept moving, my mind one hot red blank, and at the top, winded, set my hands on my knees.

Just be calm, I coached myself. Which set me off, swinging and cursing at nothing.

"Are you all right?" a guest, Pam, said. She was out walking.

I was shocked to be caught in it.

"Wasps," I told her. "I hate wasps."

But there wasn't a wasp anywhere—though, in a way, that's where it had all started.

In my truck, parked outside the Rambler's, I was still worked up. Moses, braids, rounded shoulders, sweeping, those sausages in the window, now suggestive, letters in gold script, *Eagle's,* a condemnation. One moment I had my head resting on the steering wheel, in supplication to it, the next I could barely sit, my mind racing.

I imagined them together.

I tugged at my hair, rattled my pen on the dashboard. Just when I thought I was getting it stuffed back in, it gripped me, like a fist.

"Okay," I told myself. "It's all right."

But it wasn't all right at all. I had to get out of the truck. I made a point of not slamming the door, and then at the last second, kicked it closed, went around front, and kicked out a headlight. Went to the other and, with my bare fist, punched it. It broke all right, cut my hand, too.

But that did it, blood, wrapping my hand. Moses shuffling, afraid of me. That made me laugh. I'd gotten too tame.

Then back in the truck, my hand wrapped in my T-shirt, blood. I jabbed my pen into the lot of it, made a few notes on my pad.

I had the week to finish out, just that, the "Little Box Full" dinner to throw, Saturday night, and it would be over. It would be over, and then I'd think about the rest of it.

Years back, the dinner had been in celebration of the payment of annuities, all in silver dollars, which had been sent up from St. Paul in wooden boxes around the end of August. Now it was a night of drinking, and ostentatious shows of goodwill. The bigger the better, and the resorts, trying to attract return and new customers, outdid each other.

I threw the biggest.

I made a note to ask George and his brothers to come. And to make that work, I'd invite Charlie. Charlie wouldn't pass up a meal. I tallied heads. Fifteen—Jorgenson's—Seventeen, Kastenbaum....

The list got longer. All those who'd worked at the lodge had to be invited. The Highclouds, Terry and Simon, Mardine's niece. I winced at it, the list longer by the moment. It was as if, all over again, I was at the top of a hill on a bicycle, a rattly old bicycle with bent wheels and badly patched balloon tires, looking down a narrow rutted path, so steep it was nearly a fall, stomach shrinking at the thought of it, at the end, an abyss, what those guests could eat and drink in one night, and, after the dinner, Len.

But I had to do it, throw the dinner; it was the one bargain these high-season people got.

And we'd have the occasional passerby, too. Tens of them. The island hoppers. Chicken, for them. Clank of bottles, boats spinning drunken circles, laughter. In my mind, I saw it as an oblivion of expense, coming to absolutely nothing, and worse yet, anyone could stop by, anyone, all night.

I made a phone call from the booth on the corner of Main and Elm, back in that business persona, like slipping under the bark of a tree, arranged for everything I couldn't buy in Pine Point to be flown in: steaks—the finest marbled porterhouse, prime rib, and sirloin; imported cheeses—Brie, Muenster, Gorgonzola; greens—endive, arugula, redleaf; sweets, from a patisserie in St. Paul—petits fours, mille feuilles, gateaux; coffees—French roast, mocha, expresso; *wines*—I cringed, thinking what they would cost—red for the meal, something solid, a good French wine, Pouilly-Fuissé. Or maybe just a larger selection of B & G?; some German white for dessert; linens, the finest, embroidered, rented; stemware, fragile, and some of it to be broken, surely.

The receiver crushed between my ear and shoulder, I watched one car after another pass by, kicking up yellow dust, rubber through town, and making a U at the end of Main, park: station wagons, sedans, older couples, families, a crush of people at the Ben Franklin now, where the owner had set up a museum.

I wondered if Len had bought up Main.

In the center of town was a statue of a Viking. From where I stood, the shield caught the morning sun, a burst of gold. A boy, shinnying up the Viking's leg, stretched out to touch it, where it had been worn mirror smooth by decades of just that.

Wonder—how I wished to have it back!

"Get down from there," I heard his father say.

The outfitter was still on the line. "Hello. Hello. Is that it?"

"That's it," I said, though barely.

28

Thursday. Everyone wanted to go out at once. There was that coming to the end of summer feeling in everything. A touch of color came through the pines, birch and box elder going to yellow. Red canoes glided by the lodge, the canoeists waving, and we'd wave in return.

I sent one bunch of our guests out with Hugh, on the pontoon, another in the smallest of our boats. They were surprised, Bernadine, and Robert, and Abe, when I drew them a map on my notepad and tore the sheet from the pad with a certain happy indifference.

"Got things to do," I explained.

Through it all, Clark was hovering, close by, baseball hat—red and blue, Braves—pulled down so I couldn't see his eyes under the visor. He was gawky now, cutting himself off midsentence, then rushing, only to cut himself off again. *Are you going out—I mean, later? If you have time, maybe... never mind.*

He pestered me all morning, scooting up close, then backing away. I was worried at times that I'd lose it, strike out at him.

"All right, *goddammit,*" I said finally, down at the dock. "What— is— it?"

"You want to go into town tonight?" Big, awkward smile, almost simpering. "Just tonight, what do you say? It'd be like old times. Just you and me—"

Was it fear in his voice, or shame, or a kind of apology? Whatever it was, I couldn't stand it. It was like standing ankle deep in filth.

"Sure," I said, to stop him.

I would call it off, later. Sorry, Clark, things to do. It would go on like that, and would stay like that, and it made me sad to think about it.

Where Clark was concerned, I would always have things to do.

And I did. That afternoon—a propeller on an outboard sheared off on the sandbar across the bay, in deep water, and so I had to tow the boat back, and since we had no shear pins, we were down to two small boats, and that terribly slow pontoon; lures, live baits, a sprained wrist—and into the evening, a cut, and stitching it with monofilament; sterilizing the line in boiling water, Betadine, my hands bathed in it, orange and wrinkled. But I was happy to do it, all of it, even to focus on that good, clean operation—was comforted by business, and ritual, and a quiet hope.

Maybe we could just get to the end of it after all?

On the porch after dinner, they were playing cards and swapping stories about one wildcatter they all knew, Jack, who'd underbid them in a construction contract. The women studied their cards and gave each other wry glances.

Just like that, the lights went out. Mardine shuttled out candles.

"Who knows what evil lurks in the hearts of men," Eddie laughed. He seemed much more himself since Owen had left, a better person.

"I'll fix it," I said.

I went into the kitchen to check the fuse box. Buss fuses, a small glass window in each, a small bar there, the bottom fuse melted clean through. I lit a cigarette, thinking. Six big fuses: teal blue, like oversize buttons. A lever, the size and shape of a thumb, on the left of the fuse box. Two things could have caused the fuse to melt: resistance—of the kind that had started the boathouse fire, which made me worse than nervous. Or someone had pulled the lever down, then put in the burnt fuse. But then, *all* the appliances would have stopped. And what would the point be in that?

I stood there, trying to remember: One moment we'd been laughing out on the porch, the older guests playing a rubber of bridge, the kids chasing each other down on shore, and the next it had been dark.

There was something critical in it, and I couldn't think what.

What quality of darkness, what sounds?

I had to remember, but couldn't. Or was I just being anxious, overconcerned? I checked our fire extinguishers, then took Mardine aside, her eyes darting, alert.

"See anything odd?"

"Like what?" she said.

But now the lights worked fine, though there was a faint pulsing, just the faintest, and on the porch, bright laughter, cigar smoke, the paper patter of cards, the *ploosh* of kids tossing rocks into the lake from the ridge, distant laughter. Crowded there on the porch, but happy, I thought: the brushes in the generator.

I put my boots up on the window ledge. That was it. Just glazed brushes.

They must have gotten damaged the week we put the cabins up, I thought, the generator running day and night like that, too hot. But now, the new fuse in, all the electricity we could want. The island coming alive, the lights I'd strung along the shoreline, in series, carnival-like, early evening, and the night birds calling out on the lake.

I took some consolation in that.

Tomorrow, we'd throw the big dinner, people would swing by out of nowhere, drinking and going off to Barney's Ball Lake Resort, or farther up the lake, to the Northwest Outfitters; they'd sing, in the dark, drunken show tunes. Ballads. The year before, someone had belted out "Some Enchanted Evening," in a rich, resonant baritone. We'd all laughed. All night there'd be guests, coming and going. The lake would be alive with people. There'd be expressions of goodwill. Tables laden with food.

I felt, boots up, the guests laughing behind me, just for a moment, almost shamed. I tried to work up a feeling of gratitude. After all, the dinner was a potlatch, really. A giveaway. And the more one gave, and in good conscience, the better one's luck following.

I believed in that, and thinking it, remembered what my mother had called it:

Nabdanwin'tibik, Night of dreams.

Back then, if you walked through the woods, in the dark, here and there would be shrines, lit with candles: tobacco, sweetgrass, and cedar, for the Thunderbirds, the above spirits; and to appease the manidog, the below spirits, plates of meat, fruit, coins. And for the in-between, for us?

Charms.

There'd be charms, of all kinds, hung up in the trees, made of birch bark, human hair, elk teeth. Love charms, vermilion dust in buckskin packets; or fertility charms, birch bark bundles, a fetal rabbit inside each. There would be bone whistle charms, to take away sickness, root charms, to ensure safety and success.

Walking through the woods, and knowing the charms, you were struck by the whole of a people's hopes. Of a people's wanting.

Of a people's dreams.

>> ◇ <<

"So?" Clark said.

I was listening to the talk behind me, income tax, tax shelters, the like. It had been pleasant to lose myself in it. I did not want to go into Pine Point now, with Clark or anyone else. I did not want to go anywhere, and last of all into Pine Point after dark.

"Gwen?" I said.

Gwen had her back turned stiffly to us. She gave me a wave, craning her head around. There was something stricken in her face.

"Go on," she said, which so surprised me I couldn't think of an excuse not to.

Clark stood on the bank down to the dock, ducking and bobbing, nervous at it all. "Come on, I already told Mardine," he said.

"All right." I rose to it, as a pike might rise to a flashy, triple-barbed spoon.

>> ◇ <<

Clark bought another round, a beer for himself, 7Up for me.

"Putting that on your expense account?" I asked, as he laid a bill on the bar. "Like flights, those sorts of things? A little *East Coast* business?"

"Right," Clark said, an instant blossom of red in his cheeks. We'd been there for an hour or so.

We were packed in, those behind us reaching over our shoulders for drinks.

Clark dodged out onto the dance floor, mimed having someone in his arms, tangoed to Johnny Cash, which had people laughing. He dipped his partner, kissing her, this imaginary girl. This leggy, beautiful girl, whom I now imagined to be Gwen.

At the bar, he put down his beer.

"So, I guess you'll have to kill me now," he said, matter-of-factly, grinning.

"You and a few other people," I said, cold bottle in my hand.

Clark went back out to the dance floor. There were fifteen or so couples at it. Denim, pearl-buttoned shirts, fancy appliqué blouses and skirts. Dipping and spinning, turning on high-heeled boots, the floor humping with it. Those strings of lights like stars, overhead, the ceiling green with bills. Clark was dancing with one of the Highcloud girls, Irma, big around as she was tall, but a good dancer. Then he was back, beads of sweat on his forehead, just long enough to belt down a beer and go back out again.

I waited, all of an interminable hour, waiting to get to it with him, then got so angry I couldn't sit. Now he was back at the bar, tossed back a glass.

"I'm leaving," I said.

"Fine," he told me.

I put a tip on the bar and, turning to the front door, saluted Moses, and Moses tossed that white towel over his shoulder, skipped down to where I was sitting, something theatrical in it.

He reached under the counter. The lights flickered, went into a frenzied pattern, first in trains of light, whirling around the room, then in pairs and groups. You couldn't not watch them.

People came in from the parking lot, so I couldn't get past them.

Moses rolled out the barrel of tickets, a dented fifty-gallon drum on lead pipe, everyone shouting, packed in around him.

Moses spun the barrel, then mimed pulling a ticket out of it, held up his empty hand, flash of teeth.

"Hey!" someone shouted. "That's mine!"

Everyone laughed. Moses spun the barrel again, reached in, and pulled out his hand, nothing! Again. Clowning. Standing on the barrel. Everyone shouting. He did that three, four times, and each time the shouting got louder. Each time I felt more angry. What was he trying to prove, anyway? I was sitting on the edge of my stool.

It was hot in there; I felt a sudden suffocation, a panic. I gripped the stool, feeling myself rise away from it, my head prickling. What was it? Moses gave the barrel one last spin and, thrusting his hand into it, pulled out a yellow ticket, holding it over his head, bright as a small flame in all that dark.

There was a crescendo of voices, expectantly rising in pitch.

The door opened in front and in came George. Moses was throwing out names of BIA functionaries we'd hated, DIAND agents, nuns at Our Lady.

"And the winner is...Sister Redempta!"

Everyone booed. I was on the edge of it, some irrational fury. I had to get out, now, but the door was blocked.

Moses held that ticket up, moon face, braids, as if to read it, squinting. It was dark. We were all packed in. I jumped up off my stool, jabbed through, arms poking, to the barrel, where Moses stood holding the ticket behind his back now.

I grabbed for it, and he dodged. Everyone laughed. Which only made me more angry. I jumped up, snatched the ticket out of Moses' hands, and holding it up to one of those strings of lights, shouted,

"Two Persons!" even as I realized the ticket was mine.

I had not bought a ticket.

>> ◇ <<

I was doing my duty, so as not to engender more bad feelings, tearing those bills from the ceiling, buying round after round, when the front door thumped open and Gilby strode in, black vest over low-cut leotard top, black jeans, her hair knotted and tied back with cobalt cloth.

There was a pause, like a quick, surprised breath, and everyone went back to it.

"Hey, you two," Gilby said.

She dropped down beside Clark and, nodding at Moses, ordered a drink, rapping her fingernails on an empty glass, a crystal, musical note. The juke was playing, and it was hard to hear over it.

"It's on Paul," Moses said, loudly.

"What's wrong with him?" Gilby said, motioning to Clark. He had his chin on the bar, was stirring the ice in his drink with a miniature sword.

"He's drunk," I said. I couldn't leave him now, and he was belligerent about going.

"No, I'm not," Clark said.

"You two have a lover's quarrel or something?"

I gave her a nasty stare.

"Are you drunk, Clark?" Gilby asked, a teasing lilt in her voice.

Gilby motioned to my cigarettes. I nodded, surprised at myself, at these small liberties; she would always have me, in a way, and knew it. She struck a match, smoked, toyed with Clark's hair, copper bright, even in all that dark. Clark smiled. We were pressed up against the bar, someone nearly falling on me, knocking my soda over.

"Somebody win the draw?" Gilby said. She nearly had to shout.

Clark grinned. "Paul did."

"Oh, *lucky him,*" Gilby said, setting her hand on Clark's thigh.

I went outside.

In the parking lot I shot the breeze with George's brother, Simon, kicking my boots in the sand. I was free to go now, but didn't. I ran my hand through my hair, looked one way up Main, then down the other.

"Something eatin' at you?" Simon asked.

The kids were making a racket, skating on the end, that dull, wooden rolling. Laughter.

Waiting like that, I was reminded of those teenaged years, wanting to talk to a girl but afraid to, and mooning around, poking at them, finally, cracking dirty jokes, it all coming to nothing to those girls but irritation. And for us? A kind of unavoidable humiliation. We'd thought then we'd outgrow all that.

The better part of an hour went by. I had expected Clark to come out. What was he doing in there?

I turned my back to it, frustrated. Up the sandy road that led to the Rambler's, by the big pines there, and the ramshackle homes, came my old man, my sister, and Gerry, who was scuttling, something shifty there.

"Heya," I said.

My old man turned to me and said, "Hey, yourself. You oughta git, Paul."

There was something barbed behind what he'd said; it caught my attention, but then Larissa skipped over and kissed me on the cheek. "Don't look so glum," she said.

Raw cologne, cigarettes, mint gum; smell of hot radiators. Car talk. There were ten or so of us there in the lot. A bird called off in the dark. I checked my watch. Eleven-thirty.

I was furious with myself, waiting. What was Clark doing in there? Dexter Skinaway, one of the Rambler regulars, came out, glassy button eyes, that compact, angular jaw, drunk as usual.

"Gerry's telling some bullshit about you," he said.

"What's new?"

He leaned against my truck, glanced over at me. "You really selling out?"

"No," I said.

"Honest?"

I put on a very irritated face. "And how would he know?" I said.

Dexter washed that down, shrugged.

"Ask him yourself." And laughing, he added, "I told 'em they'd have to kill you first."

I went inside, intending to do exactly that, ask Gerry. I didn't see Gerry anywhere, or Clark or Gilby. I stood at the bar, about to ask Moses where they'd gone, when I glanced up into the mirror and my heart kicked.

Len, in his booth back of the pinball machines, craned his head around, grinned—*gotcha.*

The front door whomped closed. A chill ran up my back, like two-twenty, sat on the top of my head, tingling. Electric sputter.

I used the Men's, and there, hands shaking, doing my business, thought what to do. Moses, no doubt, had unlocked the back door, to let Clark and Gilby out—and like that, Len had come in. Now it was locked again. I looked out the window. Up the road, and in the dark, under the elms, a big Ford sedan spun around and parked. Two men in workclothes came up from the lot and got in. Clunk-clunk, of doors. Another waited under the window, smoking.

I chalked up my stick, lined up the cue ball, and ran the seven down the rail, intentionally missing, but blocking the pocket. I had time between rotations and got two beers at the bar. Moses was only too happy to do it, snapping the bills from the ceiling. I hoisted one beer, put down some of it, then went back to the Men's with both, and after locking the door, dumped one of them down the sink.

I looked out the window again, thinking to climb out it, but the big guy was still waiting there. Two cars were parked up the road now, though in the brush where you wouldn't see them unless you looked.

I filled the empty bottle with water and went back to the table with both, gave the beer to George, drank the water.

Heat. Smoke. Smell of body odor and cheap cologne, moons of sweat under my arms. Cold sweat. My toes aching in my boots, my heart skipping beats, I won another doubles with Simon, working that old ruse.

Two Bottle. I was making a pyramid, on the top of the pinball machine nearest, six there now, girls in yellow bikinis and high points for Surfin' Safari runs. All the old-timers, their backs to me at the bar, were amused, knew what I was doing.

I dropped my stick, made an almost sloppy shot, put down another, the water in my stomach sloshing.

"Ah, crap!" I said, missing a bank shot, giving up the game.

I took a seat by Dexter, who'd rounded up his own bottles there at the bar, felt Len's eyes boring into my back, almost hungry. I'd heard Dexter had lost his license again, had had his car impounded. Charlie was cracking down on wilding, joyriding with a case or two, convertible, preferably.

I bent down close, said in a low voice,

"What would you say if I gave you my truck for the night? It isn't a ragtop or anything, but it's got a big motor in it."

"Why would you wanna do that?" Dexter scrunched his face up, mischievous.

I felt something like a reprieve there.

"I'd like you to lose a couple rednecks and an apple or two out in the game farm.

"Think you could do that?"

Dexter smiled, twenty kilowatts. "Gimme the keys," he said.

We went out the front door, Dexter skipping down the stoop, quick, a shadow, dodging, as I'd asked him to, into my truck. He spun the truck around, punched on the lights. Whoever it was that had been waiting outside the window cursed—"God-dammit!"—bolted to the nearest of those two cars, and they pulled out after Dexter.

There was the sharp rap of that truck engine, then seconds later, all three of them, the truck and the two cars, engines roaring and sputtering, pulling hard, headed up 525, into the reserve.

"Shut that door," somebody shouted. "You'll let the smoke out."

I dodged around under the window of the Men's. It was dark, and blue spots swam in my eyes, until the trees began to materialize out of the darkness, an upended refrigerator and an old mattress there.

In a minute Len came around from the front.

"Hey," he whispered, feeling along the side of the cinder-block foundation, blinded. "What happened?"

I reached for his hand—thick, fleshy—gave him a sharp, angry tug, levered his hand behind his back, his hand crushing mine, pain so bright I nearly let go. He knew right off who it was. But there the Two Bottle paid off. He was expecting me to be much slower, and drunken.

I tore my knife off my belt, pressed it into the wattle of fat under his chin. Everything was suddenly very sharp, and necessary, and clear.

We were in it now, and it was not going to let up.

"Let's get in your car," I said.

29

I had Len park back of the Chuckwagon, now within reservation lines. It was an Ember's kind of place, open all night, catered to drinkers. Inside, orange vinyl upholstery, round stools, the parking lot marked in drunken red lines you couldn't fit a car between. Alice Pukwan sauntered out, hair greasy in a bun pinned over her head, a no-nonsense mouth dabbed with coral red.

"Let the window down," I told Len.

He did that.

"Hey, Paul!" Alice said, nodding from another car. "Be with you in a minute."

I didn't trust my voice just yet, so I waved, then rifled through Len's wallet, on my lap, as if I'd lost something, the knife there on the floor. Ten kinds of plastic, IDs to clubs in Chicago, telephone numbers, a picture of a woman that was not Janice.

"The wife?" I said, tossing the photo on the dashboard.

Two more wallet-sized photos, a girl in a red graduation gown, smiling, a boy on a small dirt bike, the number 7 on the front.

"So you got kids," I said. I put one of his business cards, *Corzalla, Barthelowe, Ltd.*, in my pocket.

"Just in case after this is over I have to look you up—or just your family."

Len grinned. His hair was brushed up from the side of his head, comic looking, from our scuffle. Under those lights, I could see his scalp.

Alice rapped her pen on the driver's door, surprising us. She handed menus in.

"How's it goin'?" I said.

"Not so many tourists this summer." Alice pumped the fabric of her dress. "Too hot."

"This is Len Barthelowe," I said. "He's up for some kind of real estate deal. Thinking to buy. I told him, down by Wheeler's Point has the most potential. What was it?" I said. "Paper plant?"

"You're just full of laughs tonight, aren't you," Alice said, studying Len now.

"What was it, Len?"

Len said nothing. I jammed the heel of my boot down on the top of his foot. Len grunted.

"Get a good look at him," I said. "He's a real mover and shaker, this one."

Alice adjusted the bobby pins in that bun of greasy hair. Len's big, thick fingers crawled slowly under the seat, and I brought my heel down again.

"You're joking, right?" Alice said.

I told her I was. I was getting that behind glass feeling. It was all coming at me, how it would end.

"You know what they say around here," Alice quipped, with a sharp laugh. "Shoot a land developer, save a tree."

"That's what we say," I said, laughing too.

Len affected a smile. The collar of his shirt was dark with sweat.

"Well, what'll it be?" Alice said, pencil ready.

I rambled off a list. Papa Burgers, Ranch shakes, Old West fries. Hot coffee. Alice went back in; the cook, one of the Fisher kids, orange smock, hair in a net, glared at us through the window.

"I want to know who's working with you," I said.

Len snorted. It was quiet there in the car.

"You think that's funny, huh?"

"I have nothing to say to you," Len said. He had a chemical aftershave smell. Hulked there, those big hands and thick, hairy forearms.

"What if I said, I'm going to have to take you out in the woods. Sound familiar?"

"I don't know what you're talking about."

Alice came back out, and I paid her with a hundred from Len's roll and told her to keep the change. Len's face turned almost lavender.

"You're kidding," Alice said, delighted.

I pulled the lid off the coffee and set it back of the steering wheel, in front of Len, where it fogged the windshield.

"No," I told Alice. "Might sell some property. I'm celebrating."

Alice snapped that crisp one hundred, as if to make sure it was real.

"Hey, thanks," she said, and skipped inside.

I bit into my hamburger. Len grabbed for something under the seat. I caught him in the mouth with my elbow, his head bouncing back off the headrest.

"Let's get this clear," I said. "I don't know what you're up to, but I want it to stop."

I was breathing hard. I had that gun now, a revolver. I pressed it against his side.

"Eat," I said.

Len somberly chewed on his Papa Burger. I cheerfully pointed out the special sauce. Fried onions. Double patties, cheese.

"It's all part of the Chuckwagon family of burgers," I said.

Len's nostrils flared. A drop formed out of the condensation on the windshield and zigzagged crazily into the vinyl dashboard.

Len ran his tongue around the side of his mouth, to his front teeth.

"What's it all about?" I said.

Len put his hands on the wheel, grinning to himself. It put me off. I could see where all that was going. Smiling, I knocked the steaming coffee off the dashboard onto his lap. Len flailed behind the wheel and I hit him again, then thought to go at him the way I had Gerry, only harder.

"You don't get it, do you?" I said. "I know about Al. And I know you and your goons were out there in the woods last November.

"My son *died out there!*" I said. "But that wasn't supposed to happen, was it?

"What was supposed to happen out there, Len? You tell me right now, or god so help me I'll blow your fuckin' guts out right now, right here."

Len's face had turned a bright red, his look of shock almost convincing. His shirt was brown with coffee. Alice came out.

"Everything all right?" she said, but could see it wasn't.

"Fine," I told her.

A car pulled into the lot, the top whirring down, and Alice went over. I could see, by the set of Alice's back, she was thinking about us.

"Tell me!" I said again. With my free hand I picked up the knife.

He went for the gun, down on the mat, and I cut him, across the back of his hand. He was bleeding on the upholstery. Sweet blood smell.

"How about I mess up your kidneys, how would you like that?" I said.

Len kept that grin on his face. His teeth were bloody from the cut on his lip.

"Say it! You were out there!"

His nostrils flared. There was a mole on his neck he didn't shave around, his pulse leaping under the skin. He felt it coming, too, but there were all those people in the lot.

"Start the car," I said.

It came out of me with all that went with it, how it was going to end.

A cruiser pulled into the lot. Rough bark of radio. Like a dream, an accident, some odd saving fate. The patrol car looming out of the dark, olive green. Charlie, tired, looking for a coffee and some chitchat with Alice, circles under his eyes, but a sharp, now penetrating look.

He'd picked up on it just like that, seeing us, the whole thing.

He tucked his shirt in, gut straining the buttons, crossing the lot, suspicious. I set the gun and knife on the mat, back of my feet.

"Want you to meet a friend of mine," I said. "Len Barthelowe, Charlie Groten."

The two shook hands.

"We met before," Charlie said. "Nasty cut there. How'd you get it?"

It surprised me a little, how much heat Charlie was giving off. He was all business, his pistol ready at his side.

"Changing a flat," Len said, smiling that too-polished businessman's smile.

"Is that so," Charlie said.

There was a red circle on Len's knee. I handed him a couple napkins with the Chuckwagon logo on them: an Indian on horseback shooting arrows into a covered wagon, which just happened to be on fire, a local joke.

"So, what brings you up here?" Charlie asked.

"Fishing," Len said.

"Really. Maybe I should have you get out of the car? You had a few too many to be behind the wheel?" Charlie cocked his head to one side, looking up and down the length of the car. "Where's your registration?"

Len handed it over. Avis, the whole package. I noticed the back of Len's head was nearly flat. There were moons under his arms. A bead of sweat ran down from his hairline and into his collar.

"I'm here on business."

"Oh, business," Charlie said, in a nasty singsong voice. "And what kind of business would *that* be?"

Charlie set his hands on the door, bent down.

"Marine sales."

"Marine sales, what?"

"Outboards, boats—"

"Boats," Charlie said. "What *kind* of boats?"

"All kinds."

"Is that so? *New* boats or *old* boats?"

Now Len was grinning again. He did that thing with his tongue.

A few more cars pulled into the lot. Red faces, wild hair. It was closing time. The night at the Chuckwagon was just starting. Charlie tipped his hat, held up Len's license.

"Be back in a minute."

He got a coffee at the window, chatted with Alice, then got into his cruiser. I held the gun up in the light. The gun was a Smith & Wesson .38. Blue steel, and heavy, cross-hatch handle.

"What if I just blow your brains out, right here? How about that?"

Len's eyes widened.

"Whatever you're up to, it's gonna stop. Say it."

Len just glared into the windshield. Emil Debundunk came

across the lot, pigeon-toed, light on his feet. He leaned into the car through the window, smelled of patchouli.

"Heya, Paul," he said.

"Hey there, Emil."

"Nice gun," Emil said.

I told him I thought so too. Emil wanted to know if I could help him move some La-Z-Boys across the bay with my launch. I told him I'd sold it.

"Hey, I know you," Emil said, looking at Len.

"No, I don't think so," Len replied. There was a wedge of muscle in his jaw.

Emil sized him up. He did a good business in the fall guiding for whitetail. He was a very sharp guide and didn't miss things.

"You were down at the BPOE a while back, weren't ya? Last fall, in November. I seen you there a few times. He looks like a real killer, don't he?" Emil joked. "All dressed up like that? String tie and everything?"

I said, "When was that, Emil?"

"November. Third week? Or was it opening? Hell, I can't remember."

I aimed the gun at Len's head, made as if messing with it, careless.

"It isn't loaded, is it, Len?" I said. "Where's the safety on it?"

Emil reached in. "Hey—watch it there, you got your safety off already."

Len sat bolt upright in his seat, as if he made a smaller target that way. I could see the Chuckwagon sign through the driver's window, past Len's profile.

"So, you fishing?" Emil asked.

"Walleye," Len said.

While Emil was jabbering on there, I took aim; squeezed. The gun let loose a roar, kicked in my hand. Len jerked back in his seat, eyes wide, sucking in hard, short breaths, panicked.

"Ah!" he said. "Ah!"

I squeezed off two more shots, Len jerking each time, the echoes coming back across the lake.

Charlie hit his lights. Bright blue-white, blinding. Everyone was out of their cars and moving.

It was all commotion. Curious, excited faces. Finedays, Dibikamigs, Morrisons.

"Somebody shot somebody!" "No, somebody shot at a car going by." "No, the out-of-towner, he shot out the sign." Now the sign read:

uck agon

Couples were sliding up to the big, cement bumpers in front. Kids wheeled in on bicycles, jabbered in knots, pointing. I explained to Charlie,

"He was just showing it to me."

Charlie had the gun. "And it went off?"

"*No,*" Len said.

"'*No,' what?*" Charlie said.

Len tried to explain, but all Charlie did was frown. It was clear Charlie wasn't having any of it. He didn't once look at me, working Len over.

"You stay put," he said, "both of you."

Charlie went back to his cruiser, the gun swinging from a finger. There were all those kids, gawking. Rough squall of radio, Charlie running a Vehicle Identification on the rented car. For the first time I noticed it was an odd color: burnt orange.

I said, seated beside Len,

"I don't have to tell you what will happen if I see you up here again, do I?"

Len did that thing with his tongue, ran it around the front of his teeth.

"You don't have anything to say, huh?"

"No," he said.

I got out of the car and went up and by Charlie's cruiser.

"You know where you can find me," I said.

30

Gwen, in the kitchen, had her hair done up in that turquoise towel. Her hands were white with flour and her apron was spotted red with cinnamon. The kitchen smelled yeasty, and sweet. Sticky buns for breakfast. I sat back of her on a stool.

"So where is he?" Gwen said. There is a vein that throbs on her left temple, when she is angry, and it was throbbing.

"I don't know," I said. "Should I?"

"He's your friend, isn't he?"

I knew exactly what she was getting at, making my friendship with Clark seem something to argue between us, and I wasn't going to go for it. Not tonight. She punched the dough down again, cut it in half, then pounded it down. The table rocked slightly and I got off the stool, took the newspaper by the phone, folded a few pages of it, and put it under the shorter leg.

Just then, I felt like that table.

"I told you what I thought about your swimming out there in the dark," I said.

"And I told you what I thought about your coming in at all hours."

She tossed her hair back, but it wouldn't stay, fell down again.

"Gwen—"

"No. No more excuses."

"Just listen," I said.

"It's a little late for confessions, isn't it?"

Her mouth pursed, she slapped the dough down. We had three days to go; just three days, and I wanted to see the thing through. It was our only hope.

"What is there to confess?" I asked. I didn't want to hear it.

"Why don't *you* start?"

"Where would you want me to?"

She cut the dough with a large, serrated knife, dropped the rounds in a greased tin tray, flung open the oven, and slid them in. She did that with three trays, then stood back of the counter, her hands on her hips.

"There," she said.

"*Please* don't swim out past the buoys for the next couple days," I said.

" 'Please.' I like that." She tucked a strand of that unruly hair into the knot she'd made of it in back. "Is someone going to drown me?"

I said, "Gwen—"

"Or is it that you don't want me wandering around in my swimsuit. Your wife's too fat now, or something."

I wasn't going to respond to that. But now I looked. She had put on some weight. I was almost shocked at what went through my head.

The oven boomed with the change in temperature, a hot clang. I wanted to say—please, let's stop this. And I couldn't be right about the weight.

"Did you have a good time with Clark?" she said.

"No," I said, "should I have?"

She looked at me across the counter. There was something hurt and angry in the set of her mouth, something wounded. Still, she had the most lovely eyes, now a cobalt blue. They seemed to change colors like that.

"Paul..."

"Yes," I said, my heart sinking.

"Make him go away." She set her hands on her hips, her back to me.

"Who?"

"Clark."

I tried not to smile. It was an odd victory, that moment, and a loss. "Why?"

"Because I don't want him here."

"It will all be over on Monday, anyway."

"No, *now.*" She was cleaning up, stacking the mixing bowls, arranging spices in the cupboard.

"You mean, we'll just get him up, and send him away. Like that, you mean?"

"Yes," she said. She turned to face me, nothing equivocal in it.

"Right now."

"Yes, right now."

I wondered what she was talking about. "He's not here, anyway," I said. I expected her to say, Well, then where is he? But she didn't say that. She said,

"Yes, he is. He's down there with your *friends,* Paul."

Friends? And, too, I hadn't once thought Clark would do that; bring Gilby up after all that had happened, all that had come between us.

"I want them out."

"I can't," I said, almost pleading. "We don't need to make a scene now, do we?"

"I don't care. Get them out, *now.*"

Gwen set her hands on the countertop. Tan. Sinews. Her mouth was ugly in a way I'd never seen it.

"First thing in the morning," I said.

"Fine," Gwen said.

She rushed out the back door of the kitchen, but not to our cabin, not to the point. Not to anywhere I could find her, which had me cursing myself, all that dark, endless night.

31

Morning. Sun, too sharp. I had everything to do, and was doing none of it. I was exhausted, had slept, finally, in the boathouse, on the workbench, in a sea of sharp carpenter's tools, ready if someone came in during the night.

"Where is she?" I said to Mardine in the kitchen.

Mardine, hands turning loafs out of bread pans, said, curtly, "Swimming."

"Since when?"

"About four."

Clark stepped into the kitchen. Blinding morning light, unfocused look, hangover, and then some.

"She's not talking to me," he said, in an affected, jolly voice.

"You've been a complete ass, Clark," Mardine said, at the grill, scrubbing, "and I'm not letting it go by this time."

Blue ceramic pitcher of pancake batter, bacon, in white butcher paper, newspaper-colored cartons of eggs. She broke an egg on the griddle, chopped at it with her spatula.

"Where is she?" I asked Clark.

"Who?"

"Don't act dumb," I said.

A look of surprise registered on Clark's face. I think he got it then, what he'd done. I'd told Clark down in the Cities that after Bobby'd died I'd had a pathetic and melancholy little fling but had not told him who it had been. Why should I have?

"Hugh took them in," Clark said.

"What do you want to eat?" Mardine snapped.

"I don't think I'm hungry," Clark said, and looking pitifully between Mardine and me, went out.

I got a call from the outfitters in Pine Point and made a run into town. Clark insisted on going, to help, he said. We got all of it in the back of the truck, heavy boxes of silver, those steaks, fragile cases of wine. Stemware in cardboard boxes like honeycomb.

I circled Pine Point, looking for that burnt orange sedan, but didn't see it anywhere.

>> ◇ <<

Later that afternoon, the guests out on the bay with Hugh, I went back to the generator, to escape Clark. He was hovering again, though worse now, hands hanging at his sides, pathetic.

When he got near me, I wanted to hit him.

From the shed, I could see Mardine in the kitchen window, working, hands as efficient as levers on some machine, hair pinned in a tight black bun over her head. I had her shut the current off from the fuse box.

We had twenty, sixty-volt backup batteries, and when they kicked in, the voltage regulator, shoulder high on the wall of the shed, immediately buzzed and got hot with all that amperage.

It reminded me, just then, of bees, which put me in an even darker mood.

I waved for Mardine to shut the batteries down, too, and that buzzing quit. My ears rang with the quiet; the shed felt dangerous. I hated that place. The generator shed was oily, and smelled of hot carbon, ozone, and burned oil and diesel and wood. Twice the shed had caught fire in the past, and I'd been lucky to be near, where I could get to it.

Everything in that shed felt poisonous, and I avoided it, generally, for that reason. Even the walls, the roof, the floor, were saturated with a burned, electrical-mechanical smell. It bothered me, and always had, that the main shutoff switch back-looped into the kitchen, into that fuse box. That was so if the generator stalled in a rainstorm, say, you wouldn't have to go out into the shed to turn on the batteries.

And, too, it was a safety precaution, having that switch in the kitchen: If the concrete floor under the generator were wet, and the batteries were on, all one had to do to be electrocuted was touch the generator housing. Sixty amperes, you could weld with that.

So why had those engineers put the diesel restart button exactly there?

I'd asked Frank, the last owner, about that. Got the wrong generator sent up, he told me. The electricians had already finished and gone home, so they'd wired the rest of it themselves.

Just make sure the goddamned batteries are off when you're in here, he said.

I looked at my feet. Red wings, scuffed on the toes, but thick neoprene soles. The floor was covered with reddish pine needles and yellow poplar leaves, all dry.

Still, it made me uneasy. I made a point of not letting my knees touch the floor.

But then I got down to it. I'd brought out my toolbox, and after a few minutes, I forgot about the awful smells. There was something cockeyed in the generator, but I couldn't see what. Then I was down on one knee, rough concrete, to hell with it. Heavy, iron-green legs of the housing, nickel-plated shims. It got darker in there, suddenly.

"Jesus," I said to myself. "It'll probably fucking rain now."

I glanced up, and in the window, just an opening in the pine wall of the shack, was Clark.

"Mardine sent me out with this," he said.

He snapped on a light; for a second there I was blinded. Startled. My heart galloped. For a second I thought he'd snapped the batteries back on somehow—expected those sixty amperes to run through me.

"Bring that in here," I said.

I was lying on my back, aiming the flashlight into the maw of that generator. Coils of shiny, shellacked, copper wire, steel and copper armature. I would have to remove the housing to get at the brushes.

I turned the takeoff shaft from the diesel. There was a spray of brass dust on the cement. There'd been some resistance, something nonconductive between the brushes and the armature. It looked like sand.

"What is it?" Clark said.

"Here," I said, and handed him the flashlight. "Shine it in here."

Now there were parts all over the floor, carefully set on end, so as not to get dirty, and Clark, reaching for the flashlight, managed to send them caterwheeling into every corner of that shed. Metal on cement, cursing.

"Clark," I said.

"Goddammit," he said. "It's wrecked, just every goddamn thing."

We were on our hands and knees, looking for those parts. I wanted to be anywhere but stuck in that shed with Clark.

"Listen—" Clark said, stopping to look up.

"What?"

I was wishing Hugh had come out, instead of Clark, because he was good with these things, and because, now, I worried Clark would finish what civility we had left between us.

"I'm ruined," he said.

"Ruined, huh?"

I chuckled at that. It was this very way he had of stating things that had so amused me for so long. "This arrow's stuck in my side," he'd said, all those years ago. "Think my insides'll come undone?" All said in that wounded, inquisitive voice, that arrow wobbling in his stomach like some oversized dart.

It was part and parcel of our friendship.

No, I'll call it love; because that is what it was. I know that now. All those years, his oddball humor saved me from my sometimes killing seriousness.

"I did something I shouldn't have," Clark said.

He got a look on his face, one that made me want to forgive him all over again; he looked lost, that boy grown old, still silly, but weren't we all? Instead, I needled him. Jealousy has that way of getting to you, no matter how levelheaded you are. I hated him just then, truly.

"You could be a little more specific."

"I gave in to something. She made me do something...."

"She *who?*"

"Gilby."

I laughed, rocking back on my haunches, a brass fitting in my hand. "Is that all it is?"

"It isn't funny," he said miserably, but I couldn't help myself.

Well, I thought, Gilby had done herself one better. Of course she'd known Clark would tell me what they'd done, if it was something he couldn't stand, later, and if not the specifics, the gist of it.

"People do all kinds of things, Clark," I told him, remembering how Dexter had seemed after something more than a joyride, had been back there with George, in the dark, earlier. "You aren't having trouble sitting," I said, a little meanly.

"Shut up," Clark said.

"Ah," I said. "I see."

"She shouldn't have had him come along."

"Was this somebody new... to this... *whatever*, like yourself?"

"I don't think so," Clark said.

"Clark," I told him. "It's only a problem if you think it is."

"You think so? Maybe it isn't for you."

His face bunched up, and I was afraid he was going to cry.

"I'd been drinking."

"No excuse, Clark," I told him. "That just won't wash with me."

I had all the parts now. I set myself to repairing that generator. Clark lent a hand.

"I put that money I was talking about in your account," Clark said.

The lunch bell rang, three times. The light was filtering down through the trees. I was putting the last of it together, tightened it all with a ratchet and a nine-sixteenths socket. I looked up from the housing.

"Clark," I said, "you didn't. Not really. And don't say that again; it's too late for that."

"All right, I didn't," he said, then covered his face and had himself a good cry.

I felt like laughing. I wasn't going to give in to any of it; all that was over and done with. I'd feel something about it later.

"Everything is just... so... *awful*," he said.

"Don't be so hard on yourself, Clark," I told him. "You're just an amateur."

I shut the toolbox, looked around the floor of the shed to make sure I hadn't forgotten anything.

"Amateur what?"

"You're just an amateur bad guy." I grinned at him, slapped him on the back, as if we were just acquaintances. "You, my friend, are such an amateur bad guy that it's funny."

At that word, *friend,* he smiled.

"Really?"

It was an awful, broken smile. I felt positively evil, and had to get away from him, from myself around him, before I did something I couldn't forgive myself. I took a tug on my cigarette, crushed it under my boot.

"I've got things to do," I said.

32

Up the lake, past the buoys, and to Barney's, there were fireworks. One after another, a winding line of gray smoke rising into all that blue; a flash of light, and a *pop!* Boats wallowed up the channel through the buoys, then sped off. Guests dove from the boathouse roof, women and men alike, big around the middle, but laughing, while others talked on shore, read books, drifted in our canoes across the bay, arms hanging over the side.

Here was the end of it.

Around two, someone sent up balloons—red, white, and blue—notes dangling from strings under them. They caught in trees, and if you could get to them—guests climbed, some who hadn't climbed in twenty, thirty years, their hands and feet pitch-sticky, and scratched—they'd come down. Some of the balloons had fortunes on them.

On one note was scrawled, *Migayenin minawin,* Blessings and long life.

There was the smell of sweetgrass, and cedar smoke, the Midewiwin, up around Snowbank, throwing a potlatch, too. I had a list I'd made out, and I followed it like you'd follow a map.

The slightest deviation from it made me crazy, and one thing done, I'd move on to the next.

All of it was in preparation for the dinner now, breaking bags of ice in the freezer, humping dry supplies up from the pontoon, uncrating comestibles.

When Gwen and I crossed paths, she would not look at me.

Evening coming on, I got the grills out, pipe legs bolted to their rounded bottoms, filled them with charcoal, then huffed a case of beer up to the ridge for our guests. They were all sitting on the ridge, the twenty or so of them. Judy and Dick Clough, the Simmonses, Eddie Hawes, the Kleinmeiers, Fitzgeralds, Tafts. I knew them all.

To the north, those rockets went up—there'd be that augering line of smoke, a flash, and seconds later, an echoing, airy *pop!*

Clark was up there. He had them laughing, this Clark I once knew. He flashed them his boyish smile, though there was something desperate in it now. A story, a joke. "You hear about the Norwegian farmer who loved his wife soooo much, he almost told her?" Laughter. He looked the picture of life, those hands flying every which way, carrot-red hair, now bright, green eyes.

"Yo, Kimosabe," he said.

It had been a joke between us for years, our role reversal. I mimicked pulling six-guns, and he took a few shots in the chest.

"When's dinner?"

"An hour or so," I said.

On the way back down to the lodge, I was surprised to feel something almost like—hatred, at the laughter behind me.

Or was it—envy, that in the midst of it all, he could laugh like that?

. . .

Just before dinner, a number of people not in our party came by on pontoon boats, and in six-man Bayliners, and outboards, crummy Larson fishing boats, an old, wood-hulled rowboat with thole-pin oars. I had two galvanized steel bathtubs full of ice down by the dock, bottles of beer poking out like brown bobbers. I popped beers for the Morrisons and Yellowfeathers and the Strong Rocks; the Finedays and Highclouds. The kids got 7Ups.

The kids ran this way and that, around the boathouse, the dock, laughing, reaching for each other, brightly colored cloth turned in a breeze, chasing itself.

Watching them, I got that packed-down feeling, a kind of tightness in my chest. The canoes glided in, light on the water, bumping, then the boats, and Hugh with the pontoon, with the last-of-the-season crowd. All in the dreamy, late-afternoon quiet. I ran a long, ninety-weight chain through the mooring loop in the bow of each of the boats, rhythmic, clattering, each hull a sounding board, echoing across the bay, poked the chain through the big iron eye set in front of the boathouse, turned the chain back on itself, and padlocked it with a final snap.

Now, no one would take the boats out on the lake and drown. Nor would the Pillager or Big Grassy kids, looking for something to do, steal the boats or canoes, and my guns, all but for that pump Remington under the bed, I'd locked away so no one could so much as think to use them as noisemakers as they had in years past.

Years back, following the Night of Dreams, or Hump Night, as the kids called it, we'd move south, the season over, to White Earth, and the forests that remained there, to timber work.

But the night before, the kids, out of resentment, or frustration at themselves, or at life itself, ran amok on the lake. I'd done that with Al, hair torn back, full tilt, laughing, flying low in pitch blackness in a boat we'd stolen, cold damp air, and the disappointment, finally, of waking somewhere.

A small, flat-bottomed skiff zigzagged in around the point, up by the buoys, now high and white in the late-afternoon sun. Gerry tethered the skiff and came clunking up the dock, jumped to the beach, where Hugh and I were turning the canoes and boats over, so they wouldn't fill if it rained. Sandy rasp on metal hull, gasoline, wet paper smells.

"Just gotta see Larissa," Gerry said, breathless, going by us, climbing to the lodge, his hands on his knees, pumping his legs.

"Now, what is he doing here?" I said, watching him go into the lodge.

"Hey," Hugh said. He heaved the last canoe over. "What did you expect? You got Larissa working, you don't think he'd show up for a free dinner?"

I didn't like the way he said it; as if he were angry with me.

We had reached that false lull between afternoon and evening; an exhalation, before setting to the main event. I checked my list. Everything I did now was a part of a motion to end the season.

I repaired a toilet (sanitary napkins) in cabin 7. Shoveled the ashes out of the trap in the lodge fireplace, coughing, hands black, smelling of burned pine and newspaper. Polished silverware, pungent chemical cleaner, fingers wrinkling, Hugh, quiet, glowering, and thinking I didn't know what, beside me.

Gerry was in for it now, too, bullied into cutting carrot roses by Mardine, and taking her insults when he ruined them.

What, do you have toes for fingers? Mardine said in the old language. *Are you trying to grow mushrooms under your nails? Scrub! Here!* she said at the sink, holding out a brush! *Achhhh!*

What helpers! And Spawning Trout there—she pointed to Hugh. *Right, you. I'm talking to you. Get your hands out of your pockets!*

Hugh pretended he didn't understand her.

I'll give you a swift kick, Mardine said.

I went down to the boathouse, new smelling still, cheap particleboard inside. Worked the better part of an hour mothballing outboards—pulling the spark plugs and squirting in thirty-weight oil, then tightening the plugs and turning the engine over. We'd need only the pontoon and one boat after tomorrow.

Done, I climbed the side of the boathouse and sat on the roof, the lake there quiet and beautiful as always, in repose, it seemed.

Hugh and Gerry came down the path, foreshortened. Gerry balding, Hugh those braids down his broad shoulders, that cocky angle he stood at.

"I'm watching you," Hugh said.

Gerry grinned like a Halloween pumpkin. He had his hands in his pockets, turned his back to Hugh, shuffling. Every time he turned, Hugh followed. Hugh put his face in Gerry's. I don't know what it was he said, but Gerry recoiled at it.

He nearly flew back up to the lodge. I whistled, and Hugh saw me there.

"What did you say to Gerry?" I said.

Hugh shook himself, surprised. "I'd cut his nuts off if he gave us any trouble."

"Nice."

"I don't like him," Hugh said.

"Any particular reason?" I was falling painfully into my anxieties.

"He's wearing a watch."

I laughed at that. "A regular banker, that Gerry," I said, but it wasn't funny. Gerry never wore a watch, and I wondered why he was doing it now.

>> ◇ <<

At five, the lot of them came down from the ridge and Mardine threw the door of the lodge open. Drinks, until dinner. I sprayed the charcoal with lighter fluid, oily, petroleum smell, touched a match to it. Flames leapt up. I grilled mushrooms filled with crabmeat, vegetables in tamari, barbecued venison strips marinated in red wine.

Mardine brought out our old RCA and a stack of 78s, and people danced.

"This is silly," Joyce Kleinmeier said, "but it's nice."

Buzz of conversation. Laughter. There were a few good dancers among them, and they whirled out eastern swing. Some of the older guests did the Big Apple, called out to that old tune—

Pennsylvania Six Nine Oh Oh Oh!

Sinatra, Roger Miller, Nat King Cole, crooning, big as lost love itself, cast the evening in sweet nostalgia. I mixed drinks, and the light faded. The moon rose ghostly in the west, a luminous zilch. Some guests, lying on the mossy ground, played cards, drinking. They'd wave each other over, chunky class rings, the women in dangling earrings and mouths bright with color.

Gwen was lovely in a cobalt, off-the-shoulder dress. Pearl necklace. Graceful, swift movements, that Irish black hair tied in a braid down her back, that slightly skewed smile, sensuous.

I was madly in love with her, all over again.

But working. Cheerful tinkle of ice in empty glasses. A bell. Juniper scent of gin. Rye. Lime. Soda. Hugh and I mixed drinks, dressed in black. Bow tie. Cummerbund. It was silly, but part of it.

Across from us, on the hillside, Gwen let her head drop back, laughing. Delicious line of neck, bare shoulder, hint of breasts, those extraordinary, blue eyes.

White, white teeth.

Then, a hammering, distant. Coming up from the south. In a wide, heavy arc, the big boat swung up the channel, roaring, throwing up water, a spray of bright silver.

33

It was an impressive, powerful boat, of a kind that had once been popular on the lake, wood hulled, low slung, powered by a car engine. The windshield caught the sun and threw back a bright red flash. The driver spun in a circle, tearing up gouts of green water, the engine hammering and impressive in its awfulness.

Then the boat pulled up to the dock, forked red flag flapping from a post on the bow like a snake's tongue, and I went down to them.

I gave Gilby a hand up. She kissed the side of my face. Smelled of lilacs.

"Hello, Paul," she said.

"Hello," I said, Len climbing out, George coming out big behind him.

I caught the bow with my shoe, tossed a rope around the cleat there, then cinched the boat so it came snugly up against the dock.

The boat was an old Chris Craft, recently refinished, the brass fittings sparkling gold and shinier than new, the mahogany hull reddish brown and lovely, tapered to the stern, there, a second seat for passengers.

Red leather upholstery. The gauges on the dashboard all replated nickel and flawless.

But the steering wheel was as I had known it, even down to the pitted black, Bakelite surface, the horn in the center with a thunderbolt slashed across.

I reached across the seat, pressed the horn—it let go a loud, compressed *rauuuuuup!*—as Dr. Piper must have done countless times.

As I'd dreamed I would someday.

I came up the path, around Gilby and George and Len. There was that regular-irregular iron *clank!* and a pause, *clank!* of horseshoe on post, and laughter.

A score. "Ten all!"

The older guests danced, under the pines, the lodge behind us, big as an oceanliner, catching the last of the sunlight, looming out of the trees. Gwen, taking orders for highballs, as the older guests called them, saw Gilby, Len, and George. She stood, jade-green bottle of Tanqueray in her hand, just that moment, frozen stiff as Lot's wife, and I saw it was no use going to her now, Gilby, tugging Clark out to dance, that false girlishness of hers, George studying me, from behind the guests, Len, dropping into the middle of them, our Aetna Insurance people.

They were drinking and talking business, winter trips.

"I hear those safaris are something," Len said, cutting in.

"I'd say!" Bernadine Boettcher said.

"I'd like to shoot a lion," Len said. He winked, as though he were joking.

Bernadine, beside him, looked shocked. "You can't do that these days."

"Who says," Len said, winking again. "Just gotta grease the right wheels."

The men all laughed.

Then Clark wandered off, and Gilby danced with George. There was something odd in it, because he was paying her no attention, and it maddened her. Maybe George was giving it back? She was wearing some low-cut thing, you couldn't *not* pay attention, with her dancing in that honeyed way of hers, but George was looking off.

He looked at me. A sober, serious face, saying what I couldn't tell.

I bent to the grills. The record player dropped another 78.

Our group from Boston came down from the ridge, scuffling on the path and laughing—"You didn't really, did you?" a woman tittered, and it all picked up again. Sweaters now, a fire in the lodge fireplace. Loons calling out on the lake, everywhere the buzz of outboards, the *shhhhut!* of fireworks, explosions.

The dancing went on. Someone had started the others on a dance circle.

"Abe!" one of the guests shouted. "Show us how to do that old dance. Come on!"

I liked this Abe. He had a sharp sense of humor, reminded me a bit of my grandfather, Nita. It surprised me how he could dance, ropy-armed, legs akimbo, but all in time. His wife was good too, spun her skirt out, a billow of geometrical diamonds.

They were taking turns. At the grills, I listened to the music, looked over at Gwen. She was leaning against the lodge, as if to pick something up, but her chest was heaving. She was sick; I stepped out to go to her and she ducked inside.

I looked to see who was dancing in the circle, Clark and Gilby again. Clark spun Gilby out and caught her. They looked the pair, dipping and bowing, Clark smiling as if he were enjoying himself, though I knew, from his incessant blinking, just how hard he was trying.

A few more boats came in, Charlie with them, and the night swelled, and like that, took on a life of its own.

Dinner. Inside, all thirty, thirty-five of us, under that high, high ceiling, dark varnished wood, candlelight. Through the windows, a girl, on the bank, ebony braids, stopping, turning, a boy chasing, the two going around a tree, falling, while back of a table, taking an order, Bobby Darrin on the RCA, red gingham curtains, a guest's lifted face, skis on the wall, pictures of snow-covered lakes, trophy catches. Barrette in platinum hair. Gerry slinking in with a full plate. Low voices, a burst of laughter, pouring drinks, filling water glasses, Gwen, lifting platters at her shoulder, spinning, smiling.

Hours went by in a blur.

Bell-like ring of one glass, then many. Abe proposed a toast.

"To the Two Persons!"

Everyone laughed, then clapped. Gwen smiled, her face reddening. A woman in a dress that positively crackled when she crossed the room, stooped over a table. I brought Joe Strong Rock in, and he sang, in that ululating voice, a blessing for the year, Larissa watching from the kitchen. Then Abe sang something, I forget what.

I threw the door open, brought them all in, what the hell. The Highclouds, Finedays, everybody, free everything. I hadn't done that in all the years I'd run the resort, so why not the last? I was sure of it now.

So I poured out our best, most expensive liqueurs, in tiny, thumb-sized glasses. Bolted one myself, then tossed the glass in the fireplace, the glass breaking, and then everyone was doing it, laughing, glass shattering, all those brittle disappointments, frustrations breaking.

Then, in the corner, an arm-wrestling match, George winning, Len holding up George's arm, flash of stainless-steel watch. Mardine, in the kitchen, flame in a pan, then in the room, a flaming dessert, smell of caramelized sugar and rum and cream. Flame in glasses, on Lois Habek's face, blue glow. Flame in the windows. Charlie, there with the Yellowfeathers, hands held up and apart. A fish story.

This big.

Moses, as if underwater, coming up alongside the windows, head bobbing, slick braids, then gone somewhere. Over the lake, a burst, a flower, yellow and blue light, and the following, reverberating—Kaboom! We had all the windows open, and the noise of the fireworks came at us, thumping the air, so that you startled at it. And more, a burst, red and green and silver. A condensed, white flash, something violent as a mortar explosion.

The windows, the glass on top, rattled, mosquitoes clinging to the screen below. Charlie, lighting a cigarette, blew smoke on them.

"Stupid skeeters," he said, "don't know when to quit, do ya?"

White tablecloth. Tiny electric lights, constellations of them, overhead, blinking. Time passing like that. Mardine coming out of the kitchen with yet another cake—Waldorf red cake, white icing, small slices. Everyone cheered, and the lights, just then, got brighter, then went out. I could hear that the diesel had stopped, the night sounds louder for it.

All candles now. Clank and scratch of Charlie's Zippo. Tobacco.

"You need help?" he said.

"No," I told him. "I've got it."

I checked the fuses in the kitchen. Blue buttons. Nothing wrong there. Then made sure the batteries were off. Took the flashlight on the wall and went out to the generator, the moon high and full in the trees. Clark was waiting outside.

"Hey," he said.

"Go back in with the others," I told him, but he followed me to the shed.

"All right," I told him, "you want to help? Hold this."

I gave him the flashlight. I thought to say, Don't touch anything, but didn't. (Even now, I ask myself, just then, in that moment, why didn't I?) Clark got down on his knees beside me.

We were like two penitents, me in black tie, Clark in his navy dinner jacket. We stooped beside the generator. Everything looked fine, industrial-green housing, the power lines snaking off into the dark. Why had it just quit like that?

A clammy wet came through the knees of my pants. Some gray thing was orbiting in my head. Outside, the record player started up again and I thought—*what?*

There was that angry buzzing behind us, the voltage regulator.

"I'll get the reset," Clark said.

There was that second when Clark rocked forward—slightly off balance. And I thought—*no.* Reached for him—he would have to stop himself, he would have to catch himself, grinning like that—didn't he hear it now, that battery hum, and the turntable?

"*Clark!*" I shouted.

—set his hand on the generator housing, and his eyes rolled into his head, teeth snapping shut, twice, as if biting something in two.

The music stopped.

I was on my hands and knees in the dark, the flashlight, angled away, that buzzing behind me. Cursing, I lifted Clark, his head hanging, as if broken, and I ran him outside.

I put my mouth to his, frantic to get him breathing, his skin already the color of putty, his eyes half open, as if sleepy. Pounded on his chest. But it was no good, any of it. I started the diesel, pushing the button in with a stick, got the lights going again, so no one would come back to check on me.

The music came on again, Sinatra.

Then it was cool, and quiet, except for the rattle of that diesel.

I took my time, kneeling beside Clark, one moment so swollen with rage, I thought to just go inside for Len, the next, eyes glassed up, tried to still my breathing.

34

Len was at the table in the corner. He looked up as I came in, eyes widening, shutter-quick, in surprise; he picked up his glass, sipped from the rim, carefully setting the glass back on the table. Gerry came out of the kitchen with a piece of cake, and seeing me, dropped his fork.

"Just had to get seconds, did you?" I said, brushing by.

A burst of laughter came from the tables along the lakeside windows. George had divided the guests into two groups. They were playing dewclaws, a kind of ring and pin game. George, even with his catcher's mitt hands, shot another dewclaw off the bone splinter, catching it, just one, and everyone cheered, shouted out the score. Now, "Eighty seven!"

Abe was playing against George, on his face a look of fierce, perplexed concentration, his gray hair in disarray, collar unbuttoned. Charlie next in line, that nervous twitch of mustache, smiling. The Highclouds and the Morrisons there laughed at Abe's neophyte attempts at mastering the game.

I pulled out a chair beside Len and sat, both of us facing the others, candlelight, laughter, Charlie missing at dewclaws now, eyes hard on it—there had to be some trick here—a shout of scores, 62–17, Mardine and Hugh clearing the tables, quiet, efficient, Gerry standing behind George, as if he were taking an interest in the game.

Len rapped that class ring of his on the table. "Bring your policeman friend into it," he said, "we'll burn you out. All I have to do is signal, and this place'll go up in minutes."

The wind was blowing in from the northwest, down from the point, cool and pine scented; all but one window to our left shut against it.

I put my hands to either side of the table setting there. Crystal stemware, geometric patterns, plates, gold filigree, roses around the rim, matching silver, fork, spoon, knife, steak knife, napkin, folded in a complicated spray of linen. I rapped that steak knife on the rim of the plate, bone china ringing.

There was a peal of laughter behind us—"Oh, Alice, you *didn't,* did you?"

I saw exactly how I would move, feinting, right. He would catch my hand, at the wrist, but I'd've switched, would have the knife in my left, would cut him across the neck, would cut down to the bone.

"I wouldn't," Len said, matter-of-factly. "It'll be the same if I don't—if I *can't*—signal, see? A lot of people would get hurt."

Charlie, across from us, kicked back from the table, conceding the game, dancing fingers over his head, "They failed me!" all of them laughing, George making a bunched-up, serious face, shooting out three dewclaws, just like that—One—Two—Three—catching them. Abe waved Len over, his arm a hook.

"Your turn, Barthelowe," he shouted.

Len placed his hands, heavy class ring, wedding band, those thick fingers, on the table. He'd worked that impassive command back into it, the set of his shoulders, business as usual.

"Later," he said, "I want you to meet someone. I want you to come down to the boat, and I want you to be friendly."

He moved away from the table, broad, thick shoulders, melon head, that bald spot, suddenly avuncular, even pleasant looking, moving into the heart of it.

"All right, all right, I'm comin', you buncha crazies. What is it? Huh?"

At a table now was Gilby, a girl with painted nails, waiting. She'd been waiting some time, and it was wearing thin.

"Ach, it's harder than it looks," Charlie said, in a loud voice, "give it another go, Len."

In candlelight, Len made another attempt at getting a single dewclaw to spin off that bone spur. When the others were all shouting, George leaned down over Charlie, their heads side by side, as if to better see the game. Charlie said something, and George, craning his head around, glared at me.

I mouthed, Outside, but he acted as if he hadn't seen it. I looked around to see where Gwen was, trying this thing on for size. Gwen was in back, swatch of blue, at a table with Marlyse Dobbs, Regina Satterfield, Marilee Kaufman, colorful birds. I hoped she wouldn't see it, what I was going to do.

I went outside, set a 78 on the RCA. The cord ran in through one of the windows, under the screen, and inside I plugged it in. Tony Bennett, singing brassy, bruise blue. I pulled Gilby up, danced her to the front door, hit it with my shoulder, going out.

Gilby had muscular, purposeful hands, moved quickly, following my lead.

"Bored?" I said, forced her out, on the bank, spun her back in, some dark, and old, enchantment in it.

Our hands were like clay, or leather gloves. I pressed her to me; we were like two hateful things.

"You like this?" I said.

On the bank there, I kissed her, full on the mouth, made a big show of it, roughly, crudely, forced my tongue into her mouth, for George. Gilby pushed me away.

"*God,* what's *wrong* with you!"

She slapped me, open-handed, so hard my head was jerked to the side, a confused, hurt look on her face. I reached for her again, and she ran down the bank, her legs knocking into each other, all that hurt in her, and now confusion, and I went after.

At the boathouse I caught her arm, spun her roughly around.

"Stop it," she said. I shook her, and she kicked me.

"I hate you," she said.

I spun her around, locking her arms against her chest. I didn't like to hurt her like that.

"Get out of here, Gilby," I said. "Now."

I forced the keys to Charlie's boat into her hand and she slashed at me with them, was ready to give it another go, until George came down the hillside, jingle of change in pockets, heavy, thudding footsteps.

I reached for her again.

"Paul!" she shouted.

She went up the dock, glancing behind her, George coming on, and wanting no part of it, dropped down into Charlie's boat. The engine started with a cough, and she spun out and away. George came down the last of the hillside, hulking out of the dark.

"What the fuck was that about, Paul?"

We were both breathing hard. The boat went out between the buoys and onto the bay, turning in a long, wide arc, and went out of sight.

"It's not what you think it is," I said. "I had to get you down here."

George stepped toward me.

"I had to know if you were working some angle with Charlie. Are you?"

George gave me one of those slow, frustrated looks of his.

"You're really something, Paul," he said. "I mean, you could have just—"

I told him, no.

I took George around shore and up through the pines to the generator. That diesel smell, engine hammering, wind of the fan blade and smell of leaky radiator. Clark lay on his back, eyes staring up at nothing.

George blew out the side of his mouth, disgusted. "Ah, god."

"It was Len," I said, angry again.

"It *wasn't* Len," George said, "but he's in it. Gerry and Moses were back in the kitchen, both of 'em. Could be either. You can't prove anything, though. Think about all those people up there in the lodge. Anyone could have done it. You'd have ten stories if you went after it now."

"So who's behind it?" I said.

"Why do you think I didn't come after you for that *stupid* stunt you pulled?"

"With Parker?"

The music floated down the hill, now Nat King Cole. "Unforgettable," the voice, disembodied, seeming nearly to hang in the trees.

Laughter, slap of screen door, the *shuuut-pop!* of a bottle rocket. I cringed, I was nearly expecting the north island to go up in a burst of flames. I knew Moses was out there. The wind blowing from the north now, it would be the end of everything, a fire now would take it all, would put us out in the water, everyone, without the boats, and then what? Drownings? Or people getting burned?

"You and Charlie are after Parker, aren't you," I said. "It's Parker who's behind it all."

George put the heels of his hands to his forehead, blinking.

"You know, Wonder Boy, considering how smart you're supposed to be, you surprise me at times. But then, you don't know much about anything around here, do you? Kind of cut yourself off there, didn't you.

"Yeah," George said, "Parker's got half the north end tied up.

"Took out a few people to do it, too. It wasn't just Al—but he was one of the hardest. Just the same, no one'll give anything up on Parker. He's too connected.

"So we got nothing. Zilch. A suicide, a couple accidents, that's all it amounts to. Charlie thinks it's somebody trying to break into the casino racket here. I think Charlie's nuts, but whoever they are, they got Len out here to fix it."

"That afternoon my boy died—"

George let his head drop back, sick at it; he didn't want to have to be the one to tell me.

"Len planned it. And he brought Gerry—"

I must have been staring; so that's why Gerry had been so crazy at the house.

"But they were after me."

George gave me a flat, disgusted look. "I think that's what they had in mind, but when Bobby got hit, and you took off with him like that—I mean, he was injured, right, and if someone hadn't filed an accident report, what would it have looked like?

"So Len fixed that, fake IDs and all, got two stoolies to come in and fess up."

I stood there for a moment, stupefied.

"You went for it," George said, "the whole accident thing; that's what they were waiting for. Then they came back to kick out your props.

"I mean, you wanted to ruin somebody, and make it look like everything just fell apart, how would you do it? And, see, they had all that working for them.

"And you almost did it, didn't you? That afternoon at Parker's? You almost gave it up."

I wasn't going to answer that. I was having trouble breathing.

"Who did the shooting?"

"It was just Len and Gerry out there—coulda been either."

George nudged Clark's body with his boot.

"One thing's for sure, though—Gerry wasn't cut out for it. He was screwin' up all over the place—left his tracks up at Kennebeck Lake—and tonight?

"We'll have to get Charlie out here."

"No," I said. "Charlie so much as steps outside now, Len'll turn this place into a bonfire. He's got Moses up on the point."

The shed light sat over George's head, a yellow sun. Here was another George now. I could see the possibilities turning in him, his eyes distant.

"So what do you want from me?" George said.

And so I told him.

I threw the door of our cabin open but did not turn on the lights. I got down on my knees beside the bed, rough wooden floor, reached under it. I slid out that pump twelve-gauge, cold metal, warm, walnut stock. I tossed the gun, sideways, to George and he caught it.

Moonlight, shadows, a dream, but not. He tripped off the safety, gave it a sharp pump—*cher-clack!*—swung it in my direction.

"Five shells or seven?" George said.

The gun looked small in his hands. He balanced it expertly. He lifted the barrel, so that it was pointed right at my middle. I imagined the blast of it. Maybe I'd got it all wrong. After all, with Len now, I could imagine anything.

George scowled, "Christ, TP!" he said, "you know, you can't tell your friends from a fucking hole in the wall. Anyone ever tell you that?"

"Yes," I told him, someone had.

Outside, George, enormous and quiet on his feet, rushed up through the trees, traversing the hillside, paralleling the ridge, toward the north end and the point.

If Moses wasn't there, if George couldn't get him back to the lodge—I'd have to deal with that.

> > ◇ < <

I was sitting with Abe and his wife, talking about old times, when Frank had owned the lodge. I was sweating, trying to follow it, while I tried to think what to do. An hour had gone by and George wasn't back.

I'd given George my Remington, without realizing I couldn't get to the others.

"We always stopped in Fort Francis on the way up then," Abe was saying. Leah, his wife, winked. "There was that beer stand. With those frosted glass mugs, and they were soooo cold, the beer froze in there, on the sides. Wrapped the hamburgers in tissue paper.

"Had...what do you call it? That bread?"

"Fry bread," I told him.

Abe grinned. "I always ate too much fry bread."

I lit a cigarette, and shaking the match out, looked the picture of nerves. Leah waved the smoke off, so I got up and sat by the screen.

We talked like that, a distance apart. The dark in the room like some irritating cotton. Faces lit in candlelight. Gwen, at Charlie's table, would not so much as look at me, carefully drank a glass of water. Len, face lit up, pretending enjoyment, had those thick-fingered hands over his head, was telling a joke.

Everyone at the table laughed, Charlie most.

Nearly midnight, some twenty or so guests were still up. Some lounged on the hillside, some were telling stories inside. Inside, it was dark, and quiet. Gwen was at one of the windows overlooking the lake, her arms on the sill, watching nothing, chatting with the Greenbergs. Charlie in the corner was smoking another cigarette, on his second pack. Gerry, in the kitchen doorway, was drinking too much, was a regular study of twitches there.

The others were playing cards, a drunken game of spoons at one table. Poker at another.

"A run," Tom Boettcher said.

They were all waiting to climb the ladder, and at midnight, go over the roof to drop down the other side and make a proper end of it.

A lucky end. That was the tradition.

Len checked his watch. Something hard settled in his face. He waved me over and I went back there, bent over him as if to talk.

"I hope you haven't done anything stupid," he said.

I said, putting my mouth to his ear: "Fuck yourself, Len."

He nodded, as if I'd said something amusing. Rucked his hair back, big fisted, and laughed.

A boatload docked, a pontoon, up from Moose Point Lodge, and I put out sandwiches. People were diving from the boathouse into the dark water, some I didn't know now, broad swan dives, belly flops, cannonballs. A jackknife. One *ka-ploom!* of water after another. Then the remaining lot of them, still dressed, toppled into the water, shouting.

I went inside, meaning to help Hugh and Mardine, but instead sat a distance from Len, working myself up to what I wasn't sure.

Leah, playing cards, looked up from her table. "It's almost midnight," she said.

I took everyone outside, in the dark, the pines so high you felt you were at the bottom of some green well. We climbed the roof, rough cedar shakes, the drunks in their wet clothes, smelling of wet cotton and wool and beer and an almost salty, wet leather smell. We were all up there, packed in. Twenty-five or thirty of us.

Gwen was facing into the wind, and the wind blew her hair back and over her shoulders. The air was damp, blowing hard, and some of the guests shuddered, waiting.

"Here it comes," Leah said, her watch raised, so she could see it in the dark.

"Here what comes?" said Abe beside her.

"Yeah," Tom Boettcher said. "Here comes what?"

"Spread out," I told them. "Don't want to damage the roof."

I could barely sit, balled my hands into fists and jammed them under my arms.

The wind whooshed in the trees. All over the lake, fireworks went up, silver glitterings and flashes of light, fountains of yellow and red fire, and green whooshings and crackling firecrackers, like a sputtering in a pan, the whole island lit up.

I waited for that catch, that incendiary whoosh that would send us running, to the lake, and the burning that would follow.

"Make a wish," Leah said.

We were all up there, packed in, shuddering and wishing and thinking and the night coming at us; I could almost not bear it, and then it was midnight, truly, and there was a paroxysm of noise, guns now too, and I heard them going off, handguns, rapid short bursts, and shotguns, that explosion, and gap—pump, bang! pump, bang! three blasts, so near that Leah said,

"Where did that come from? Is someone on the island, shooting like that?"

And I lied, a hardness settling in me, "It's just more of the same," and it just went on, even as I was saying it, bursts of fire, explosions overhead, burst after flowering burst of color, magenta, chrome yellow, vivid cobalt blue, chrome green, now airhorns, and shots fired again, boom! boom! boom! everyone cheering, happy, and sad, and some laughing.

Abe and Leah danced there, a little awkwardly at an incline, a fox-trot. He called her "Ginger," Leah returning, "Fred."

They'd done that every year since I'd taken over, and for some time before it, Frank had told me.

Then, on the backside, I held the ladder, aluminum creaking, hollow clatter of footsteps, I wanted them to rush, to be safe, to go down near the water, but said nothing, and they climbed down, in the near dark, Len, gritting his teeth, and glaring. Ten or fifteen yet to go, Charlie, scuffling, hating heights, coming at me, big in the belly and balding, a sheen of nervous sweat, always that face, bulldog jowls, and blear eyes, and Gwen last. I caught her arm.

"Don't," she said.

I kissed her and she pushed me away, hands hard and angry. She went up the backside of the lodge, with the others, and where the path led off to our cabin, went up a distance and stopped, looked at me over her shoulder, a perplexed, anxious look.

"Gwen," I said.

She was taking me in. I must have looked ridiculous, that monkey suit, dirty, bow tie askew, then turned away, walking up the path to our cabin, and I thought, Just as well.

There was all that to do down at the lodge, and it would be easier without her watching me, without feeling as if I'd done something awful.

I scrubbed dishes—George would have to come back—the washer broken again. Used the galvanized tubs. One, hot water, suds, scrubbing; rinsing in the tub to the right, handing another plate to Hugh, who dried, red-checkered dish towel, the RCA behind us, cycling through yet another stack of 78s, now Vera Lynn.

We carefully washed and repacked the stemware, green Styrofoam popcorn, cardboard boxes, sticky strip of tape, snipping it short with scissors. Did the same with the silverware and china.

It took forever, twenty boxes, crumpling newspaper, stacking; every few minutes, I found some excuse to check on Len in the dining room.

After a time, we stood back of all those boxes, a small brown castle in the middle of that mint-green floor.

"So what do you say," Hugh said. "I think we pulled it off."

"Right," I said.

Mardine came in, checked on her bread, rising off to one side of the counters.

"Len wants to talk to you," she said.

I went out past the cardplayers, Charlie, and Abe and Eddie, and a few others hunched over a table, beers, Charlie smoking, Len excusing himself, motioning me with a wave of his hand outside, to a table, wicker chairs.

"Sit," he said.

So I did that, sat across from him, and right there played my trump card.

"Haven't seen Moses," I said.

Len smiled, self-satisfied, sipped from his glass. I got a sinking feeling, Len crossing his legs, one of those tasseled shoes of his up. He polished the side with a napkin.

"Nor that pretty wife of yours," he said, glancing up at me, giving me a winning smile.

I was instantly, painfully awake.

"Excuse me," I said.

"Take your time," Len replied.

Up the lodge stoop, rushing, feet distant under me, my breath strange, into the kitchen, bright light, too bright, unreal, Mardine, big at the sink, a bear in gingham, jabbing at dishes, shaking her head, Hugh and Mardine joking, Hugh jabbing her with his elbow.

"Where's Gwen?" I said.

Her hands on her hips, Mardine gave me a positively nasty look.

"She's swimming," she said. "Where did you think she'd be, after what you did?" She didn't say Gilby.

I ducked out behind the reception desk. I was crazy with all of it.

Do something, I thought. But what?

I sat beside Len. A quiet was settling on the lake, a blue-black, late-night dark.

"You assume things you shouldn't," Len said. "That's your problem."

Now and then, he craned his head around, checking the south end of the bay. He turned up his watch, heavy metal band, thick glass face.

"You have about—oh, I'd say—thirty minutes."

He pointed through the trees. Out on the bay were two lights, one red, one green, as if in one star. Bow lights. They went up and past the channel.

"She's quite a swimmer, your wife. Isn't she."

I sat in that wicker chair, a strand poking into my back, out front of us, the trees a rough scrim vaguely green on the horizon, and all that water, black as vacuum.

"We're gonna play a little game tonight," Len said. "I know you like games. One light means one thing. Two lights—I guess I'll just have to flash, on off, something like that—means another."

His eyes slid around, fixing on me.

"Pretty dangerous out there on a night like tonight, Hump Night. Someone swimming. A boat doesn't see someone in the water when it's so dark out. You didn't think about that, did you, Paul?

"You didn't think much about any of it. You've got no planning sense. Just one boot in front of the other, like all you people up here.

"You don't deserve what you have." He scratched his neck. "You should be running...forty, forty-five cabins, an island this size. And all this old...crap, this—thing behind us. It'll all come down. Half-assed boats. Too many trees."

He pulled himself up in his chair, leaned over the table, excited now.

"But we're not talking about that, are we? We were on swimming. How people get hurt Hump Night.

"I heard you took someone in a few years ago. Someone who got run over."

"Who told you that?" I said.

"Oh, I know all about you. But about swimming, a boat runs over someone, and, hey, since they don't even know, well, they don't stay around. Do they?"

One year, Hump Night, some kids had come charging up the bank. They'd been skiing, in the dark, drinking, and swinging around to pick up their buddy, who'd fallen, had run over him and nearly cut his leg off. I'd put a tourniquet on that kid's leg, just a teenager and scared sick, but he'd bled badly in the water, and he died on the way into Pine Point.

I watched for Gwen, out on the bay, the buoys phosphorus white, open water beyond that, limitless and dark and full of awful possibility.

"I timed her, when I was up," Len said. "Takes a little over an hour. And she's made it longer. Hasn't she?"

Gerry lumbered out from the lodge and sat at the table.

"Get the fuck out of here," I said.

Gerry glanced over at Len.

"Siddown, Gerry," Len said.

I lit a cigarette, my head a tangle of unworkable solutions.

"What do you want?"

"I'll give you, let's say," Len said, "seven-fifty, for the works. Which, I understand, should cover things."

"But it would still be on my paper."

"It would have to be. Can't sell it to me, remember? I'm the *wrong color.* Not a timber—"

I gave him a flat, unequivocal stare. The N word sat between us.

"Why don't you just say it? Or are you afraid Gerald here will take offense." I turned and smiled meanly at Gerry. I'd give him one last chance.

"You're a *nigger,* aren't you, Gerald?" I said.

Gerry looked away, as if he hadn't heard me, a hopeless case.

Inside a cheer went up. Charlie was shouting something or another.

"So, did you approach Al with this... plan, too?"

"He didn't like the idea," Len said.

I laughed at that, imagining what Al would have said.

Len lifted his watch. "She should be turning around out there, right about... *now*—"

I looked behind me, into the lodge. Warm, yellow light, low rumble of conversation, punctuated by laughter. Mardine and Hugh, cleaning up.

"Moses is dead," I told Len.

"That won't help you now," Len said.

His hand shook just the slightest when he reached for his glass. "But then, you didn't think I'd ask Moses to do something like this, did you?"

Len leaned closer and, his face in mine, said,

"Maybe they won't kill her—"

I thought about all that Gwen had buried in herself to survive already, that childhood thing she'd kept from me, but that I'd guessed at.

Gerry was laughing to himself, at me. I punched him in the face, so hard I felt his cheekbone give under my knuckles. He went over backward in his chair, arms flying over his head. He righted the chair and sat again.

"It would be better to cooperate now," Len said.

We sat, Gerry mumbling, holding the tablecloth to his nose, a red blossom in that white cloth. Right there, it occurred to me what I would do. All I needed was a little luck, and the strength to go through with it.

I stood, carefully setting my chair against the table.

"All right," I said. "But I want to go out for her, and I want to do it now."

"Fine," Len said.

He took up the big flashlight, the one I'd had in the generator shed, and flashed it twice. He did that again, and the boat moved off, as if turning south toward the government docks. The green and red lights winked out. But I knew that lake, every turn of it, every island—including Horseshoe, which they'd ducked behind.

> > ◇ < <

Dockside then. Len nodded for me to get in the back of Dr. Piper's boat, to take the jumpseat. Gerry tossed the rope from the bow cleat and got in behind the wheel, still holding that cloth to his face.

We were a grim little group, pretending to be enjoying ourselves for the guests in the lodge.

The boat started with a deep, shaking roar.

"LT-1," Len shouted over it. Harsh, burned exhaust and water smell, marine grease, hot iron. "Four hundred fifty-five cubic inches."

Everyone in the lodge turned to look, amused faces, ghostlike in that candlelight, a few of them waving, Charlie pressing his face into the window there, as if he was longing after something he wasn't quite getting.

We backed away from the dock, that smart red flag flapping in the breeze, the moon behind us in the trees, motored out away from the hook of shoreline, dark, ragged pines. The boat charged out onto the bay.

Ripple of moon on black water.

I felt myself smiling. The sky opening, one dark layer after another. I looked right up into it, all that dark, cool air pummeling my face. We were just the three of us, out on the lake, late at night, taking in the cool air, broad, open water, on each island, those shrines, now lit like fireflies, blinking, through the trees, hundreds of them, insistent as voices.

And when Gerry steered the boat up the channel, the buoys there looming phosphorus white, and high, each big as an upended early-model Cadillac, turned, in a wide, lazy arc, the other boat, out on the bay, waiting, bobbing in all that dark, behind horseshoe, I settled into it.

"There's a quarter-mile stretch here, through the buoys," I shouted. "Let's see this thing go,"

Len tapped Gerry's shoulder. I had them both in front of me, Len just to my right.

"Bring it up!" Len said, turning to smile, and I grinned.

The boat sped up, thrum of hull, engine rumbling. I set my left hand alongside my thigh, then felt in the dark for that port there.

All older inboards with rudders operate on cables. There was a port, in the hull, to make servicing those cables easy, and while Len was smiling to himself, I reached in and took hold of that cable. Pull back, the boat should turn to the right, pull forward, the boat would veer left.

I tried that—the boat seemed to waffle, as if on a wave, and Gerry gripped the wheel tighter.

"Is that all the faster it'll go?" I shouted.

We were halfway up the channel, approaching those buoys, high and white in the moonlight now.

"Gerry was always a lightweight," I shouted. "Huh, *fuckhead?*"

Len grinned, tossing his head back. He poked Gerry's shoulder.

"Give him a piece of it," he shouted.

The engine kicked, the boat leaping out of the water. We were flying, on that propeller and rudder, high and flying, in the dark. The first buoy loomed larger, then larger, flashed by, just yards to our right, the whole boat powerful, and surging forward, massive; up by the third buoy, I brought us closer, Gerry would never admit he wasn't doing it intentionally, wouldn't admit the boat was getting away from him. The fourth went by, engine churning, the boat digging in and cutting through that water, just as I had always dreamed it would, and when the eighth buoy loomed up, white in the windshield, the hairs on Gerry's hand, on that pitted, Bakelite wheel, Gerry wondering what was wrong, the thunderbolt, lit now, hairs, luffing on Gerry's hand, glint of moon on windshield, on hull, Len, smiling, white teeth, wide expanse of bay, chuff of water under the hull, one green light, in the dashboard, temperature—*cool,* water-muffled roar of engine, the wash of sound, violent thrum under our feet, flying, in myself, all quiet, somehow, in that great, wall-less room, a voice, Nita's, chanting—

anindi abigwen manido? Odeima abigwen. Odeima.

where is the dwelling of the greatest spirit? In the heart is the dwelling—

anindi abigwen manido—

the eighth buoy, there, beside us, *now,* pulling back sharply on the cable—

An explosion—

Slamming though glass, rubbery thump of bodies, high and over the lake, flying, rush of cool air, turning lazily, weightless, end, over end, over end, and skipping, water abrasive, shoulder, head, hitting again, like cement now, slap of water, in nose, eyelid torn back, and that final, hard, hard wet slap, and lying on my back, smell of oil, and gasoline, and that roaring in my ears.

A boat, closer, voices, "Jesus Christ!" then pulling away.

Floating, on my back. Stars. A darkness, not in the night, but in my head. Behind me, breathing, desperate slappings, crying, then nothing.

I lay back, going under, water in my mouth, thought, *There.*

But here were more splashings. Hard, rhythmic breathing.

I went under again, better this way, ripple of lake, the moon distant, wavering over that skin between lake and sky. So quiet down there, and just then, a hand catching me up, powerful.

"*Don't move,*" Gwen said.

She had me under the chin, in a carry, across her back.

"I'm sorry," I said. "I'm sorry for everything," I said.

"Shhhhhh," she said.

"It's all right now," she said.

"But it isn't," I said, "It was never all right."

"Shhhhh," she said. "Don't try to move. I've got you," she said. "I've got you now."

BOOK III

35

We were late. But we were always late then, because of the difficulty I had moving, but I was happy. Out and away from the government docks, cool spring air, I steered our new launch up the Grassy Narrows, toward Pawaganak Bay and the lodge, Gwen and Hugh in back, Hugh, checking out his partial, in the launch mirror, having just gotten his teeth fixed in St. Paul on my ticket.

Every moment, passing the Kennebeck Lake channel, skittering as if on wings by Snowbank Island, Old Woman's Fire, Opwagun, was something new.

I'd been inside all winter, first at Fairview, and then trying to do carpentry, not too successfully.

Here the sky peeled back, morning pink skin, and under it, an infinite blue. Just to taste the air! Snow was still in it, and damp earth, wet moss. I felt a kind of resurrection. Late May, the season started, Barney's Ball Lake Resort open, cool weather, already a record catch, a twenty-six-pound lake trout, we were returning, early morning. Six-ish.

The sun popped up over Bear Island, bright as all hope.

Gwen, unbuttoning her shirt, fed Claire. Hugh, smiling awkwardly, looked away.

I steered the boat out onto Makogan Bay. Here was all of life again.

Each island rose up, higher, broader; trees, tall and green and inviting, the lake turning back on itself, more water, another island, tamarack, spruce, birch growing out of basalt and granite, backlit, the sun bright on the water, the water deep blue-black and mysterious with life.

I got the odd sensation I wanted to climb down into it, and stopped the boat.

"What is it?" Gwen said.

Claire was in the crook of her arm. A blanket embroidered in the old way—floral patterns on black background—a present sent to us by Mardine.

"We're going to be late," Gwen said. "You know how Charlie gets."

Charlie had called to say he had something to discuss with me, his voice positively sepulchral. So I wasn't rushing. I wanted this moment to last—home, perhaps for the first time, ever, the lake something miraculous.

"Paul?"

"All right," I said, meaning it, turning a full circle, trees, a hummock of snow in the lee of an island, jays calling, got us started again.

But Charlie did not come that morning, or that afternoon, and I waited. And waited. He did not come that evening, or the day after, or the day after that. After a time, I just got down to it. We were busy, had twenty-five guests up, the Rasmussens, Goldbergs, Ike Washington, and a couple families. I rose at five, and then, as is my ritual, checked the cabins and generator, a brand-new GM, stopped in the boathouse, where I poured a cup of coffee, and the sun rising, put together baits.

All of that my hands knew: the knots, six turns around the leader, through the loop, and cinch. A kind of meditation. Pork rind. Fathead minnows. Spinners. Poppers. White and yellow live bait containers. Gas premix ratios. Setting needle jets on stubborn, too-old engines. Shear pins. Lithium grease. Speed or troll props. Half-float bobbers, sinkers, open-faced reels (only for the experienced). Monofilament line of different sizes and weights and colors, blue green, clear, green. Smoking, at the end of the dock. The mornings, again, infinite, the days long, each a meditation on grace.

I loved all of it, but was waiting for Charlie.

Every day was a waiting. He'd have to come, to finish things. Late May, then June, cold water, good fishing, ferns looping out from under rocks, trout, near shore, mating, silver, rainbow-sided and fat with roe. Shallow declivities in the sand, a fish there, guarding her eggs, and in the bulrushes, damselfly nymphs. Even the mosquito larvae in the brackish water, in ponds, on low spots, melted snow, were mysterious to me.

"See?" I'd say, pointing them out to a boy or girl. "If you look really closely, you can see they're underwater. So how do they breathe?" I explained how they had a kind of snorkel. All of that seemed miraculous to me then—even the mosquitoes.

At Fairview, I'd been in an oxygen tent for a month, so just breathing without pain seemed miraculous. And so did the play of light on water, smoke rising from a cigarette. Flame. Clouds, flat bottomed and floating on nothing. The moon at night, Gwen, something healed between us, and Claire.

George stopped by Friday of that third week, carpenter's belt and cement-stained jeans that looked like pancake batter had been tossed on them.

"Let's go," he said, and we did.

He took me to the northernmost shore of the Angle Inlet. More of the bay lease—mine. Now a rust-red barn sat in a hollow of waxy-leaved poplars. There were stables, dark-sided log affairs, bales of yellow hay stacked blocklike on the south side. Ten horses. They had names like Jupiter, and *Ikode*—fire—and Waboos, who'd distinguished himself by biting guests when they tried to feed him.

I followed George up a path. It was a high path through oaks, and at one point became so steep I had trouble climbing. I was trying not to get angry with myself, George some distance away, and getting further so. I couldn't bring myself to stop him—like some beetle—scuttled there at the steepest, sandiest point, fuming, enraged at myself.

"I'm gonna have to call you Pegleg Two Persons," George called down.

I waved him away. I angled that almost useless leg under me, a kind of angry red swelling in my side that was getting worse. I thought I might be sick. I wasn't to climb anything for another few months, but I couldn't wait.

"Hold it there," George said, "wait."

I was breathing hard, ready to give it another go. The path was horseshoe rutted. Here and there, horseapples. Green, fresh. I liked that, the everydayness of it. To someone who has known horses as a child, it is a kind of perfume, all that. Horse froth, currycomb, salty, sweaty hair, twitching tail and mane, flop of excrement, at the water trough, beautiful ridged hooves, that wonderful, ground-thump, cantering or running, the rush of leaves and trees, gripping the horse between your knees, flying.

But on that hillside, green sumac to both sides, stuck, hip on fire, and that pumping sensation in my stomach, I was going nowhere. George got his forearm under my armpit and lifted.

"Wait," I said.

For a second, I thought he was going to subject me to the indignity of just carrying me up. We looked at each other. George, a head taller, towering over me, blue-black crew cut, pearl-buttoned western shirt, carpenter's belt and those ruined pants.

I had that awful salty, copper taste in my mouth. Then that passed.

George tugged up, under my arm, and I got my leg under. It took forever, but he didn't help me more than I could stand.

From the top, the Angle Inlet stretched out for miles. Riffle of silver water. The Nin'godonin'djigan just north of the upper shore.

"All right, tell me," I said.

There was an expansiveness in the moment, high and over the lake, clouds, white and billowing, the roll of land, magisterial, to a far distant line where blue and gray met green, the horizon.

I'd heard how the divers had found Len and Gerry in two hundred feet of water. But Moses?

"I'm not going to tell you," George said.

"But you have to."

"No," he said, putting the palm of his hand to his forehead, a visor, "no, I don't.

"Let's just say, like Moses said about Al, *he's just run off.* You understand?"

I said nothing. The clouds scudded by on the horizon, big as dreams.

"You want that gun back?"

"No," I said.

"You'd never find it now anyway. Besides, you know what water does to guns."

A horse whinnied from down below, swinging creak of the barn door.

"You've been away a long time, Paul," George said, "a lot's changed up here."

"Was my old man in it?"

George laughed. It was a bright, sunny laughter. "Your old man saved your hide, Paul. Who do you think set Charlie and me after Parker?

"It was Gerry there at the house, gave it away. Panicked."

George kicked at the hard ground, made a circle, and crossed it.

"So?" I said.

"Just our luck, Parker got greedy. Otherwise, who knows how far it would've gone? Sold Al on some shitty loan or whatever, a lean on the Rambler's, and Al went out with that boat, up to Kennebeck Lake, panicked.

"They were all waiting for him, had all that planned. Only Gerry, seeing how they messed Al up, got wet feet, was jabbering about it in the house later."

"So why didn't they just take Gerry out?"

"They would've whacked Gerry, but how'd they get your allotment in Pine Point then, all that land, if not through him? Through your old man and Larissa. Greedy, see?"

"And Parker?"

"We've got absolutely nothing on him."

I was tempted to tell George what I knew, but was saving it for later, ammunition. Or maybe, just then, it was a kind of talisman, in my pocket.

"Why didn't Zozed come to me?" I said.

"Your old man," George said, "he knew you wouldn't have anything to do with him—said you hated his guts. And besides, what would you've done that Charlie didn't do? After all, he checked into things and got nowhere, and that with all his cop connections. See?"

"Gilby?"

"She went off to the Dakotas."

"Well—" I said, letting go a not altogether relieved breath.

"So," George said, a hook in it.

"What?"

I watched a boy take a horse out of the barn, a glossy roan quarter horse, high, proud tail.

"We're in this together now," he said.

"Who *we?*" I asked.

"Us Big Grassy; all us people up here."

And I said, "*Nikan,*" brother, "we'll never let go, will we?"

George's face lit up at that.

Yet in the cabin, nights, I did not sleep. Not through the night. Claire cried, and I would get up, and do the usual, bottle-feed her, sitting in the chair by the window overlooking the lake. Gwen, later, would rise and touch me, gently, on my forearm, and I'd go out.

I'd stand under that pine there, the biggest on the island, get ready for the day, and Gwen would come out in her suit and stretch. She was still swimming early.

But that tree. One morning, just to see what Bobby'd liked so much up there, I climbed it. High, near the top, seventy feet up or so, the heel of my bad foot slipped, I jammed down, and teetering over backward, fell. Hit something. Came to, my neck painfully pinched between two branches, my legs doubled over, knees in my face, so that blood ran down into my head, and my eyes felt swollen.

I had fallen, fifteen or twenty feet, and had gotten caught there. I tried to right myself, and nearly fell again. Something was loose in my hip. Now it really ratcheted when I tried to move my leg at all.

I felt something was watching me. Had gone off a distance, but was still there.

I got down finally and took stock of myself.

All that was just magical thinking, I told myself, that Al's shadow still marked me, that maybe Bobby's did, too, that I saw, now, worlds in bracken water. You can't run a place like that, a lodge, and be spaced out all the time, taking pleasure in watching fish on the lake bottom, big-finned and Buddha-like, being strange in a tree, thinking the world is alive, populated with spirits, and that stones talk, or that the dead remind us of our obligations.

Or can you?

Late June now, and still waiting, the lilacs in Pine Point blooming, lavender and white buds, fragrant. Main Street not crowded, but happy with traffic, always someone at the Ben Franklin, glowing yard-high red sign, where Jim Wilson had added the remains of Dr. Piper's Chris Craft to his museum. In the center of Main, the Viking's shield throwing back sunlight. Rusty bicycles on the roof of the Rambler's, in daylight, those colored bulbs like some odd fruit. Charlie, in his office, always on the phone, receiver in one hand, pen in the other, right where Highway 525 exited the reserve, his dented cruiser out front.

Or not.

At the Tribal Office, just across the road, Parker hunched over his desk as I passed, watching me go by.

Gwen and I had this conversation about Charlie late one night.

"He can take everything away," I said. "*That's* why I just *can't* tell him. He'll bring all the rest of it up. He'll want to know about the boat—where Moses went."

"He won't ask about any of that."

I said, anxious again, "Why? Why do you think that?"

Gwen pulled the quilt around her middle. Claire was crying and she fed her. Claire was looking at me and it just hurt. I couldn't stand to lose a child like that again.

"*Why* do you think that?" I said, insistent. "Why do you think he won't just dig into all of it?"

"Because I just know things," Gwen said. "Because I know Charlie in a way you can't.

"He had a family down in the Twin Cities when all that happened.

"If you listened sometime, maybe he'd tell you about it," she said.

Then, one morning, instead of getting on her suit, Gwen bundled up Claire, and even after I'd used Mardine as an excuse, how Mardine couldn't do all that herself, run the place, just Hugh, and the new kid, Delbert, to help, there was no getting around it.

"I have to go now," Gwen said. "And I want you to take me."

It was a cool, cloudless day. Gwen smiled at me from the bow, holding Claire, Claire bundled in that floral blanket. In the morning sun, Claire's hair shone a coppery red. Hands, eager with life, into everything.

Then, driving in from Pine Point, the land rising up, always north, into the Nin'godonin'djigan.

> > ◇ < <

That November morning, the year before, we'd risen early. Coffee. Joking around. Bobby had just turned eight and was anxious, running from table to kitchen to table again, the way kids do, all excitement and expectation.

"When are we going?" he said, for the fifth time. "Are we going now? How come we're waiting? I don't want to wait."

Gwen had set a plate in front of him. "Eat," she said, a command he tried to follow.

I told Bobby, five minutes. "We'll go in five minutes."

"A minute's already gone," he said, shoving pancake into his mouth.

It was an unseasonably warm day, south winds blowing. Sun filtered through the windows like gold. I would sign the deed for the sale the following day and was feeling a kind of euphoria. All that hassle with the tribal council was over.

The place was mine, finally, I thought. How could I have thought that? *Mine?*

"What are you grinning like that for?" Clark said, poking me.

I hooked Bobby in my arm, squeezing him, but didn't say.

"Where we going?" Clark asked.

We'd be hunting north of the Angle Inlet. I hadn't shot a deer for a few seasons, claiming bad luck. The truth was, I'd lost a taste for it, felt something precarious in my being on the island, as if I might upset some deep and sensitive balance. And that was irritating me. All the big hunters around, kidding me, so that every year, I lied.

"Didn't see anything," I'd say.

But now, Bobby was going to be with us, and I didn't want the joke to attach to him, how the Two Persons had gone soft and blind. He'd been shooting tin cans for a month, .22 longs, and he was good. That's what I was thinking about, and there was something else, too.

Just a small worry. He was a healthy kid, but he had those allergies. Ragweed, pine pollen, nettles made him sick. Worst of all, though, he was allergic to bee stings, so he would bolt if one flew anywhere near him.

Joking there with Clark, I tried to decide if I shouldn't just wait another year to take him along, for that reason alone—that he couldn't force himself to stay put.

And, too, Gwen had been dead set against it earlier.

He wasn't to carry a gun, and he would just tag along.

I said, Fine. What could go wrong?

Now Clark was retelling a story I'd told him—a Trickster story.

"See, the dog came at me," he said, "and just when he was going to bite—you know, his hackles up and everything—just when he lunged for me?" Clark reached for Bobby, hands claws, and Bobby jumped back. "I put my hand right down his throat and caught his tail, turned him inside out, and ate him!

"A hot dog!"

"You did not!" Bobby said, and the three of us laughed.

From the kitchen, Gwen gave me one of her significant looks. She wanted to change her mind, put her foot down, but didn't say so.

"What do you get when you cross a gorilla with a camel?" Clark asked Bobby.

Bobby got this thoughtful look on his face. "I don't know," he said.

Clark winked, playing uncle. I said, rolling my eyes,

"A dromehairy."

"You ruined it," Clark said, explaining the joke to Bobby.

I gave Gwen, there in the kitchen, one last searching look. I was waiting for her to do it. To come to me, to say no, for her to play the killjoy.

But Gwen didn't turn, busy at the grill, and like that, the floor hollow under our my boots, we went out. Out into the open, out into the morning.

I remember, that morning, on the way in, he had to do his business, and so we stopped at an island, high backed, heavily wooded. He scrambled into the pines.

"Remember, if you flick it more than once you're playin' with it," Clark joked.

Bobby came down minutes later. I was already back in the boat, waiting, when I heard them laughing. Clark had swung Bobby onto his shoulders, and they came down to the boat like that, hugely tall, laughing.

"Pick me a cloud," Clark said.

"What flavor?"

"Grape."

"Pineapple!" Bobby shouted, delighted at this game.

"Motorcar!"

"That doesn't have a flavor!"

"Who says?"

"I say!"

"All right, you two," I said.

I was happy, for a moment. And then a certain bitterness took hold. Clark, it occurred to me, was closer to my son than I was. It had always been like that, and it cut me.

> > ◇ < <

We were climbing up the hillside on the north side of the Inlet. I had Claire on my back. We'd taken the truck in from the government docks, parked it, now hundreds of feet below us, just as Clark and I had that morning.

The hillside was steep, and awful, and even with that birdcage brace on my leg, my hip wasn't worth much. Claire fussed. She weighed only eighteen pounds, but even so, now every step up, my hip snapped back into the socket with a sickening, plastic *pop!*

Up ahead of me, Gwen went very slowly, with a certain unstoppable intent, and didn't speak.

Here was the highest mass of stone north of the bay, all at that odd, vertiginous angle. It was as if the ground had lifted up and come to rest like that. My hip hurt so badly, I began to glide—climbing.

Always that afternoon.

> > ◇ < <

"What are you in such a rush for?" Clark said.

It was warm, and we had our jackets wrapped around our waists. We'd picked up my truck at the government docks, then driven north into the Nin'godonin'djigan, and were hiking in from the road now.

There was that fall grass-in-the-sun smell. The red sumacs, the oaks still red brown. Bobby rolled his pants up.

"Don't do that, Bobby," I told him. "You know about the chiggers."

Clark strode up beside me. Bobby, climbing behind us, fell and slid a ways down.

"Traverse the slope," I told him. "Go up and across it."

But no, he had to come on, right on up, and fall again. I was *making* him fall then, I thought. He was falling for me, just like I'd done with my father, with those rice sacks, had done with everything those years. I was furious with myself, but couldn't stop it.

"*Bobby,*" I said, in a curt, controlled voice. I scuffled down to him.

"*What?*"

He was sweating, face flushed, just a boy.

"Listen," I said. Clark was watching.

I ached to swing him up into my arms, the way I had years before. I wanted to kiss the top of his head. I wanted all that had gone bad between us to disappear, like smoke.

"Hey," I said. "Would you like to shoot my rifle?"

He was all eagerness then, and I showed him how to hold it, and there was a stump there, and when he fired the rifle, it kicked back, tearing a hole in the quiet, and he stumbled and fell.

He threw the bolt back, loaded up another shell. I stood behind him, wrapped my arms around his. I knew it was the wrong thing to do the second I did it.

"Don't jerk the trigger, this time *squee—*"

But he jerked at the trigger, and off balance, he fell back into me, dropping the gun, hard little shoulders, knocking me away, unable to stop himself from trying to devil me, going up the hill, angry at himself, at everything. I knew that feeling exactly.

I swept up the gun and headed off after him, but not before glancing over at Clark.

"Hey," I said. "Don't move the truck without coming for me. Just in case. Okay?"

Clark nodded.

I met up with Bobby at the top of the hill, just in time for him to catch Clark waving, and Bobby waved, in a way that got to me all over again.

"You all right?" I asked him.

Bobby shrugged and headed up the path. He already knew how it worked:

Clark would double back to the road, where he'd pass the truck, then circle in from the west, so that the deer would come our direction, right through a wooded area that a deer run funneled through.

Bobby and I would be on the other side of the trees, waiting for them.

Some time later, we crossed a field of high, yellow grass, the wooded area just ahead of us, and stopped for lunch. In the middle of the field was a stunted cedar, a stone wedged into the branches, down low, so that the branches, growing, had wrapped around it, deformed. We stood looking at that tree. Why had someone put that stone there? Bobby asked. He was squinting, his head cocked to the side.

"It's a marker," I said.

"Of what?"

"Anybody's guess."

Far off, on a ridge, maybe a half mile distant, on the west side of the deer run, two hunters went by, in fluorescent orange ponchos. One held his hand up, though not quite waving.

I remember thinking it was odd they'd found the place—it was remote and hard to get to; but then told myself at the worst, no matter how noisy they were, along with Clark, they'd drive the deer to us.

> > ◇ < <

Gwen and I reached the tree. We were both breathing hard, sweating. Claire, on my back, was pulling on my hair and kicking in her seat.

"Let me have her," Gwen said.

I paced back of the tree. Though still stunted, the rock there, it was green now, as was the whole hillside, and the ridge. Jays called in the pines back of us.

"Now, tell me," Gwen said. "I have to hear all of it."

It was hot. Late afternoon. I got out our lunches and Bobby did not eat his.

"I hate peanut butter and honey," he said. "Why does she make these things?"

"I made them," I said, which darkened the mood further.

We sat in the sun, our backs to each other, a fair distance apart. I'd wanted it to be a good thing, this outing, but it wasn't. Bobby put a stick through his sandwich and flung it out into the grass.

"You'll want that later," I told him.

"No, I won't," he said.

"Fine," I said.

I pulled my cap over my eyes and stretched out. I wasn't sleeping exactly, but time passed. I got up on one elbow, and there Bobby was, looking for that sandwich. I remember taking a certain pleasure in it, one that also made me feel ashamed of myself.

I was tempted to say, Hungry? but didn't.

I got to my feet, stretching. Bobby picked up the sandwich, bit into it, and right then he made an awful, surprised cry,

"Accch!" spitting.

"*What?*" I said, irritated all over again. I thought he was just complaining.

He pointed to his mouth, then was digging in his mouth with both hands. I felt a charge of something I'll call terror run up my back and stood.

There were wasps all over him, lighting on his face, his arms, his hands.

He was swinging wildly at them, and before I could so much as take a step nearer, he bolted up the deer path and I threw my gun down and ran after him. The deer path was narrow and muddy, and the brush—since I was taller—tore at my face in a way it didn't at Bobby's.

"Bobby!" I shouted. "Goddammit! *Stop!*"

He tore on up that path. There was a rise ahead, and the sun cutting bright and diamond sharp through the trees, I gained on him, until at the top, where the deer run emptied into the valley below, I was little more than an arm's length away. Right there, coming over the ridge, and down, Bobby lifted bodily off the ground, as if he'd been kicked in the air, spinning, and even as I caught him in my arms, I heard the rifle report, and saw below us, the two men in orange, one standing, his rifle hanging from his hand, in shock, the other, thickset, coming at me.

Bobby was hiccuping. He'd been hit in the shoulder; already I was covered with blood. The thickset man was charging at me, still a hundred fifty yards or so down the valley. I thought to scream some obscenity at him—or just wait to see his face. The shooter. To see who they were.

But I thought—the truck.

Just get down to the goddamned truck. If I could just get to the truck. *Oh, Jesus Christ, just there, we could drive into Pine Point in minutes.*

I came out of the trees and onto the road.

Ankle-deep sand, ruined telephone line, hanging from poles, each smaller, as far as I could see, in both directions.

A dented blue car I'd never seen, the hood up, parked alongside the ditch.

Ten miles. I tripped, blundered, turning, so as not to fall on Bobby, when I did, then got to my feet again, finally, and legs palsied, all those miles later, bawling, angled across a field of waist-high oats, to old Henry Selkirk's.

"Henry!" I shouted in his yard. "Henry *goddammit* come out!

"*Goddammit Henry!*"

Henry burst out the door, the sun blinding, started his old truck, drove, trees flashing, the whole world in that rush of light and trees, Bobby in my arms, into town, and at Our Lady, followed me inside, gave me a push, to go with those doctors, letting them take Bobby, and when I came out of there, I said, to Henry,

"Don't you wanna know?"

He drew me into his arms. Those big, scarred hands of his on my back.

"I'm sorry," he said, and I lost it.

Later, I heard from Mardine that Henry'd known Bobby was dead when I'd come into his yard. Driving us in was the least he could do, he'd told her.

I stood back of that tree, the rock there, limbs twisted around it, holding Claire. I had never heard Gwen shriek before, a high, tearing sound that just ate into me, and I just cried at it.

It went on for some time, and then some, and the only help for it was remembering that smile Len had given me in the boat, then how we'd hit the buoy.

Still, that was little consolation.

We stopped at the Chuckwagon and got milk shakes. They'd fixed the sign, but the uniforms were still the same.

"Are you okay," Alice said, setting her hand on Gwen's shoulder, and she was in it again.

"No, she's not," I told Alice. "But that's all right. Go on. It's all right," I said. "Go back to work."

We had another week of cool, rainy weather. Green ponchos. Rubber boots. Smell of vinyl. Guests' cheap rain gear tearing, wet wool and cotton, and happy enough, the fire going in the lodge fireplace, good fishing, and reading afternoons in the rain.

I was talking with a guest one of those afternoons, arch of lodge roof overhead, the sibilant patter of rain, the comfort of being inside, everything through the windows rain-glazed.

"It's so quiet," this Carol said. She was up with her husband, both of them from New York.

"Yes, it is," I said.

I was reading, Aurelius's *Meditations* again.

Carol got an impish grin on her face. "Tell me," she said. "Just tell me, *really*. Doesn't it get *boring* up here? I mean, doesn't this—" she made a sweeping motion with her hand "—just drive you crazy?"

I took it all in, high, open ceiling, the old, oak furniture, the beaded leggings on the wall. The fireplace. Rain-streaked windows, knock of pans in the kitchen.

"Doesn't it?" she asked.

"Yes," I told her, "sometimes," and left it at that.

Just after the Fourth, Charlie stopped by. I met him down at the dock, tied his boat to one of the bumpers, and gave him a hand up. Now his boat had an official-looking gold star on the side, big as a dinner plate. That was new. It scared me.

"You always had gray in your hair, Paul? Or you just get that?" he asked.

Inside, I poured him a cup of coffee. Our last group had just left, and it was quiet, the old clock on the mantel making that *cluck-tick, cluck-tick.*

"You've put on some weight," I said.

"I suppose you don't get lost anymore, huh?" Charlie gave me one of those slanty smiles. "Walk in circles with a leg like that. Oughta get yourself a parrot."

I shook my head. "Very funny, Charlie."

Another boat pulled in at the dock. This one, all business, men in black windbreakers, polished black shoes, the whole bit. They wasted no time coming up the hill, marched really.

I was stunned, then fearful.

"*Don't shake,*" Charlie said, one eyebrow cocked, meaning, you listen to me now. "And *keep your mouth shut.* I would have warned you, but I didn't know when they were coming myself. Don't talk back for once in your life. I saw the whole thing up here. I'm the eyewitness about what happened that night. Okay? I give it first, you just say—that's the way it happened. Sorry, not to bust your bubble, but it's me they're gonna believe. You know it, and I know it, so I'm doing the telling. So zip it.

"I didn't want you to think about it, or do anything dumb.

"I'm on your side here, Paul, believe it or not."

"Really," I said.

We were all up in the lodge porch when they left, late that afternoon. The morning had been an almost unbearable barrage of questions, most of which Charlie answered just as he'd promised he would, but I hadn't counted on him to twist the truth the way he did—which he did more than a few times.

"Good riddance, you fuckers," Charlie said, watching them go.

The boat went around the south shore and out of sight. We went out the front then, free, headed down the bank, Mardine, Gwen with Claire, Hugh and myself.

The whole island had greened in the rain, an almost preternatural, vibrant green.

Hugh and Mardine went around back, for firewood.

"Tell him," Gwen said. "I want you to do it now."

The sun came out from under a cloud. Gwen, lovely, and quiet, but suddenly, smiling, white teeth, and those blue eyes, china blue, gave me a push.

The baby's hair had come in, caught all that sun. She was going to be a redhead, all right.

"Hey, how about that?" Charlie said. "Almost as beautiful as her mother."

"I think more," Gwen said.

"Can I take her?" I asked.

I took Claire in my arms. I bounced her. She was tugging at my hair. Charlie and I went the rest of the way down to the dock.

"You know they'll be back," Charlie said. "Parker'll find somebody to mess with you."

He dusted off his shirt, short-fingered, thick hands, an exasperated look on his face.

"Listen," I said, "I've been meaning to tell you something."

It was hard giving anything up to Charlie; it had been a point of pride for so many years not to. And the color line was one we never crossed, not like this. But now I'd do it.

"You know those markings all over Al's body?" I said. "That you had me look at?

"Henry did that for me. Something with the stripes, under or over, on his cheeks. A Potawatomi'd do 'em over. Something like that. Henry told me all that.

"That gets us nowhere." Charlie sniffed, rubbed his hand over his chin.

"All that with the boot, too, it's all just conjecture, nothing, zero without physical evidence Parker was there that night.

"Can't prove nothing."

"But that dust all over him," I said, "that artemisia—Henry probably called it mugwort—" Charlie was nodding now, "—did it have graphite in it, and wood shavings?"

Charlie glanced up, interested.

"How'd you know that?" he asked. "We couldn't make sense of that for anything."

I bumped Claire on my knee. She had a hand in my hair; I kissed her.

I stopped all that, gave Charlie a hard, long look. I wanted him to understand me, that we were striking some bargain.

"All right," Charlie said, glancing off across the lake. "Tell me."

"It's on Parker's desk," I said. "I was in there, middle of the summer, about a loan. He sharpened a pencil into a jar. The *wrong* jar—his medicine jar—he was so nervous. I knew he dusted himself, did that night they killed Al, too. Did it right there, at Kennebeck Lake, to put the shadow off.

"Old Parker was afraid of *djasakid,* like Al," I said. "You go over to Parker's, at the Tribal Office. Bring George and one of those agents if you want.

"That stuff that was all over Al's body? Same as Parker used on himself. I've gone by that office a few days every week this summer.

"Every time, I got close enough to make sure it was there."

"Is it?"

"Got the jar on his desk. Left side, by the telephone."

"You'll swear you saw him do it, sharpen his pencil like that?"

I took that in, imagined facing Parker. It was a sobering thought.

"Don't do us any good deeds here," Charlie said, offended at my hesitation. "We all know what that kind of thing comes to."

"No good deed," I joked.

"Goes unpunished," Charlie added, mouth twisted into a grin. "I mean, you got the council eatin' out of your hand now."

"That's George's thing," I said. "George and his subtle ways."

We both laughed.

"So you'll do it?"

"Yes," I said.

Charlie got into his boat. Belly over his middle, worn work boots. But he was excited.

"You know," Charlie said, peering up at me, big gutted, and not so mean looking now, almost friendly. "I'm not sure if I should be afraid of you, or if I should admire you. It's a real toss-up."

I undid the bowline, tossed it back to him. He started the engine. Something lifted there.

"Don't do either."

The sun came out, bright over the trees. Clouds bumping the horizon. The light was almost blinding, everything seeming to glow as if from inside.

"When'd you think of all that with Parker?" Charlie said.

"Flat out on my back, at Fairview down in the Twin Cities," I said.

"You'll call me if you have trouble?"

"You know I will," I said.

"Hey, god bless," Charlie said, reaching over the gunnel, and gave me a handshake that, even for the complicity in it, meant something.

Gwen came down, as if gliding, blue eyes sparkling. We watched Charlie turn south, around the island, rather than going out by the buoys. I'd been doing that for some time, too. Everybody did. There was that winding up, outboard hum, and he was gone.

"I can take her," Gwen said, reaching out.

I stepped over to Gwen. She was looking away anxiously.

"It's all right now," I said.

The baby was crying. I kissed Gwen, and she did not stop. The baby was looking up at me. Blue-green eyes and those tiny hands. I was crazy about that kid.

"Paul?" Gwen said.

"What?"

I kissed the top of Claire's head. She was a funny baby, already, and I could see more than a little of her father in her.

"Come on," she said.

We got into one of the boats, just a blanket, and a little dinner, the whole lake to ourselves.

9 780743 406321